THE
TURNING
CHRONICLES

THE
TURNING
CHRONICLES

A TRILOGY OF DEATH, LIFE AND RENEWAL

JUDITH PEDERSEN-BENN

MILL CITY PRESS
MINNEAPOLIS, MN

Mill City Press, Inc.
322 First Avenue N, 5th floor
Minneapolis, MN 55401
612.455.2293
www.millcitypublishing.com

ISBN-13: 978-1-63413-053-0
LCCN: 2014949510

Image Credits: Linda Scarth
Cover Design by Biz Cook
Typeset by Sophie Chi

Printed in the United States of America

ONE

Grandmother's Story

I *woke to the sound of voices filling our small home. Father's* friends had brought precious food and water to share. I watched as they sat on the floor and formed a human circle. One by one they began to tell stories of Grandmother's life. I laughed when I heard how she had made up funny songs and cried at the sincere expressions of gratefulness and loss. Some were still angry with her over things she had said to them and, of course, she had made mistakes. Piece by piece Grandmother's life was laid out for all to see. She had been a strong woman who spoke her truth and she was well loved. Our gathering lasted until our hearts were filled and our souls found rest. We thanked Grandmother for her presence in our lives and for the stories she left us. Blessings were offered for her journey into the spirit world, and then we rose to take her to the place where all dead bodies go. Walking single file, we must have been quite a sight carrying Grandmother's body on our shoulders. We were taking our grief outside and risking our lives, but this did not occur to me until much later. People on the street stared, but no one tried to stop us. Perhaps

Grandmother's presence was still protecting us. We went to the place where fires were kept burning day and night. There I saw a column of fire rising up into the sky. Its heat burned my face, and I noticed those who placed Grandmother's body onto the fire had singed eyebrows. We watched as the fire burned away the last remnants of her body. With tears streaming down my face, I sent my final blessings for her journey. Father gathered me in his arms and held me close as we made our way home. I looked over Father's shoulder as he walked, but all I could see was gray despair on the faces of those we passed, suffocating black smoke, and a dismal sky above us. I was reminded once more of Grandmother's final story.

✦ ✦ ✦

I was born into the arms of the Corpsety, a hideous mass of gray despair that had given up all pretense of beauty. Grandmother often told the story of how my mother's young, malnourished body had given itself over to birth me. But it was not me she blamed, for Grandmother knew the Corpsety killed her daughter as surely as if it had plunged a knife deep into her heart. Grandmother had a long history with the Corpsety and it was evil in her eyes. And so it was in mine.

Grandmother arrived soon after my mother's death, and from the beginning her presence in my life was a gift. She delighted in telling me stories of a time when there was no Corpsety, a time when a beautiful and proud people who called themselves Free wandered from place to place looking for food and water. They were always moving, she explained, but never alone. They lived surrounded by a family of wanderers. A resting place might be made of leaves, grass, or dirt; it didn't matter much to them. Their feet were their transportation, and family was their home. The Free People played and worked and lived together in a timeless stream of life and movement. "Are we free?" I asked one day. "No, little one, we are not." I didn't think we were, because our way of life was completely different. We ate canned food and hardly ever went outside. I had a family but it was small, and I couldn't imagine living without the protection of the Corpsety. I was confused.

How could Grandmother know about a way of life so different from ours? "Were you one of them?" I asked. She shook her head no. "Well, then the story must be made up," I countered. She looked at me and sighed, "There are some things, little one, that we just know to be true. This story is very old. It was handed down to me by my great-grandmother, and she received it from her great-grandmother, and one day you will pass it on to your grandchildren so it will not be lost." I felt bad about accusing her of making the story up. I promised to pass it on, though I couldn't imagine myself with children much less as an old grandmother.

The Corpsety dominated our lives. We lived in it and it lived in us. As best my grandmother could tell, the Corpsety arrived about five thousand years ago. She knew this because there had once been libraries and schools where people could go to discover such things. Now the libraries belonged to the rich and powerful Corpses. Grandmother had been a servant to a Corpse with a library, and there she had learned how to read. Although her master was a good man, she was fond of saying the Corpses had long outstayed their welcome on earth. Under her tutelage I grew up with a healthy disrespect for Corpses and the Corpsety. Grandmother had given me the vision of an earlier time of joy, beauty, and Free People, which I much preferred to our life in the Corpsety.

For the most part my life was uneventful. I spent my days inside. It was dangerous to go outside where people with desperate eyes wandered through streets filled with filth and disease. Just the thought of their ghastly faces gave me nightmares. Grandmother and I spent our time cooking, cleaning, and playing games, and on special days she shared stories of the Free People. I didn't understand much of what she told me, but I loved to hear her sweet voice and lay against her soft body. I was safe in the cocoon of home.

My father was gone from sunup to sundown working hard to provide the food we ate, the water we drank, and the roof over our heads. Our ramshackle one room was drafty, cold, and ugly, but it was ours, and Father intended to keep it that way. Sometimes he had friends over and they would talk about the Corpsety in hushed voices. Grandmother thought I was too young for these gatherings and sent me off to bed behind the ragged curtain that separated the rest of the room from our sleeping place. She must have known the curtain was no match for my youthful curiosity, but perhaps she hoped I would nod off to sleep if the whispers grew harder to hear. On those nights I lay awake and silently watched the frayed curtain move with the rhythm of their whispers. Only last night my hungry ears caught the breath of a sentence: "The Corpsety is our sinking lifeboat." I sat up on my pallet, frightened at the picture the words conjured up. I knew about water. Water untreated by the Corpsety was so polluted it could eat the flesh away from anyone who dared to touch it. Only untreated water was big enough for a boat. Treated water came in bottles and cost far more than food. Yes, I knew a thing or two, and I didn't want to be on any boat that was going to sink into that water! I stifled my desire to bust through the curtain and ask what they meant, because I didn't want to disturb Grandmother. I was afraid she might ask Father's friends to go away, and I didn't want to lose my place behind the curtain of their words. I would ask Father about the sinking boat in the morning. Surely he could ease my fears, for if Grandmother was my cushion, he was my rock.

I woke to find Father already gone. I had overslept, and now my question would have to wait. I blamed an unsettling dream for keeping me from waking. I dreamed that Grandmother was floating above me. I was trying to make sense of this when I realized Grandmother was still in bed—which was odd, because she always got up early to fix my father a cup of hot water before he left for work. I crept over to the bed where she lay sleeping, trying to be as quiet as a mouse, but then I saw a roach on the wall and just had to smack it. Grandmother woke with a start. Her blue eyes, usually sharp and twinkling, were dull and glazed. "Grandmother, what's wrong?" I asked. It took her a long time to answer, but when she did there was a faint smile on her face. "Come here, little one," she whispered. "Let me see you." She gazed into my eyes for the longest time and a shiver went down my spine. "You have the look," she told me. "What is that?" I wanted to know. "I don't rightly know how to explain it, but your mother had it too. You see things differently, my child, you see things others do not see, and even at your age it shows." Just saying this seemed to exhaust her and she fell back on the pillows.

What in the world she meant by "the look" I had no idea, but I was more concerned about her looks at the moment. "Grandmother, I'll get you some warm water and a biscuit," I called out as I ran to the corner of the house we used for a kitchen. My hands were cold and shaking as I tried to light the small fire burner we cooked on. I watched the tiny flame move under the pot and fidgeted with the end of the burner to make it hurry up. Carrying the water and biscuit carefully across the room, I noticed a crack in the plate had widened. It seemed everything we had was either cracking or breaking.

Grandmother was awake now but shivering. She took a few sips of the warm water but refused the biscuit, motioning for me to eat it instead. I attempted to take a bite but it stuck in my throat. The biscuits we ate were dry and tasteless, even on a good day, which today most certainly was not. I ran to get the thin blankets off the pallets Father and I slept on, hoping they would stop her shivering. Only Grandmother slept in a bed. After my mother died and Grandmother came to live with us, Father insisted she take the one bed we owned. Grandmother had protested, but Father won out. He had a commanding presence, standing over six feet tall with a full head of long brown hair and dark, piercing eyes. When she saw he was not going to back down Grandmother accepted his gift, but not without letting him know she wanted no other favors. She proceeded to take care of Father and me with great devotion, paying us back a hundred times over for the small comfort she received from the bed. Grandmother was the heart and soul of our home and we loved her greatly.

The blankets and warm water seemed to revive her a little, and she asked me to come and lay down beside her. Happily, I climbed into her bed. I hoped she would tell me a story. Storytelling was Grandmother's passion, and I thought a story might make her feel better. "Mariah," she whispered, "I want you to remember the story I'm going to tell you because it may be the last story I have to give. I know you are too young to understand, but I want you to remember this story, and someday you will know what it means." I was worried about grandmother calling me by name. She always called me "little one," never Mariah. She seemed to sense my discomfort. "Little one," she whispered, "look at me, for I'm going to tell you what I know of the Corpsety. When you are grown and people are calling you Mariah, I want you to remember what I've told you, for the story I have to tell will not be found in any books and few will dare to tell it." And so she began.

The promise of the Corpsety's greatness blinded our ancestors, the Free People, to its reality. The Corpsety was their great shining star, their chance at immortality, their opportunity to rise up above all the other creatures on earth. Even when all the Corpsety's promises had been broken, the Free People held onto them because, by that time, the Corpsety was all they knew. It was their sinking lifeboat. Oh no, I thought, here is that lifeboat thing again. I heard Grandmother's voice calling me back, "Mariah, stop daydreaming, you must listen; I haven't much time." Long ago the Free People gave up their wandering life when the

Corpsety's siren song called. *Come to the Corpsety, it sang, and you will have plenty to eat without having to wander from place to place. Come to the Corpsety, it cajoled, and you will find safety from the whims of nature, for the Corpsety will build buildings that last forever, dam rivers for their power, and build mighty fortresses to keep you safe. Come to the Corpsety, it crooned, and you will be secure in the nest created for you.* And they came. Slowly at first, but eventually they all came." In the beginning the Corpsety was not so different from the natural world the Free People had lived in. It was nestled among hills, mountains, streams, and magnificent forests. Above it was a clear blue sky and beneath it was rich, brown, solid earth. Surrounding the Corpsety were plants and animals of all sizes, shapes, and colors. The Corpsety promised to be a perfect paradise. But nothing is perfect, and anything that seems so is bound to be poisonous and rotten to its very core. This was a lesson the Free People had yet to learn.

Having fallen under the spell of the Corpsety and its promise, the Free People spread the message far and wide. Soon the Corpsety didn't even have to recruit. Few were able to resist the Corpsety's magnetic field of promise. This was the first in a long line of dirty deeds the Free People were tricked into doing for the Corpsety. Eventually its reach was so wide that, at its peak, no human on earth was untouched by it. Such was the power the Corpsety wielded over humankind.

Even now you can still hear wondrous stories of the Corpsety. Stories that tell of glorious, golden monuments; of towering buildings that rose into the heavens; of gigantic granaries holding surplus from cultivated fields spreading as far as the eye could see; of knowledge so vast it was stored in libraries; of machines that could fly in the air and swim under the water; of reaching out beyond the stars and capturing the heavens. All this and more the Corpsety accomplished. But the stories forget to mention how its creations existed solely for those who were rich, powerful, and privileged: those who were called Corpses, for they were devoid of humanity. The Corpsety was, in fact, their vision, their dream of what life on earth should be like. Everyone else served them. The choice, the freedom, and the dreams of those who were not privileged had to be given over to the Corpses.

The Corpses had started out as Free People, but somewhere along the way they lost their respect for community and for life itself. They became obsessed with the idea of creating individual wealth and power. Leaving the wandering life behind, they settled in places with abundant resources, built permanent shelters with rock walls for protection, and began to plant seeds and keep animals. The Free People gave them a wide berth and took no interest in their affairs. For a while they coexisted like this until the Corpses discovered they could not achieve their desires without the labor of others. It seemed they needed the Free People after all—but for their own purposes. The Corpsety's siren song was their brilliant strategy to attract laborers.

At first the Free People did not respond. Their ears were shielded from the song by the warmth of joy, community, and freedom. They wanted no part of the Corpse's vision of life; they were happy and contented. But, the children grew curious. Their tender ears could not resist the Corpsety's call. One by one they grew up and made their way to the Corpsety. The distraught parents followed, hoping to protect their children, and were swallowed up by the Corpsety. In the end only a stalwart few continued to wander, and when death came for them they left behind nothing but their stories.

The Corpsety's siren song had blinded the Free People to the cost of entry. The cost was high because it included their all: their labor, their time, their sacred relationship with others and with nature, their joy, and finally, their souls. In return they were promised safety and security. Never mind that it was a promise that couldn't be kept. The Free People had come to believe that the Corpsety gave them life when in fact it was meting out death, a slow, painful death that eclipsed joy and replaced it with misery.

Great monuments and buildings were built with Free People's labor, but not for their pleasure. They labored in the cultivated fields but were the first to die of starvation. The vast stores of knowledge were jealously guarded and used to keep Free People separated from one another. Machines which held such promise were used to make war and keep Free People from rising up against the Corpsety. Did the Free People understand what the Corpsety would ask of them when they arrived? No, of course they didn't, and this was the tragedy. Nothing in their previous lives of wandering in small groups and looking out for each other could have prepared them for the viper's nest they had entered. Thus began the Free People's descent into the darkest of times. A time when the sunlight was squeezed from the sky and only a dull, gray memory of its existence remained. The era of the Corpsety had been born.

The dullness continued year after year, century after century until the very fabric of the earth began to collapse. Wild animals lost their places to live and began to die off. The forest, whose greatness supported the whole of life on earth, began to falter and wither under the demands of the devouring Corpsety. The brown, fertile soil which housed the wealth everyone depended on began to dry up and blow away due to a lack of nurturing. Even the great oceans and waterways lost their ability to provide life. Filled with poisons and filth, their capacity to clean and renew was destroyed. The sky was so full of dust and pollution that simply breathing required great effort. The Free People wept and mourned the losses. They knew something was wrong, greatly wrong, but they didn't know what to do. And so they did nothing.

The true promise of the Corpsety had come to pass, but it was not the promise of safety and security. Instead it was the promise of death, destruction, and suffering that comes from wanton greed and corruption. For any time more is taken than is needed, and beings are enslaved, the natural balance of the world is broken and madness is released. This is the promise that no human can change no matter how hard they might try.

Even while life on earth was unraveling, the rich and powerful Corpses expanded their grasp on life. Great nations provided people with previously unheard of levels of wealth. Good food was wasted though people were starving, monstrous houses crowded out farms and forests, factories burped out enticements while oozing sludge into oceans and groundwater. This largesse of greed and wastefulness didn't last long. In a short time the people of those great nations were themselves enslaved. In the end, the Corpsety was divided into two groups: the elite Corpse and everyone else. The Corpses ruled the world. They lived in extravagant houses on the tops of hills and mountains. Their homes were fortified by walls and heavily guarded. Because they had land, the Corpses had access to fresh food, meat, and clean water. There was little interaction between the Corpses and the Free People, who no longer called themselves free.

Those who provided labor for the enterprise of the Corpses led a singularly bleak existence. The Corpsety had given up all pretense of security and beauty. With the loss of the forests and trees, clean water, and other living beings, the Corpsety was exposed for what it was: a stark, dirty, ugly beast. Noise from hundreds of machines that ran day and night assaulted the ears. Clouds of black smoke poured out of smokestacks, giving a pall of grayness to all it touched. The sour smell of production and garbage overwhelmed those who entered, while those who lived in the Corpsety hardly noticed. Laborers were charged outrageously high prices for crowded, drab dormitory rooms that kept them indebted to the Corpses. Those who rejected the dormitories had to compete for abandoned, ramshackle houses which were unprotected. The only food available was tasteless, processed food made in the factories. Clean water was tightly controlled and could only be purchased from the Corpsety. The cost of food and water could easily take up all of a worker's pay, leaving nothing for anything else. Outside of the Corpsety no other jobs existed. Those without work had to scavenge in the trash pits for the Corpse's leftovers. These Trashers had an impossibly hard life, and there were stories of people who became so thirsty they drank polluted water and died horrible deaths. But the people were not completely without influence. In their agony, they labeled those who oppressed them Corpses and the city they had created the Corpsety. Over time these names stuck, and even the wealthy were unable to erase them.

"How did people get banished to the Trash pits?" I asked, but got no response. Grandmother had drifted off to sleep. I lay there for a while before deciding to get up and figure out what to do next. I ate the biscuit Grandmother had refused and tried to start a fire in the small burner. Should I go out and find Father? I was fearful of the Corpsety and the scary people lurking around every corner. Father had cautioned me never to go outside without him, but I was screwing up my courage to do just that when I heard the front door open. I held my breath and peeked around the curtain. There I saw my father's outline at the door. I ran to him, crying, "Something is wrong with Grandmother." He sat me on his lap and wiped my tears. "Shush, Mariah, I came home because I had a feeling something was not right this morning."

We walked over to where Grandmother lay sleeping and watched her closely. She opened her eyes and didn't seem surprised to see Father even though it was daytime. Grandmother told him to sit down on the bed while she directed me to a far corner. I moved toward the dusty corner but not so far that I couldn't hear what she was saying. "Thomas, there is something I want to say. I was wrong about you. My daughter saw what I could not. You are a good man and a wise man. My desire to save my daughter from the perils of the Corpsety blinded me to your goodness and to her calling. I am sorry for judging you harshly and for any pain I have caused." "Grandmother," Father started to say, but she silenced him with her hand. "I don't have much time left so I don't want to spend any of it on needless arguing. I have looked into the soul of the little one. She has the gift to see the future and hold the course until the future is realized, just as her mother did. I understand now why my daughter had to leave the master's house. You must take action on the plan you and your friends are talking about. Use the guidance of the little one to help you. She will know how to lead the way. You have my blessing. I know this is what my daughter would want." She finished speaking and lay back on her pillows.

"I promise to do all that you have asked, Grandmother, and I thank you for your blessing," Father whispered as a tear rolled down his cheek. "Come, little one," Grandmother called as she motioned for Father and me to climb into bed with her. Grandmother spoke of the blessing of returning to the Great Mystery and the realm of the spirit. She called this the eternal cycle and said it would take her back to a place of wholeness where everything is possible. After she finished talking we lay quietly together. Snuggled down between my grandmother and father, I felt warm and secure. Sometime later Father gently shook me awake. "She's gone, Mariah, Grandmother has gone to join the Great Mystery where your mother went before." It was true. When I looked at Grandmother she was peaceful but not breathing anymore, and she was getting cold. We pulled the covers up over her head and moved out of the bed. It seemed suddenly very quiet and cold in the room.

Father started a small fire and I watched as he washed

Grandmother's body. Gently, I helped him dress her and lay her on the bed. We stood quietly as the tears fell from our bowed heads. "Your story is safe with me, Grandmother," I vowed, "and I will never forget it." Then, I asked Father about the words Grandmother had spoken to him before she died.

Father's usually solemn face softened and took on a faraway look. He explained how unhappy Grandmother was when her daughter left for the Corpsety to be with him. "I can't blame her for that," he told me. "Your grandmother had an unusual life. Would you like to hear her story?" Without waiting for my response, he began to tell the story of Grandmother's early life. "She had been chosen as a young child to live and work in the house of a Corpse. It was a kind of slavery, but fortunately she had a kind master who let her play and learn with his children. She had a good life as a servant and she was allowed to stay with the household even after she conceived your mother. Grandmother never spoke of her child's father, but I suspect it was the master's son. She had planned for your mother to continue living in the refuge of the master's house as she had—indentured but kindly treated and well fed. Her daughter learned how to read and write and had a happy childhood. But she was headstrong and not content with the life of a slave.

"She escaped to the Corpsety because she wanted to see how others lived. It was in the Corpsety that we met and fell in love. When your mother announced, 'My destiny is in the Corpsety,' Grandmother was heartbroken. She could not understand why her daughter would want to live in such a hateful place, and she was afraid for her. After your mother died giving birth to you, I visited Grandmother to give her the sad news. Without saying a word she put together a small bundle of things and left her master's house forever. 'I want to be with my daughter's child,' she told me. I never blamed her for holding me responsible for her daughter's death. After all, she was right the Corpsety was a terrible place. Now, Grandmother has moved on to the spirit world, and may the Great Mystery bless her soul's journey," he whispered as more tears rolled down his brown cheeks. I watched him cry and my eyes filled with tears, too. I was crying because I missed my grandmother and because I loved my father.

TWO

Walking Away

Even though night had descended, the small group returned to our home after Grandmother's death ceremony. Once again, they sat in a circle listening as Father shared the prophecy Grandmother had given, of my abilities to see and hold the course, and of the need to leave. His words lit a silence under us and for a short time it seemed everyone had lost the power of speech. Father watched while the others sat with their thoughts until a flood of words broke the silence. "We should listen to her advice." "No, it's too soon." "I'm not ready." "We'll never be ready." "Can we really do it?" It went on like this late into the night until I fell asleep on my father's lap. Somehow they managed to agree. They would leave the Corpsety as soon as possible. No one really knew what it was like outside the Corpsety. The outside was known as "the Wild" and it was clouded in secrecy. The Corpsety had declared the Wild a wasteland of desert with polluted water and unknown dangers. Fearful stories had been spread by caravan drivers (those who transported things between Corpsetys) about dangerous animals with teeth and claws that tore flesh. Even worse were the unseen perils they hinted at. Leaving the Corpsety would mean facing the Wild with no protection, no heat blocks to keep us warm, and no security. At least in the Corpsety we could get meager food, water, and heat as long as we worked. The Wild offered no such assurances.

Leaving would be difficult, but not as difficult as trying to get back in. The Trash pits surrounding the Corpsety were inhabited by criminals and outcasts the Corpsety had banished. Security was tightly controlled in an effort to keep them from reentering. Once we left, there would be no going back. Still, Father and his friends decided they were willing to brave the unknown Wild rather than live any longer in the prison of the Corpsety. They were brave and maybe even a little foolish, but they were committed. At night Father pored over books that had belonged to my mother. Books were rarely found among the workers, since most could not read and because Corpses held tightly to their libraries. My mother had taken these books before she left in order to teach Father to read. I guess you could say she stole them. Each night Father read the books out loud to me, and I was happy just to listen to his voice. Most of what he read didn't make sense, but the sound of his voice was soothing and lessened my longing for Grandmother.

The books told stories of life in the Wild, of natural remedies, and of the "ancients," a people who lived long ago according to the natural laws of cooperation, conservation, connection, and community. Father repeated these laws over and over again to himself until they left an indelible mark on me. "We must learn how to live by these laws if we are to survive in the Wild," he told me. "Were the ancients the Free

People Grandmother told me about?" I asked. He replied, "Maybe, just maybe they are, Mariah, and free is what we hope to be too."

That night I had a strange dream. I was surrounded by a group of people with wild, unkempt hair, strange clothes, and smiles on their faces. "We are the ancients," they told me. "We are in your blood. We are in your bones. The ancient ways are not dead but alive in you and in others. It is your task to bring our ways back so that life can begin again." Then they put their arms around me and I felt a wonderful sense of joy, peace, and wonder all at the same time. I woke in the night and blinked my eyes to make sure I was home. There was the familiar torn curtain and Father lying on his pallet, and yet, the otherworldly sense was still strong in me. As I drifted back to sleep, I could feel the arms of the ancients around me, and I had a feeling it would always be so.

I watched as Father's friends discussed how to proceed and noticed a funny thing. Each time there was a disagreement the group would stop and do something called "shaking," which seemed to help. "Why do you do that?" I asked. "It's a way to release tension and clear your head," Father answered. I wanted to know how he had learned how to do this. Father sat me on his knee. "Your mother taught me how to use movement and breathing to calm myself. Would you like to learn how to shake, Mariah?" I nodded my head and he showed me how to stand with my knees slightly bent, letting a shaking movement begin in my feet and move all the way up to my head. "I'm tingling," I shouted. Laughing, Father told me to stop and tell him what else I noticed. My mind was free of thoughts and oddly calm.

"I feel weird," I said. "Ah," he said quietly, "That is a good start, a very good start."

Days, weeks, and months passed and I began to have doubts about leaving. Maybe people were backing out because the trip was too dangerous or too difficult. I spent the days alone now that Grandmother was gone, and it wasn't much fun. I was bored, and the talk of leaving had sparked a desire in me for excitement. One night as I waited for Father to come home his friends began to arrive. By the time Father returned I was frowning. He took me aside and apologized for not letting me know, and then he spoke to the group. "I invited you here tonight to settle on a plan and a time for our escape." A flurry of words came after he spoke. It was pretty much as I had guessed—some were afraid of the dangers and felt they would not survive the challenges. Father asked them to consider why they had risked their lives to come to our home tonight. Our crowded little house went quiet as he waited for someone to respond. After a long silence, a woman shyly spoke up: "When I am with all of you I have hope and I can sense the Great Mystery in my life." Her words must have echoed in the hearts of others because the group nodded and affirmed her words. Everyone agreed that in the vile Corpsety hope could only survive in the connection of community.

"Have we waited long enough for a decision to be made?" Father asked. I looked at the faces around me and saw hopeful excitement as well as fear. The question hung in the air until Father said, "I am willing to leave now, will anyone join me?" Twenty-five people came forward. Although many had chosen to stay behind, twenty-five willing souls would be enough. "It is settled then," Father announced. Those who chose to stay behind shuffled toward the door with sad eyes and stooped shoulders. They were not yet ready. "We will return for you if we are able," Father shouted as they slipped out the door.

Now, the planning began in earnest. We would each bring enough water, food, biscuits, and canned meat to last for several weeks. A bedroll, layers of clothes, matches, candles, and any tools we owned were all we would take with us. Cean, a young group member, offered up boxes of tablets the Corpsety used to purify water. Father brought one of the boxes closer so he could read the label. "Cean, you are right," he said in amazement. "These tablets do purify water." Cean beamed with pride as Father handed the box back to him. With these tablets we could travel without the fear of polluted waters. Our plan was simple. After leaving the Corpsety we would walk until we found a place that suited us. I looked around the circle at the small group of adults and children about to set off for the Wild. We were looking for a way out of the downward spiral.

The group set a time to leave in two weeks. It would take that long to secure the extra food and water for the journey. I watched as the small group said their good-byes. Who were these people I would be travelling with? I had only listened to their voices through the curtain. What would it be like to live with them? We would be entering into the unknown in more ways than one. I drifted off to sleep that night with their faces in my mind's eye but dreamed of things I had never seen. I dreamed great groups of green trees full of life and clear running water with power and energy. I saw dark times ahead but also times of joy and light. It was a magical dream, and like the other one I kept it to myself.

Father sold the meager furnishings of our room to buy extra food and water. We were ready. On the appointed day we said good-bye to the house that had held us for so long. The house belonged to the Corpsety we were leaving behind. The day was warm and the sky was dull as usual. I almost tripped over a man lying in the street who grabbed for my foot. Father pulled me closer to him as we made our way to the outer wall. Before passing through a cracked hole in the wall, we looked back at the Corpsety. All we could see were the tall black smokestacks and the ever-present grayness. I looked at Father; he was tall and strong and I felt safe with him. "Are you ready, Mariah?" he asked with brown eyes twinkling. "Yes," I whispered. "Then, let's be the first to turn our backs and walk away from the Corpsety. Let's go!" We jumped into the hole and were outside in a flash. And so our journey began.

Father and I wandered around as we got our first glimpse of the Trash pits. They were full of rotting debris and desperate people. I could hardly tell the difference between the two. I stayed close to Father as we milled around waiting for the others to arrive. When we were all within sight of each other we started picking our way through the debris, adding bits and pieces of trash to cover the things we carried with us. We could ill afford to be robbed. Fortunately, the Trashers were too busy searching for valuables to pay us any attention.

Beyond the Trash pits the land was bleak and deserted. We stopped to rest and get our bearings and Cean took out a paper map for us to look at. "Where did this come from?" I asked innocently. Cean's face turned red as he admitted he had stolen it from the caravan. "But, I am not really a thief," he stammered, "Well, I mean, I did steal the tablets and this map, but only from the Corpsety. Was that wrong?" "Why don't you tell us your story?" Father gently prompted him. I could tell he was still embarrassed, but with Father's encouragement he launched into his story. Cean's father had taken him to the caravans when he was a boy. He was too young to work so he spent his days snooping around. No one paid much attention to him and they became accustomed to his presence. On one trip, he discovered the purification tablets and map in a leather case that had fallen onto the ground. He quickly emptied the contents and left the case where it had dropped. Cean didn't quite know what he had found, but he guessed anything in a leather case was valuable. He had intended to sell the items, but for some reason he couldn't bring himself to. Father looked at the paper Cean had produced. "This is a map of the caravan routes through the Wild," he said quietly. "Cean, you have brought us the key to our journey. I don't see how we can condemn you." Cean bowed his head in relief as the red flush crawled up his neck again. He was tall and broad shouldered like my father but there the likeness ended, for Cean was young with short reddish-brown hair and bright blue eyes. I liked the way he carried himself with grace and strength.

We headed north, for that seemed to be the place most remote from the trade caravans that crisscrossed the land between Corpsetys. Walking all day, we stopped only to eat a biscuit and drink some water. Both biscuits and water would take on a whole new meaning for us as we moved farther and farther away from the Corpsety.

The dreary mist of the Corpsety continued to follow us, but it had lost its power to oppress. We were headed toward the color of freedom, and whatever color that might be, it would not be gray. Picking up sticks along the way, we stopped for the night and built a fire for warmth and light. There were strange noises in the dark and we drew nearer to the fire after eating. The fire and company of others gave us a sense of security that lasted throughout the night.

THREE

Into the Wild

For several days we walked without much happening, and then on the fifth day we received a visitation. The dense fog we had hoped to leave behind continued to follow us. We were out of the dreaded Corpsety but had lost some of our enthusiasm for the journey. Maybe we were even a little bored. Vene, a stout, middle-aged woman with a loud voice, kept challenging our decision to go north. She went on and on complaining until we all wished she would shut up. Finally, Father called for us to stop and sit in a circle. "We are all equal here," he said quietly. "No one voice counts more than another. Let's reconsider if we want to continue heading north or change directions." He asked each of us to speak, and we were halfway around the circle when out of the fog the Wild attacked us. It was growling and snarling and trying to sink its teeth into our arms and legs. All I could see were yellow eyes. "Children in the center," someone called out, and I was pushed toward the middle of the group. The adults shouted, kicked, threw stones, and waved sticks to fend off the attack. I watched in horror as the Wild seemed to be winning against the exhausted adults. Then, as quickly as it arrived, the Wild disappeared, leaving us unhurt but with a broken sense of security. We were at the mercy of the Wild and ill prepared to defend ourselves.

It was a somber group that gathered around the fire that night. Father talked about being adaptable and called it our greatest strength. "We cannot escape life's challenges," he acknowledged. "Sickness, injury, and even death will happen in the Wild, but we will not be subjected to the needless suffering of the Corpsety." After Father spoke there was silence. Even Vene was quiet. Shyly, I decided to share my dream of trees full of green life and water that sparkled and glowed with power. "Could this be what lies ahead of us?" I asked. Father looked at me and smiled as he said, "Mariah, I don't know what lies ahead, but that is a beautiful vision for you to hold."

I woke at daylight to the strangest sound coming from the sky. The small children were laughing and dancing around me. I rubbed the sleep from my eyes and saw a green tree, almost but not quite as green as I had seen in my dream. The only trees we had seen in the Corpsety were gray. The fog had magically lifted and the sky was a beautiful blue color. The sound was coming from "flying in the air things" that sometimes came down to the ground but not for long. The children wore themselves out trying to catch them. Looking up I felt the strangeness of it all, and when I turned my eyes away I saw Father standing by me. "Mariah, your dream vision must be true, for ahead of us are green trees. You must pay careful attention to your dreams, for they have things to tell us."

The pleasant strangeness of this new visitation brought high spirits and we agreed once more that north was the way to go. I turned for a last look at the dullness we were leaving behind and said good riddance to the Corpsety's blight, which had obscured our sight. Now we were free to claim our own vision.

The sun, which was only a bright spot in the shrouded Corpsety, was now a beautiful yellow orb. We marveled at its warmth as we travelled. I walked next to Illow, who was one of the older members of the group. She was quiet and her feet made hardly a sound as she moved. Illow was tall and spindly but graceful. Her eyes were bright with intelligence and I wondered if she would talk to me. "Tell me about your dream, little one," she called out as we walked. She had called me "little one" and thoughts of Grandmother filled my heart with tears. "What's wrong?" she gently prodded. I shared how much I missed my grandmother and she told me this was as it should be. "When we love someone greatly we miss their presence at first, but if you keep them in your heart they are never far away and you are never alone." I felt her words seep into my soul and was comforted. I smiled to think that Grandmother was with me, and Illow smiled back. I told her about my dream and she nodded solemnly. "You are wise, little one," she said as she patted my head.

We walked tirelessly that day as a new world opened itself to us. Wild colors hung from the plants and delighted our eyes. Small, brown animals scurried fearlessly in between our feet and flying colors moved about our heads. If only we had known what a magical world the grayness obscured. If only everyone knew. Would this loosen the Corpsety's grip? That evening we sat around the fire. Father took out one of his books and Cean's map to show us where we were. He guessed it would take a long time before we reached the heart of the Wild. There were sighs and moans around the circle, but Lexy's laughter rang out beneath the heaviness. Lexy was young with wild red hair and a temper to match. I loved her flamboyant nature. She shouted out, "Who thought we could leave the Corpsety behind so quickly? It held us captive and I, for one, am happy to travel far away from its monstrous grasp." Roz, a friendly, middle-aged woman with boundless energy and kind brown eyes, spoke up. "We should have left years ago; what on earth were we thinking?" "We were not thinking," someone called out, and everyone began laughing. Laughter spread around the circle like a wildfire, and soon our eyes were wet and our hearts were full.

Father opened his book and began reading about the mysterious things we had seen. The flying musical things he called birds inhabited the sky and built nests in trees where they lay eggs. Our presence had caused them to leave their nests to protect their young ones waiting to hatch. "We were attacked by wolves," he explained. "Wolves spend their time hunting in order to survive." Had we been on their menu for dinner, I wondered? Remembering their yellow eyes, I hoped never to see them again. Before my thoughts could go any further, I heard Father's next words: "Outside of the Corpsety life is sacred and all beings hold value. We will have to learn to live with the wild beings in a way that honors us both." No one challenged Father, but people had many different ideas about how we could do this. Sorting them out would take time.

Illow spoke with reverent awe, "I thought I knew what the

Corpsety had taken from me, happiness, my life, my friends, but the loss of the world's beauty I knew nothing about. I had no idea what I was missing. If I die tonight it will all have been worth it." She began to hum and we joined her. A harmony of joy swirled around the circle and flowed out into the night as we added our voices to the Wild. It was hard to believe we had left the Corpsety only a short while ago. We were different people now—the Wild had touched us. I slept that night warmed by the thought of being arounded by beauty.

The next day we headed into a steep area with loose rocks and unstable footing. Our bodies tired quickly as we twisted ankles and bruised our feet on the rocks. Plants scratched our arms and legs while bugs crawled on our flesh. Everywhere we turned we were accosted and misery seemed to follow us. I stayed close to Illow. Although she was old, she had a playful spirit that attracted me. Walking was most difficult for Illow and Grund, who were the elders of our little group. They were past their prime but full of wisdom and passion for the journey. Grund was short with white hair and ears that noticeably stuck out from his head. What I noticed most about him, though, was his keen, gentle eyes. I felt grateful to have Illow and Grund along and saw in them a refuge from uncertainty. They didn't miss a thing and were always ready to hold someone in their steady gaze. Father often consulted with Grund when he was disturbed or confused about things. Grund had been a great friend to Grandmother and I remember he had spoken of her lovingly at her death circle. Grund was the kind of person who was good to have around in a crisis. He was wise, steadfast, firmly rooted to the ground, and a natural leader. He had long ago studied how to survive in the Wild. How he managed this I never discovered, but he knew things that would help us. We were depending on his knowledge and Father's books to guide us.

Grund was deep in discussion with Illow, and I moved closer to hear what they were saying. Illow was telling him about the different plants growing around us, which all looked pretty much the same to me. I followed her when she moved to pick some berries. I wanted to know how she knew about plants. Most likely she had a book, but I was curious. "I learned from my grandmother," she told me, "and she learned from her grandmother going all the way back to the people who called themselves Free." Now I was really curious. "Did you know any Free People?" "No, Mariah," she answered softly, "but in my heart I hold their memory, for it is the Free People who walk with us on this journey. They are the ancestors who will show us the way to create a new life." "Do you talk with them?" I whispered, almost afraid to hear her answer. "Yes, little one, I do, and I think they talk to you too." "I've never heard anything," I told her frankly. "Perhaps you do not know what to listen for. I believe your dreams and visions bring the voices of the ancestors to us." She smiled at me and walked on. Did Illow somehow know of my dream? I had shared it with no one, not even Father. I needed time to think about what she had said. She was a mystery, but it was a mystery I wanted more of.

Our strength was being tested as we walked. Everyone looked tired, and even the children were cranky. I loved the young ones but tonight they were, well, annoying. I guessed we would quickly fall into our pallets, but I was wrong. Father called a circle meeting. In the firelight I noticed Father's long brown hair was starting to turn gray. His eyes were still dark and lively, and I felt their gaze even though I was sitting across the circle. He asked Illow to speak. She told of berries she had found that could be eaten. The Corpsety had warned us about poisoned food and polluted water in the Wild. How could she know such a thing? The group was not convinced by her words. A discussion wound its way around the circle. Who was right? Some believed in the Corpsety while others were skeptical of Illow. In reality, none of us knew the truth of the matter. When the circle returned to Illow she offered the group a solution. She explained that she had learned about plants from her grandmother and asked to be allowed to eat the foods she identified as edible in order to see if they made her sick. She offered this as a "give away" to the group. "We will have to find sources of food in the Wild," she reminded us, "and we need to know what is safe to eat and what is not." Everyone was quiet around the fire as Father asked for agreement or dissent on her proposal. Heads nodded in agreement and we arounded Illow with hearts full of gratitude. I felt the warmth of our connection growing. Next, the talk turned to water.

"If we are careful," Father guessed, "we have six or seven days of water left." Before he could continue anxious talk erupted. "Shouldn't we have found water by now?" some demanded. I watched as fear found its way to our little group. Father invited everyone to stand and shake while Cean began beating a drum he had fashioned from junk he found in the Trash pits. We jiggled, jumped, and shook until our bodies moved beyond the grasp of fear. Sitting down again, we reformed the circle. Cean volunteered to go on ahead to see if he could find water, but Grund pointed out that he could easily get lost. Father suggested we continue to travel in the hope of finding water. No one came forward with other ideas, so Father's suggestion was accepted—but without much enthusiasm.

Another day of endless walking pulled us onward until a fatigue so great we could hardly lift our feet stopped us. We huddled around the fire briefly and then fell into our blankets. Before sleep overtook us we were roused by loud noises coming out of the sky. The trees began twisting and moaning while the wind howled around us. The ground shook and strange noises filled the air and lit up the sky. The wind took on a life of its own, causing everything to fly up into the air as it pushed and pulled at us. In the midst of all this chaos people began to panic and hysterical screams filled the air. Torrents of water fell from the sky as we stood shivering and shaken, wondering what was happening to us. We fell exhausted on the ground in a wet, cold, and miserable heap. I went to sleep with the sound of sobbing in my ears and thoughts of the warm pallet I had left behind the curtain in the Corpsety.

In the morning a huge golden sun rose to greet us. Its mellow light melted even the coldest of hearts and we entered a new day. Grateful to be alive, we built a fire and warmed our soggy blankets before we set out. As we walked we told stories of how we would live when we finally found "our place." Lexy was unusually quiet and subdued this morning. I asked about her silence and she broke into tears. This fierce redhead I thought of as fearless told me last night had terrified her.

Although she hated the Corpsety, she had doubts about her ability to survive in the Wild. Illow and Roz had been listening to our conversation and joined us. "What happened last night is called a storm," Illow explained. "They can be dangerous, but if you have a roof over your head and something that separates you from the outside you are safe. We are vulnerable now because we are traveling out in the open and have no protection from storms or animals." Lexy was shivering now. "What about that unnatural, jagged light?" "That is lightning," Roz explained. "We couldn't see it in the Corpsety because of the grayness." Illow's calm voice comforted Lexy as she assured her that we would become used to a free life in the Wild. With shame in her eyes, Lexy apologized. "I'm afraid I let my fears overtake me." "We all have fears," Illow admitted, "but we also have each other." She motioned for Lexy, Roz, and me to join arms with her and we moved back and forth, swaying gently until the movement shared its peace with us. I was glad to have these women in my life. Illow had used the word free to describe us. Would we become like the Free People Grandmother had told me about? I hoped so.

My mind drifted to thinking of the Corpsety, which seemed far away, and I wondered if we would be the only ones brave enough or crazy enough to escape its grasp. Roz must have read my mind. She began listing all the terrible things she remembered about the Corpsety: dismal grayness, difficulty breathing, lack of work and food, the shacks, the dirt and grime, a constant threat of violence, powerlessness, and wealthy, oppressive Corpses. Now we have blue sky, fresh air, the freedom to roam where we like, and best of all, we have each other. Flinging her arms open as if to embrace it all, she shouted, "If I never live another day, this has all been worth it for me." I looked into her warm, brown eyes and saw a depth of feeling and love that was new to me. The Wild was working some strange magic on us.

That night I dreamed of water . . . wild, untamed water that wouldn't be caught. I was pulled out of sleep abruptly by cries and shouts. There were people weeping and raging at nothing I could see. But there it was. During the night animals had laid waste to our supplies. Some of the biscuits were gone but, more importantly, our water supply was almost wiped out. Many of the plastic bags we had worked so hard to fill in the Corpsety were torn and empty. Now we had only the water we carried with us. Without water we were doomed.

A circle formed to decide what we should do now. First one and then another person talked about wanting to go back to the Corpsety where they had a roof over their heads and water. About half of the group got caught up in doubts and accusations and angry words began flying around the circle. Father, Roz, Illow, and Grund withheld their comments and quietly observed the process. Before it went too far, Father suggested we try shaking. Sullenly, some of the group stood while others remained glued to the ground. Cean began drumming and the shake slowly moved through us until, sitting or standing, everyone was moving. The pulse of the drum took something away and quiet settled over the circle. "We were being killed slowly in the Corpsety," Father declared. "Sure, we had food and water, but never enough. The Corpsety provided just enough for us to continue doing its dirty work. I came on this journey because I want to try to live in a different way. I want to be free to live my life and create a community where we can share our lives." Roz, Grund, and Illow echoed agreement with Father's vision. Lef threw up his hands and declared, "We don't really have a choice. If we turn around now we will be just as vulnerable. I say we go onward!" His words startled the group and they began to talk about working together instead of yearning for the false safety of the Corpsety.

I screwed up my courage and stood to speak. I shared my dream about water and told the group I thought it meant we were close to finding it. Around the circle I saw doubtful looks about the dreams of a child and I hung my head in shame. It was Illow's soft voice that saved me. "Do you remember Grandmother's prophesy that Mariah holds a vision of what is to come? I think we need to carefully consider the wisdom of her words." For now she had allayed the group's distrust, but I feared it wouldn't last. I had probably not heard the end of it.

FOUR

Water Found and Water Lost

The sun shone brightly, making us all the more aware of our thirst. We walked with the weight of lost water on our minds. On and on we travelled, hoping for a miracle. The children cried constantly but no tears flowed from their sunken eyes. Illow had to lean on others to keep going, and all of us were becoming more and more irritable. Finally, we fell to the ground. We had gone as far as we could go. We slept that night where we had fallen without even a blanket to shelter us.

I woke with my ear pressed against the ground. There was a faint sound that reminded me of my dream. In a stupor I stumbled on, not knowing where I was going. No one tried to stop me, not even Father. Was this to be the end for us? Another hot day without water and some of us would surely begin to die. On and on I walked, stopping every so often to put my ear to the ground. The sound was getting louder and pulling me toward it. I came to a large rock wall, which I managed to drag myself over. There, right before my eyes, was deep, green, and wildly moving water. The sound had found me. Here was our water source! Running, stumbling, and crawling, I made my way back to the others. When I got within calling distance, I cried out, "Water! I have seen water." Father and a few others met me as I made it into the camp. "There is water waiting for us," I shouted. My joy was contagious and the others joined in: "We have found water. We are saved." But, finding water was not the same as getting it.

Father, Cean, Lexy, and a few others volunteered to scale the rock wall down to the water. We watched as they climbed and sometimes slid to the bottom. Once the water bags were filled, they began the steep climb back to the top. Holding our breath, we watched as they struggled to find handholds and footholds. We were witness to their courage and dared not turn our eyes away. It happened so quickly I wasn't sure I had seen it at all. With a sick feeling in my stomach I looked again and saw that a young man had slipped and fallen. Father tried to reach him and ended up falling himself. We stood there watching helplessly as they regrouped, and Cean began the descent down to help Father. The young man had not moved and we could see blood staining his shirt. We were shocked to see Cean and Father put his body into the water. This could only mean that he was dead. This particular young man was gentle and sweet. His impish face and crop of blond hair were always to be seen at the front of our troupe. Many times it had been his enthusiasm and energy that kept our spirits high. A moan rose from our lips and tears began to flow. We continued to watch as the small group made their way toward us. They arrived exhausted and dirty from their climb.

Everyone gathered around to ask what had happened. Father explained how the young man had died immediately after hitting his head on the rocks. Since the small group could not carry him up the wall, they decided to put him into the water rather than let his body remain on the rocks. Some group members were angry, saying his body should have been brought back for a proper ceremony. Father had been hurt in the fall and was struggling to stand. Grund asked for silence and the group quieted. "What's done is done. It is not for us to judge a decision made in a moment of crisis," he said. He suggested we spend this night remembering and honoring the young man. Tomorrow we would hold a circle to discuss what to do next. The angry group members continued to grumble but left to prepare the remembering circle. Grund and I went to see about Father.

Illow was applying plants to the wound on his leg. Father's face was drawn and pale but his eyes were still bright. "I'm all right," he told me. Illow cautioned him to stay off the leg tomorrow, which meant the group would have to take a day off. Grund believed it would be good for everyone to rest and regain their strength. A few of us gathered around Grund and he asked for our thoughts about the meeting. Lexy spoke with her usual passion: "People are out of control, they whine and complain and get mad about impossible things. If we don't find a way to keep them in line our plans will be sabotaged." "I hate to say it but I agree with Lexy," Cean added. "The negative group members have too much influence." Roz's face carried a question: "I agree we are all affected by their negativity, but I wonder what is behind it." "Fear is driving it, Roz," Father answered, "and it's fear we must deal with." Illow nodded her head and Grund agreed, saying, "It does us no good to try to control the group, because the reality is we can't. Oh, we could shout at them, give them orders, but their fears would keep coming back to haunt us." Illow suggested we give people a chance to talk about their fears. Then, she motioned for us to leave so Father could rest. I followed Illow out.

"Why didn't we wait to talk at the meeting circle where everyone could hear?" I asked. Illow sat down and I sat down beside her. "Mariah, I think you are ready to start learning some things." Her voice had a faraway quality to it and I was reminded of Grandmother. "There have always been spiritual healers living among the people," she began. "They help others see the possibility of a way of life that is different from the Corpsety." "How do you know if someone is a spiritual healer?" I wanted to know. Illow smiled and continued, "They have a strong connection to the natural laws of nature and live in communion with others and the natural world. They use only what they need and conserve the rest while valuing community and connection as the important core of life."

Illow was quiet but I had lots of feelings whirling around inside me. It was hard to find words to fit what I was experiencing. "These laws you speak of—I don't see many people following them. In the Corpsety the Corpses have more than they need while most people don't have enough. Conflict and competition are the norm, and no one seems to be connected to anyone else. The Corpsety's way of life doesn't follow these laws and sometimes our group members don't either. How can these be laws if no one follows them?"

Illow's face was thoughtful as she said, "Remember, the role of a healer is to help others see another way. Your father,

Roz, Grund, and I are spiritual healers because we know in our bones that the natural laws are true. We gather to talk so we can better understand how to accompany others as we move toward a new way of being together. We honor the truth of life, which says, 'We will all make it together or none of us will make it.'" "Why were Lexy and Cean at the meeting?" I asked. "They are drawn to our way of thinking and want to learn from us," she explained. "Anyone is free to join us but few do. Ours is not an easy path, and it's a calling that emerges from within." "What about me?" I whispered. Illow looked at me with soft eyes and said, "I think you already know the answer to that question, Mariah." She was right. I did know the answer. The natural laws were the only way for me to live. The strange dream vision had awakened me to the wisdom in my bones. Hesitantly, I asked what the rest of the group thought of us, for I feared they might be resentful. "You may have heard them refer to us as the wise ones," she answered. "We are accepted because our voices hold no more weight than anyone else's. We do not force our views on others. We offer our presence, our knowledge, and our way of being. It is not our role to force others to change. Our responsibility is to help others see another way. We hope that separated from the corruption of the Corpsety people will once again be able to see and live by the natural laws." Then, she motioned for me to move. "That's enough for now. Let's go help with the evening meal."

My head was spinning and yet I was oddly quieted by the thought that I was to be a spiritual healer. Our meal was quick and silent since the remembering circle was on everyone's mind. We gathered around the fire and Grund began by sharing how courageous the young man had been. Others talked about his gentleness and joy in playing with the children. His passion for helping others came through in the stories and tears flowed freely as we shared our sadness at his passing. Vene was especially upset. She stomped her feet on the ground and demanded to know why such a promising, gentle young man had to die. "It's not fair!" she shouted. Group members held her close as she wrestled with the reality of his death and her anger. We continued to tell stories until our emotions and memories were spent. Grund gave thanks for the young man's presence in our lives and for the stories he had given us. The ceremony came to a close after each of us sent our blessing for his journey back to the Great Mystery.

That night I had another dream visitation which told of the place where we would make our home. The place had a stream running through its center with a thick, green, inviting forest on one side and rich brown soil on the other. Higher up was the tallest hill I had ever seen. The place sang sweetly and it called to me. I woke with the sound of sweetness in my ears.

FIVE

The Communion of the Forest

Father was carried to the circle on a pallet, looking weary but resolute. Roz invited everyone to talk about their feelings and Vene jumped up to say that she was angry about all the hardships she had endured. We hadn't planned well enough, and she feared we were going to die before finding a place to settle. She preferred the Corpsety, where at least she knew what to expect. Berd, her partner, and several others shouted out their agreement. I began to fear that people were going to leave. Then, a young couple came forward to speak of their overwhelming fear of the unknown. In the Corpsety they had looked forward to the Wild with excitement, but now they were scared. They did not want to go back to the hopelessness of a slow, sure death in the Corpsety, but they could not go forward without something to hold onto.

Father surprised me by rising to speak. "I too am fearful," he acknowledged and paused while a thick silence settled over the circle. "Everything we have encountered is new to me, and I have been shaken to my very core by the events of yesterday. But, I can face whatever comes as long as I have the support and help of everyone around the circle. Without that I cannot continue, for I am only one person, and I need all of you to be strong." He invited the group to look at the trees. "Trees live together in a community called a forest. No matter how strong or large or beautiful a tree might be it can never compete with a forest. You see, the forest is a place of refuge where trees grow together by nurturing, supporting, and protecting each other from the vagaries of wind, rain, and sun. Wrathful winds do little damage to a forest because of the support trees offer one another. Torrential rains that might uproot a single tree find it difficult to move a tree in the forest. When the sun's heat bears down and there are no clouds of relief, the trees share water and are saved. The forest is a sanctuary, a place where trees can grow and thrive. Any tree deprived of its forest is less than it could be and is infinitely vulnerable. And so it is with people too. We are all more when we are together in community. We are a place of refuge for each other when we grow and nurture and support one another. Our collective presence offers us safety from the vagaries of nature. Together we are wise, we know things that none of us could know individually because our collective mind is joined with that of the Great Mystery. We may all act as leaders or followers at times, but we must never forget that it is the whole, the community, that sustains us and provides the wisdom and strength we need to survive. In the Corpsety there are no forests and no communities, and that is why I never want to go back there."

After Father spoke, there was silence broken only by soft crying. We stopped to eat and the sharing of food lightened our mood. Back in the circle Vene was the first to speak. "The sharing today has moved my heart. It's fear that calls me back to the Corpsety and I am caught in its trap." Others agreed with Vene; there was no way around fear. Nevertheless, the sharing had worked its alchemy and loosened fear's grip on our souls. Lef, an middle aged member of the group, acknowledged that sharing made the fear somehow easier to bear, and Father smiled and put his arm around Lef. "Are we all together then?" he asked. And so it was that we decided to continue the journey together. Roz called for shaking. Simply moving our bodies seemed to generate genuine happiness, and I could see light returning to faces. In the Corpsety we didn't dance together. I was curious about why this was. Perhaps movement and joy cannot survive in a place so divorced from the Wild.

Warmed with the happiness of shaking, and facing our fears, we began to talk about water. Lef spoke first. As he stood I noticed how tall he was. His receding hair was brownish gray and he had guarded gray eyes that could throw sparks. Lef had a lot of passion, and it often got the better of him. He hated the Corpsety with a vengeance, but his fears about making it in the Wild were just as powerful. He brought tremendous energy to the group but also great fear. "We have to find a supply of water or we are sunk," he said forcefully. People nodded their heads in agreement and Lef sat down. I could feel an undercurrent of fear beginning to rise again.

Slowly the discussion wound its way around the circle. Water gathered from the river would last for maybe a week if we consumed it carefully. Scaling the rocks again to get water from the ravine was not feasible. We would risk losing people each time we tried it. Father believed we needed to keep walking until we came to accessible water, but his idea elicited groans from the group. People were tired of walking. As if it had a will of its own separate from me, my mouth blurted out that I had had another dream. Shocked at myself and embarrassed, I stood to face the group. All eyes turned to me and shakily I told of my dream vision. I described the stream winding through a flat area with a large forest on one side. I told of the broad swath of rich brown land on the other side with a great hill behind it. Then, I shared my feeling that this place was waiting for us to come to it.

A murmur started around the circle and questions began slipping out of people's mouths. "Mariah, you are a child, how do we know you are not making all this up?" "How come only you get dreams about the future?" "Maybe your dream about the water was just a coincidence." With each question I felt smaller and smaller until I wished I could disappear. Once again, it was Illow who saved the day. She changed the direction of the group's energy by asking everyone to take a few moments to consider my dream vision and what it might be telling us. "We all have the same dream language," she said, "and maybe it will speak to us too." When all eyes were closed, Illow led us through an imaginary journey where we found our settling place. After a time of quiet, Illow invited the group to open their eyes and share what they had experienced. One by one people shared their visions and how good they made them feel. Even Lef, who had a hard time settling down and getting quiet, said he had experienced an image that gave him hope. Much to my surprise, Lef and others identified details of my dream that I had not revealed. Did we truly share each other's dreams and visions? If so, then perhaps there was a Wild inside ourselves we had yet to discover.

We spent the better part of the day in discussion and still had made no decision. Father proposed we continue walking for a week or as long as our water held out. Vene wanted to know what we would do if we didn't find water. I thought Father would respond, but it was Illow who rose to speak. "We are all part of the miracle that is life," she said. "We do not know and cannot know the future in its entirety. We have no way of knowing if we will find the food and water we need or if we will die trying to escape the Corpsety. What I know is this: I am committed to trying to create a better life, a free life, a life that is lived in harmony and balance. The life we were meant to live. For me this is an honorable goal worth dying for. We have been given a sign, a vision that a place is out there waiting for us. I'm going to put my faith in that and give the outcome over to the Great Mystery where it belongs."

Illow's words were powerfully spoken and they hung over the group like a dark cloud. Her message was clear: our lives were at risk and now we needed faith. Lef stood and approached Illow. He thanked her for reminding him of the Great Mystery, the source of all goodness, and for showing him a way through his fears about dying. "The journey is our life now," he said, "and any outcome is better than the imitation life we had in the Corpsety." After Lef spoke, each group member thanked Illow for her words and agreed to travel for three more days and reassess on the fourth day. We stood in the circle with our arms around each other's shoulders while our bodies moved back and forth like a small forest bending and groaning with the winds of change. Like the forest we would offer nurturance, wisdom, protection, and support to each other. When the swaying ended, we had come to a place of acceptance. We were ready to face whatever came next.

That night we warmed canned stew and biscuits over the fire, and it had never tasted so good. In the Corpsety food tasted dull and bland, but in the Wild even canned food took on a new flavor. I was surprised by the intensity of my feelings as I looked around the fire at the faces of our group. I was growing to love them, even the ones who irritated me, as surely as I loved my father. I noticed Father's face was pale and drawn, and I hoped it was only tiredness I saw. I put my arms around his neck and told him I had prayed he would get well soon. He held me close and said it would take more than a fall to take him out. I smiled at his words; he was still the same old Father despite his injuries. I watched as Illow applied herbs to his wound and then drifted off to sleep.

The next days were a blur of walking, resting, eating, and falling exhausted onto the ground at night. Our loads were lighter but our hearts grew heavier each day we didn't find water. The children and some adults were beginning to rest almost as much as they walked. We couldn't go on this way much longer. Stopping early on the third day we called a circle meeting.

Father faced the weary group and honored their courage and endurance. He acknowledged his own weariness and opened the circle for others to speak. Many of the group members could hardly talk they were so exhausted. It was Cean who gave voice to our feelings: "I am afraid of not finding our place but I am content to know I have experienced life the way it was meant to be lived. I have pushed my body and soul to the limit and found I could carry on. I have shared everything with others and found great joy in doing so. I have made my peace with the Great Mystery and can accept whatever happens now." With solemn faces, the group roused at Cean's words and agreed to continue our journey into the unknown.

The children called for Cean to play his drum. We wondered where they found the energy? Laughing, we let ourselves be drawn into the dance under a full, yellow moon. In a strange way we were happy even though we were facing death. We were arounding each other as we embraced the unknown, and that made all the difference.

SIX

Following the Dream

I woke before the sunrise with another dream hovering over my head. Once again I found myself in the place we would call home, only this time someone was calling out "Go left, go left." I was frightened, but the dream gave me a clear sign not to go left. I saw a long curve angling to the right and I knew this was the way to go. I watched the sun weave orange into the sky as it turned itself into a fiery red ball. The strangeness of the sun's color mixed with my dream and I cried softly. Father moved beside me and wrapped his arms around my shoulders. I told him of my dream and he gave me a smile. "It's curious how your dreams come just at the right time. I'll keep my eyes open for the direction of your dream."

Illow arrived with her arms full of berries while we were eating our usual breakfast of biscuits and water. She encouraged us to try the berries, which tasted strange and stained our fingers purple. The children had fun spreading the color all over their bodies. Laughing at their transformation, we set out for the day. Just past noontime the sky began to darken and we heard thunder in the distance. Uneasiness spread to our feet and we walked faster. I looked back at the little ones and saw they were having a hard time keeping up. I turned around to tell the group to slow down and saw the curve of my dream. The curve barely had time to register in my mind when pandemonium broke loose.

The wind blew wildly while thunder and lightning rained down on us. The clouds swirled as if they were being stirred in a pot. The group veered off to the left, running for the cover of trees. Father shouted above the noise to go the other way. The group stopped and all but Vene and Berd followed Father. As the group changed direction, I heard Vene and Berd shout, "Go left, go left, the trees will protect us from the storm." Father and the rest of us continued running to the right even as we saw a huge bolt of lightning come down from the sky. It struck a large tree that Vene and Berd were standing near and we watched in horror as the tree fell on them. Afraid for our lives, we continued to run in the direction of my dream, away from the trees. When the storm clouds parted we found ourselves standing on a broad plateau facing a giant hill. Below us was a beautiful stream of clear water. The green forest, where Vene and Berd had taken shelter, lay on the other side of the stream. My eyes widened as I took in the sight and a great cry rose up among the group. Here was our place. The joy and horror of finding our place while losing Vene and Berd were beyond words. Our voices unleashed a human storm of fear, sorrow, joy, and frustration. Finally, exhausted by the storms of soul and nature, we lay down on the soft ground and let the sun work its magic on our bodies. Cradled in the comfort of the sun's gentle warmth, we came back to ourselves and to an acceptance of our loss. One by one, we rose to explore our surroundings. Illow and I went to look for food. Grund left to study the stream while others wandered off to look for wood. Father and a small group went in search of a place where we might find shelter for the night. One way or another we all began to make this place our home.

SEVEN

Home in the Heart of the Wild

Illow and I had to pass through the stream to get to the forest.
I could see through the water to the rocks at the bottom.
This water didn't seem to bear any relation to the water in
the Corpsety, which was brown, brackish, and foul smelling.
"How could this water be so completely different?" I blurted
out. Illow's face was solemn. "The Corpsety is topsy-turvy,"
she explained. "Everything there is turned upside down and is
not as it should be. Here we see the world as it rightly is, and
hopefully we can build our lives around it rightly." "How will
we know what rightly is?" I wanted to know. Illow smiled at me
and said, "We are learning, little one, each step of the way, we
are finding our right way."

In the forest, Illow looked under plants, dug up roots,
picked leaves, and studied the trees. We came out with arms
full of nuts, berries, roots, and leaves. There would be plenty
of new foods to eat with our biscuits. They might taste strange,
but we could eat them with confidence in Illow's selection.

After dinner, our thoughts returned to Vene and Berd.
Removing their bodies from under the tree would be

impossible, so burning was not an option. We would return tomorrow to the place where they had fallen and do our remembering. Their bodies would be protected under the tree until they returned to the earth.

The chaos of the storm brought the need for shelter to everyone's mind. Father and Grund had found a place nearby which was deep enough to protect us from the wind and rain. It would be crowded but adequate. Relief spread around the circle. "How soon can we move?" someone asked. "If we work on cleaning out the rocks and debris, I think we could have it ready in a few days," Father replied. Water was no longer critical since we now had a source along with the purification tablets, but food was another matter.

Someone mentioned our dwindling supply, and all eyes turned to Illow. She stood slowly. Her tall, thin body and piercing eyes held everyone's attention. She said, "Mariah and I have begun to explore the forest, and at first glance it seems to be a rich source of food. Today we found berries, nuts, roots, and leaves that are edible, and there may be other things we have not yet identified. I believe I saw trees which will bear fruit later in the year. In order for us to survive, everyone will need to learn how to identify and gather food. It's also possible that we will be able to plant our own gardens," she said with a sparkle in her eye. A gasp of surprise went around the circle. "Before Mariah's grandmother died, she gave me a box of seeds taken from her old master's house. There are seeds for corn, beans, squash, and other things I don't recognize. I don't know if the seeds are still viable, but I'm willing to plant them and see. If the seeds germinate we would have another food source and seeds for years to come. So we are not as desperate for food as it might seem." The circle came alive with buzzing excitement. Grandmother had given us the gift of life in the form of seeds! Father's voice rang out over the noise: "I can just imagine Grandmother is laughing at us right now. Will she never cease to surprise me?" Everyone burst out laughing, and some of us started rolling around on the ground we were laughing so hard. "What shall we call this garden?" Father shouted. "Grandmother's garden," a chorus of voices rang out. In just this way Grandmother became part of our new home. Grandmother's garden would be among our first projects.

I made my pallet late that night. Looking up at the stars I realized how much I would miss their company when we moved into the shelter. The stars were part of my family now. I promised myself I would continue to sleep under them sometimes. In the morning Father pulled me aside to talk. "Mariah, your dream saved us yesterday. I think the others should know." I trusted Father's judgment so I warily agreed.

We walked back to the place where the tree had fallen and taken with it the lives of Vene and Berd. The tree was enormous. All we could see of Vene and Berd were a hand and a foot. It was sad to see such a magnificent tree brought low along with Vene and Berd. We built a fire and sat down to tell their stories. Some expressed anger that they had not heeded Father's call. I spoke to remember Vene's kindness to me after Grandmother's death. Berd was remembered as a man of great talent who could fix most anything. Both were honored for their strong relationship and a passion for doing things their way. They had died as they had lived, following their own path. With tears and laughter we remembered their presence in our lives. We stood to sway together after we had given our blessings, and movement invited acceptance into the circle. Lef closed the ceremony by thanking Berd and Vene for their presence in our lives and for the stories they left us. They were in the arms of the Great Mystery now.

Walking back to camp, I got the chance to ask Father how he managed to stay calm when the chaos of a meeting swirled around him. He answered with a question: "Why do you think we have so many meetings, Mariah?" "To make decisions," I offered tentatively. "Well, you are right, Mariah, making decisions is part of the answer, but not all of it. We also meet to share our thoughts and be listened to. Each of us needs to feel we are heard and respected by others. And, meetings help us decide what problems we are facing. Sometimes people rush to make a decision before they know what the problem really is. We need to listen to each other in order to sort out all the possibilities. Perhaps the most important purpose of our meetings is to give us a place to connect with each other. A long time ago, I learned that we each have our own unique intelligence, energy, and way of seeing things. Only when we work together can we tap into this wisdom and find the best solutions. Grund and Illow taught me how to listen to others and resist my desire to tell them what to do or try to control them. Once I learned this, I could be calm in the face of most anything that came up in a group."

I was still confused. "But, what about when they are wrong?" "No one is wrong, Mariah. It's just that sometimes people can't see the whole picture. Those of us who see the bigger picture have a responsibility to stay with others until they see can more broadly." "I don't think I will ever learn how to do this," I murmured with my head bowed. "I am too impatient and critical of others." Father put his hand under my chin and pulled my face up to look at his. "Mariah, you are learning little by little. This is how it was for me too. I had to learn how to manage my feelings before I could think clearly and act wisely. It will happen for you, too, just wait and see," he said quietly. "You are already wise beyond your years."

He put his arm around my shoulders and we walked back to the camp and up to the area where the shelter stood. Everyone was working to clear the rocks and rubble, and by the end of the day good progress had been made. I prepared to spend my last night under the stars. We had arrived where we wanted to be: far away from the Corpsety in the heart of the Wild.

We adjusted to sharing close quarters, and in the time that followed we learned how to gather food, catch fish, and hunt small animals. Soon, we needed something to hold our food and water. Using leaves and mud we shaped crude containers that often collapsed under the weight of our inexperience. Laughter was our constant companion. We were learning how to create a life, and that brought us joy. Our lives took on a rhythm dominated by the rising sun, darkness, and vagaries of weather. We were never bored. In the evenings we sat around the fire telling stories and envisioning the future. It was here one night that I shared my dream about the curve and the direction to take. The other group members thanked me for sharing my gift with them, and a tiny bit of my fear of rejection slipped away. Often we heard wolves and other wild animals roving around our shelter, but as long as we kept the fires going they stayed away. In this place of relative security we began preparing for the future. The Corpsety held no future, and it was strange to think of, but here it was, staring us in the face.

What would the weather be like in this new place? We had no idea what to expect. Since we had arrived, the temperature had been mild. The sun was sharing its warmth with us. One day it began to rain, and it rained the next day and the next and the next, until we grew tired of sitting in the shelter. Our bodies needed to bend and stretch and our minds needed space to breathe, so we moved out into the rain. I was enjoying the feel of warm water trickling down my scalp when I heard Lef shouting. Running toward his voice, I came to the stream, but it was not the stream I knew. No longer was it a gently flowing body of water. It had turned into a wild torrent, determined to take back the land around it. I thought I knew the stream well. I had spent many afternoons loving its joyful ripples and gentle rhythms. The stream I saw today was entirely different, and I didn't like it. I turned to Father for comfort and told him the stream had become a monster. "Mariah, the stream will be calm and gentle again, and sometimes it will return to this chaotic state. This is the natural way of life. Life is always changing and showing us its many different sides. I am glad to see this side of the stream, for it tells me we should not locate our shelters too close to it." I listened to his words and wondered if I had a wild side that would cause me to overflow my banks and take me for a ride one day. I left my thoughts behind the moment I heard shouts that one of the children had fallen into the stream. Cean jumped into the water and caught the child. Quick as a flash, Father and Grund extended a long tree branch for him to grab.

It seemed that Father and Grund would not be able to reach Cean and then, just as he was headed for a large rock, Cean grabbed the branch and went under the water with the child in tow. Father and Grund pulled as hard as they could until Cean and the child emerged near the stream's edge. We pulled them out of the water and up on the bank, getting muddy and wet in the process. Cean was bruised and bleeding but his wounds were not serious. The child, Se, had blood in her hair and was moaning and breathing with difficulty.

Se was Grund's granddaughter. He had taken her in after her parents disappeared. This was not unusual; people often disappeared in the Corpsety never to be seen again. I had not seen Grund cry, and now his sobs filled my heart with sorrow. Grund had lost his wife and children to the Corpsety. It didn't seem fair that the river would take his only grandchild. In this moment, Father's words came back to me: "The Wild is dangerous and sometimes it takes lives, but always, always, it gives us life in return. The Corpsety takes life but gives nothing in return."

Illow came over to help. She listened to Se's heart, felt her pulse, and whispered in her ear. She directed Grund to carry Se to the shelter. Illow washed Se's head carefully and looked at the wound. She had a large gash in the back of her head. Illow used a knife to cut away her hair and put sticky goo on the wound. "What's that sticky stuff?" I asked. Ever the teacher, Illow took a moment to answer me. "This is

honey I took from the bees and mixed with healing herbs."
Illow made a place for Se away from the fire and covered her
with a blanket. "Now, we will wait with her and pray until
she returns to us or leaves," Illow said quietly. Grund joined
Illow and they sang songs and whispered in Se's ear all night.
I wished I knew what they were whispering.

The rain continued into the next day and we sat around
halfheartedly making baskets and pots. Late in the afternoon
the rain stopped and Father suggested we shake. Cean played
his drum and gratefully we began to move our bodies and shake
our souls. Afterwards, we moved outside. "Why don't we begin
to plan for the future?" Father shouted. Everyone gathered
around him and shouted back, "What do we need to do?"

Illow spoke of food. "We will not starve here," she began.
A collective sigh of relief interrupted her. It was good to hear
those words. She continued, "There is plentiful food, and as
long as everyone helps with the collecting and preserving of
foods I think we will be OK. I cannot know for sure, but that
is my best guess."

'What about water?" someone called out. Father responded.
He had read about a purification system in one of the books
using a series of canals that ran water through rocks, sand, and
vegetation. He could see purification canals running through
the community much like a stream. In the Corpsety part of the
water problem was a waste problem, he told us. We would also
need to build pits to keep our waste out of the water.

Then, Father explained that Cean would speak for Grund.
Se had made the passage back to life, but she was weak and
wanted Grund at her side. He could not deny her, and we

didn't want him to. Se's recovery was important to all of us. Cean stood excitedly to talk about shelters and shared an idea Grund had seen in a book long ago. Shelters could be hollowed out of the ground with the support of wood and stone. The group seemed supportive, and he continued enthusiastically. "Where should we locate the shelters?" he asked. The group had lots of ideas. Some wanted to locate up on the tall hill that Grund identified as a mountain, while others favored the forest. A few liked the shelter we were in now. All who spoke seemed to expect they would have their own private place. When Lexy suggested we could not possibly build that many shelters, a groundswell of voices defended the need for privacy. I watched as the enthusiasm on Cean's face withered. Here we go again, I thought. In the midst of this tumult Father spoke. "I've been thinking," he said. "We will be creating a new kind of community, a community radically different from the Corpsety where we were alone and isolated from each other." He began to draw outlines in the dirt with a stick. "Unlike the Corpsety, I expect a large part of our day will be spent outside. A common community shelter could be built between the mountains and stream. This shelter would provide a place to hold meetings, cook, care for children, and create things we need. We could also build two shelters on either side of the community house for sleeping." A murmur started vibrating around the circle and Father held up his hand to continue. "In time we could build four small shelters where people could go when they were ill or giving birth, newly partnered, or just needing time alone. If four are not enough we could build more. I like the idea of being together most of the time and being alone some of the time. This turns the Corpsety's model on its head, and I think it makes us stronger." With that said, he sat down.

The circle came alive with nervous chattering. "How could we live this way?" "We can't possibly get along living so close together!" Chaos broke out again. It seemed chaos was always close on our heels just waiting to trip us up. I looked at Grund, Illow, Roz, and Father to see how they were taking all of this. They continued to sit quietly as if unaffected. Hours went by and nothing was accomplished. Still, the wise ones listened. The group became tired, and when the last person had returned to the shelter it was late. The wise ones stayed to talk and Cean, Lexy, and I stayed too.

Cean could hardly contain himself. "Why can't they see that Thomas offered by far the best solution?" Who is Thomas? I thought. Then I laughed; he was talking about Father—for a moment I had forgotten his name. I piped in with how silly some of their ideas were. Cean wondered if we shouldn't just build our own place and let them see for themselves how wrong they are. Grund held up his hand to stop us. "What is the first natural law?" he asked. Cean sheepishly answered, "The law of cooperation." Grund looked at me and asked, "Would it be hard to cooperate with someone who had silly ideas?" "It would be hard," I admitted. "Yes, Mariah, it would be hard and maybe even impossible." Grund acknowledged that we could go our own way and create a community based on our knowledge, but that would be going against the natural laws of community, connection, and cooperation. "There are not many of us," he said. "If we break into smaller and smaller groups, how long do you think any of us will survive?" "Not long," Cean and I replied in unison as Grund continued. "We have a better chance of surviving when we work together. Once people begin to believe they can exist on their own they are doomed. The Corpsety used the fallacy of the 'strong individual' to keep people divided and weak. The natural laws promote life and survival. The natural law of connection tells us that we all rise up or we all fall down together. We intend to rise up together. That is why we work so hard to live by the natural laws even when they seem impossible. We listen and respect each person's attempt to understand a problem and find solutions. Nothing is more important to us than our ability to cooperate, work, live, and survive together. We let people talk until they have said everything they need to say; and we stay with the process until a solution is found. This is part of our responsibility as wise ones. By staying with the group, we model the art of connection and cooperation."

Illow interrupted to remind us we needed to eat and rest for tomorrow's circle. Cean and I tried to apologize for our lack of insight but Grund stopped us. "There is no need to apologize. There is no harm in making mistakes, for that is how humans learn, and you are both in the process of learning. Next time you hear a group member say something that is not well thought out or attend a meeting that drags on and on, what will you do?" he asked. I was first to respond: "I'll see myself tethered to the others so as to remember I can't get anywhere unless they are going with me." We waited in silence for Cean to respond. Rubbing his chin, he finally spoke: "I'm going to pay close attention to my thoughts and feelings, so they don't lead me astray and prevent me from hearing what others have to say." Grund nodded his head and said, "You have learned something from your mistakes and that is good."

An exceedingly strange dream came that night to confuse me. I kept trying to stand, but the ground shook under my feet and I fell down. I woke late in the morning with a sense of unease and touched the ground. Sitting up, I rubbed my eyes and saw the others moving in the direction of the circle. I jumped up and hurried to join them without stopping to eat. The meeting quickly erupted into arguing and shouting and continued that way until we broke for our noon meal.

I poured a large bowl of purple berries and sweet nuts to fill my empty stomach. Over time, I had become accustomed to the Wild's food and enjoyed the many flavors it offered. Illow joined me as I ate. "How are you?" she asked. "I still catch myself judging others," I told her. "The important thing is to recognize it," she counseled. "Just noticing your thoughts will help you to change." I was still confused and said, "But what do we wait for?" "We wait for people to come up with better solutions." "What if they never get to a good solution; do we wait forever?" I complained. Illow looked at me and sighed. "I've grown old and have forgotten how I used to struggle through meetings. Would you like to know how I made it through?" I nodded my head so hard my neck cracked. Illow laughed and shared how she had found the process easier if she became very curious. "More than anything, my curiosity helped me understand a problem from many different sides. I suppose this was not really the answer you were hoping for," she said abruptly. Now it was my turn to smile. I said, "I'm finding what I want is not always what I need." We walked arm in arm to the meeting and I found myself leaning on her. We were growing closer with each passing day.

The group had come to one conclusion. Locating in the forest would not work because of storms and falling trees. Lef asked Grund and Father what they thought about the mountain site. Grund acknowledged the value of the mountain as a lookout but suggested it would create hardships if we lived there when the weather turned cold. He pointed out how difficult it would be to stay warm in the higher elevation when the winds blew strongly. And, we would have to carry water and food up to the area. After Grund spoke there was a long silence, which lasted so long I began to feel uncomfortable. Spontaneously, people began talking again, and Lef suggested we go around the circle to see if there was agreement. At long last the group had reached consensus. We would build in the site Father had suggested. A tough decision had been made. It seemed that we could create a common future. The wise ones were right. The process does teach us how to live according to the natural laws.

We began the next day with singing. Although the songs held no words, our voices joined in spontaneous harmonies. The sound resonated in the clear morning air, inviting optimism into our circle. Once again, Father asked for discussion about building shelters. Sert, a middle-aged woman who was quiet but also forceful and dynamic, spoke up. "As you all know I am a solitary person, and don't talk much, but I like the idea of sharing living space. I do not think it will be easy for me or for any of us, and I think it's the way people are meant to live. I remember sleeping next to my parents when I was a little girl and feeling warm and secure. When we began our journey by sleeping around the fire together I noticed the same feeling of warmth and security. I hate to think about losing this feeling and going back to sleeping by myself." Before she could sit down, the circle came alive. Part of the group acknowledged the wisdom of her words while others thought it was just wishful thinking. I watched the focus shift from a few shelters to individual ones based on the idea that living together was impossible. Father asked us to identify the barriers to living together and two emerged: a lack of privacy and problems with conflict. The barriers were real, he reasoned. Then he asked how many shelters we could build before the weather turned cold and reality began to set in. The group agreed that building two lookouts, a community center, and two sleeping shelters might be possible before the cold weather came, but no more than that. I saw furrowed brows and frowns on people's faces as they quietly thought about their choices. Giving up the old ways of living did not come easily. The day slipped away and darkness fell on us as we ended our meeting, once again, without resolution.

The wise ones met again. Grund honored what a profound change we were asking the group to make. "They have been living alone, or nearly alone, for most of their lives," he said. "Making the change to a communal life seems impossible." Lexy's eyes were throwing sparks, and when she opened her mouth I was sure fire would come out. "Nonsense, they've been living communally ever since they left the Corpsety, what is all their whining about? It's not new to them at all!" "Can you say that in another way?" Illow asked. Lexy calmed down and thoughtfully began again, "I guess they don't realize they are already living communally. Why don't we ask them to try living together for a trial period? After all, they have been living in close quarters for quite some time and the problems they imagine have not come about." "Bravo, Lexy," we called out. She had given us a good way around the problem. If the group agreed to try living together this winter, perhaps we could reassure them by promising to reassess in the spring. Now that we had a plan for tomorrow, we could rest easy.

Why was Father shaking me awake in the middle of the night? I opened my eyes wide in order to see in the dark. Father was still asleep beside me. I tried to stand but the ground moved and I fell on top of Father. "Stay on the ground," Father shouted for all to hear. The shaking didn't last long but it came in waves. We could hear boulders crashing down off the mountain, and I had visions of being crushed under their weight. Then, as quickly as it had started, the shaking disappeared and we were left to stand with shaking legs. How many mysteries did the Wild hold? We had seen winds that bowed the forest, rains that turned a quiet stream into a raging torrent, and now shaking that loosened great stones and rolled them down the mountainside. I would never take the stillness of the ground for granted again.

We joined arms and swayed to calm and ground our shaken spirits, and then we gave voice to our fears. Thinking it was the right thing to do, I shared my dream about the shaking ground. People looked at me strangely, some with fear in their eyes. Father tried to quell the rising tide of voices by reminding people of my other dreams which foretold things we needed to know, but his words just made things worse. I was blamed for not letting the others know this was coming. As I shrank back from the group's intense anger, Father, Grund, and Illow came to my side to lend support. Illow spoke to the group. "Mariah's gift comes from the Great Mystery. It is not ours to judge even though we may not understand it. Her dreams have vision, but she doesn't always understand their meaning or know how to share them. I ask you to honor her gift, and I call on Mariah to tell us of her dreams so we can learn from them." I was trembling, afraid of the group's rejection, and I moved closer to the wise ones. Cean joined me and put his hand on my shoulder for support. I looked up at him nervously. This was an important moment for me in the group. Either they would finally accept me and my gift or reject me. There was some hemming and hawing but no one spoke. Cean called out, "Do you want Mariah's dreams or not?" I watched as each person hesitantly nodded their head. With relief, I quit holding my breath and let out a sigh of gratefulness. I would be accepted after all. Father ended the session with these words: "So, it is decided that Mariah will tell us of her dreams and we will listen without judgment." I had been shaken for a second time that day and my legs were unsteady. Cean gently helped me back to the circle.

The shaking earth and my dream set the tone for the day, and people were less argumentative. Perhaps everyone realized just how much we needed each other in this strange new land. Lef summarized our predicament. "It's clear we can't build enough shelters for all of us, but I don't see how we can live together." Roz asked the group to think about how they had managed all these weeks together with no privacy, sleeping next to each other at night, and working side by side each day. Once again it was Lef who offered his thoughts. "We managed because we knew it would come to an end at some point." "OK," Roz acknowledged, "but *how* did you manage?" The buzzing of voices rose. I was getting used to the sounds that went around the circle: buzzing excitement, electric shouting, fearful whispering, raucous anger, and the hum of agreement. It was as if the circle had a life and language of its own. A woman's voice brought my attention back to the group. "We were friendly but also mindful of the need to let others have their own space, and we quickly learned who liked to talk and who liked to be left alone." Another person added, "We were gentle in our approach, and when we got upset we were clear about what was bothering us."

"So we have found some good ways to deal with close quarters and conflict," Roz concluded. The group nodded their heads and Roz continued, "Why don't we try living in two shelters this winter and then reassess in the spring?" Surprised, the group considered this. The air filled with the hum of voices as they came to agreement. They would give this "trial period" their best effort and later they could debate its merits.

Father congratulated everyone on making good progress. "We will need to work hard to build lookouts, a community center, and two sleeping shelters before winter arrives." At most, he figured, "we will have a few months before the cold arrives." Now he came to the last issue of importance—protection.

"We have already agreed to a mountain and a forest lookout, so what else will we need?" Lef asked anxiously. There was the smell of fear in the air. "Eventually we will need to build underground tunnels as part of an escape plan," Father responded. Lef and the others frowned. "Escape from what?" "At some point the Corpsety will collapse," Father explained. "When this happens we will need to be prepared for those who come our way." "Surely now is not the time to worry about such things," Lef countered, and the group nodded their agreement. Father let the issue go; apparently the group could only look so far into the future.

As the circle came to a close, I reflected on how we had worked hard, shared our ideas, shared our fears, and created a plan that was acceptable to all. This process of meetings was beginning to grow on me. Sure, it had its frustrations, but it brought satisfaction too. Now we could begin the hard work of putting our plans into action.

I followed Illow as she went to check on Se and change her dressing. Se had made a remarkable recovery and was itching to leave her bed. One of the older children was taking care of Se, and she wanted to hear all about the meetings she had missed. I shared the story of our circle and before I knew it the afternoon had turned into evening.

We sat around the blazing fire that night with a round yellow moon. "Surely this is where we were meant to be," Lexy whispered, looking up at the night sky, "in the heart of the Wild, the heart of beauty." Someone started singing a lament to the moon, and Lexy and Roz rose to dance slowly around the fire. I watched as their gently swaying bodies called out a prayer of thanksgiving for our escape from the corrupt life of the Corpsety. That night I learned that bodies can talk, and my curiosity was aroused. I wondered if the reverse were true; did voices have the power to move us? I decided to tuck this question into the back of my mind. I had a feeling it would come in handy some day.

At home in the Wild, we began organizing ourselves for work. A small group began digging water canals while the rest of us helped Illow collect food and wood and dig a garden for our precious seeds. Time went by in an endless succession of work, sleep, play, and eating. The hot season had arrived and, except for those who were already black, our bodies began to darken with the sun's heat. Soon, I guessed, we would all be the same color. When work began on the shelters Grund had designed, we carried mud and stone day after day until the community center began to take shape. It was really three shelters in one: a place for food storage and preparation, a place for working and playing, and an eating and meeting space. In the front was a large fire pit with smaller fire pits inside each section. Each entrance would have a door made out of small trees tied together to keep animals and wind out. It was backbreaking work, and we were exhausted by the time the community shelter was finally finished. But, there it stood: a testament to our vision.

A large celebration was held to honor the fruits of our labors and to give us some much needed rest. As we shared food, dance, and song our joy overflowed. I was so happy dancing that my body began spinning until I found myself beyond the reach of the fire. I heard a whimper and saw yellow eyes. Trembling, I ran back to tell Father. He lit a torch and brought it to the place where I had seen the eyes. Under a blanket of darkness lay a large, badly injured wolf. Squinting in the light of the torch, it tried to move away but its body was too broken. Illow had followed us and announced, "I will treat this wolf and see if it recovers. Perhaps if we befriend it, the wolves will see we mean them no harm." She placed her hands on the wolf and it quieted. Illow sent me back to the camp for herbs and I hurried to get them. She dressed the animal's wounds and asked me to hold healing and loving thoughts in my mind. Summoning the most healing, loving thoughts I could find, I reached out to touch the wolf. It looked at me with such sad eyes that I was moved to tears. "I think this wolf has been treated badly," I told Illow. "Yes, Mariah, I think so too," she whispered.

And so it was that each day Illow and I visited the wolf, tended to her wounds, and brought food and water. We named her Wolf and I found myself becoming attached. Illow cautioned me to remember she was a wild creature and would return to the Wild once she recovered. But that was not to be. As Wolf healed, it became clear that she would never be able to run long distances again. She could walk, but her leg was too badly injured for hunting. Though we would never know why she came to us, we welcomed her into our community. She loved to sit by the fire and accompany Illow into the forest. All the children loved her, but it was me she chose to sleep beside each night and it was me she bonded to.

We continued to work tirelessly as the days passed. The canals were roughly built and water was flowing through them, two makeshift lookouts were in place, and we were beginning to build the sleeping shelters. The nights were beginning to cool and new foods were dropping from trees in the forest. The pile of wood had grown into a small mountain. But, were we prepared? We had no way of knowing what the winter would bring.

It was a happy time for me. I explored the forest and climbed to the top of the mountain with Wolf always by my side. I loved being able to work alongside the adults, and I was growing tall and strong. Working and playing outside all day had turned my skin a dark reddish brown. Some group members were getting almost as dark as Father and I, but not as dark as those with skin the color of the night. Grund said this color change was caused by the sun, but I believed it was the Wild putting its mark on us.

I noticed Father looked happy, too. His face was not so solemn and I often heard the sound of his laughter as he worked. His long brown braid was grayer but he was still handsome. Sometimes, out of the corner of my eye, I caught Roz looking at him and I wondered if he knew she was watching. Even Lef, who was usually sour, looked happy these days. He was working hard on the shelters, and in the evening around the fire I noticed he liked to talk to Sert. Was something happening between them too? I was young and had lots of questions about relationships between grown-ups. I had no idea how men and women went about getting to know each other.

EIGHT

Voice in the Wilderness

One day while the others were putting the finishing touches on the sleeping shelters, I went alone into the forest. I planned to spend the day looking for food but my mind was busy with other things. Distracted by my thoughts, I didn't notice how deeply I had wandered into the forest. I wasn't worried because Illow, Grund, and Father had taught me how to find my way. Alone, in the deep green of the forest, I was startled to hear a faint voice say, "Help me." I nearly jumped out of my skin. How could a voice be calling to me in the Wild? The fur on the back of Wolf's neck rose and she gave a low growl. "Quiet, Wolf," I whispered. Then I heard it again: "Help me, please." I couldn't see anyone. "Who are you?" I shouted. "Thunar," a voice called out weakly. Following the sound, I found its owner lying beside a tree. He looked terrible. His face was dirty and his eyes were sunken. He was so thin and weak that he seemed more like a child than a man. I had a few berries in my pocket which I gave him. "I'm going for help," I told him.

"No, don't go," he begged as he grabbed at my hand. "Please don't leave me here to die." I promised him I would come back and left Wolf to protect him. He looked warily at Wolf but didn't protest. I commanded her to stay with him until I returned, and she nuzzled me in agreement.

I arrived at the camp breathless and worried. Evening was falling fast, and I didn't know if he would survive the night. Father opened his mouth to ask where I had been all day, but my words stopped him in his tracks. "A man named Thunar is dying in the forest and we must help him." Father's face took on a look of surprise and then shock and he said, "Thunar here, how can that be?" "Do you know him?" "Yes," Father replied, "but we have no time to waste; darkness is falling." He gathered Cean and Grund and we each grabbed a burning stick. Grund explained where we were going to the others, and they promised to hold the circle until we returned. Illow gave me a hug and whispered, "You can do it, child, it's within your power." I was grateful for her encouragement because I wasn't sure I could find my way in the dark, and a man's life was depending on me.

At the edge of the forest, Father stopped and asked where Thunar was in relation to the Great Tree—the largest, oldest, and grandest tree in the forest. "I could see it clearly on my right when I was with him," I replied. Moonlight opened a path in the dark forest, and a gentle wind caused the trees to bend and groan as if they were singing and dancing. The night forest was both frightening and mysterious. Little yellow lights twinkled among the trees, and I imagined myself entering a magical world where anything was possible. Father and Grund seemed to travel effortlessly while Cean and I stumbled and struggled to find our way. Father was the first to make it to the

Great Tree where we heard Wolf's welcoming howl. We found Wolf and Thunar exactly as I had left them. Father roused Thunar and gave him some water and a mixture of healing herbs, but he was barely conscious. We put him on a wooden plank we had brought along and each of us took a corner. Grund did not like the looks of Thunar and was concerned he might die on the trip back. "It's in the hands of the Great Mystery now," Grund declared. We took a moment to say a silent prayer for Thunar.

We traveled as quickly as we could, stopping only to rest. I had grown strong and was able to carry my corner without help from the others. I was a full-fledged member of the community who could carry her fair share of the load. How good this felt! The trees began to move, and suddenly we were overtaken by a wind which pushed and pulled on us in all directions. Thunder filled our ears, and a fast-moving storm caught us in its fury. The trees lit up as they twisted and turned into a dance that brought the sky's wrath down. Swiftly, the forest had turned into a place of chaos and danger. Its magic transformed into terror. Vene and Berd's deaths ran though my mind as I felt the trees bend to the will of the wind. Would we be the next to die under a tree? Without touching a hair on our heads, the fast-moving storm moved on to drop its chaos elsewhere. The Wild sure had its way of showing us who was in charge.

Thunar hadn't noticed the storm, but like the rest of us he was wet and shivering. We picked up our pace, and I found myself becoming more and more aware of the weight I was carrying. I looked over at Cean and saw he was struggling too. I gritted my teeth and determined that I would make it to the camp without faltering. When we finally reached the camp, I was close to exhaustion. Community members came running out to greet us. Taking the cot from our hands, they threw warm blankets over our shoulders. We had made it. I looked over at Cean and we smiled at each other.

Cean and I sat down around the fire with the others, while Illow, Father, and Grund took Thunar to be cared for. It fell to the two of us to give an accounting of what had happened. We spoke of walking through the magical forest in the dark, of the storm which caught us in its fury, and of finding Thunar close to death. The group showered us with praise for our efforts, warming our hearts just as their blankets had warmed our bodies. Father and Grund returned to the fire and announced that Thunar was wavering between life and death. We joined together in a prayer for his safe passage to either side. Grund, Father, and others spoke of Thunar and his father, whom they had known back in the Corpsety. Thunar's father had been among those who wanted to leave, but could not make the journey.

By the time we finished talking it was late into the night. I turned to leave and was surprised to find Father's hand on my shoulder. "Mariah," he said in a low voice, "Illow wants you to stay with Thunar as he makes this passage. Are you willing?" I was bone tired, but it was an honor to accompany a person as they navigated the path between death and life. "I am willing, but I don't know if I am skilled enough to care for him." Father smiled at me, though his eyes remained solemn. He said, "Illow says your healing powers are strong. Since you were the one who found Thunar, we believe the Great Mystery is working through you." I lowered my eyes and agreed to be of service. Father gave me a big hug and guided me to the place where Thunar lay on a pile of dried grass and blankets. He was pale, still, and covered with sweat. Illow would stay with me this night as I needed to rest and regain my strength for the task ahead of me. Before I went to sleep, I bathed Thunar's head with a cool, wet cloth and gave him an herbal drink. The light from the fire moved shadows onto the wall of the cave, and I felt strangely serene sitting by his side with Wolf at my feet.

The days passed and I fell into a rhythm of sleep, tending, and watching over Thunar. Illow, Father, and Grund were the only ones to interrupt this cycle with food and company. Thunar often grabbed for my hand in a fog of unawareness as I bathed his forehead. I felt strongly drawn to him even though I was a child and he a man. His dark curly hair lay in ringlets around his face, which radiated intelligence and gentleness. I had never studied a man so closely, and I found him to be mysterious. On the third night his fever broke and he slept quietly. The next morning, Thunar was pale and awake, and he wanted to talk. When Father and Illow arrived he struggled to put words together. "Not long after you left the Corpsety," he said weakly, "an illness struck and many died. Food and water became more scarce. People roamed the streets in desperation looking for scraps of food and bottled water." He sat up in bed with blazing eyes and shouted, "You must go back and save the others, those who stayed behind. You have to save them." Father gently laid him back down on the blankets. "Rest, my son," he said gently, "for you came close to death and will need time to recover. We can do nothing now. The cold weather is upon us, and I have seen a white blanket on the mountain which, I believe, will come to us soon. There will be no more travel until the warmth returns. When you are well we will bring your request to the group, but for now you must rest and heal your body and soul."

I followed Illow and Father as they moved away from Thunar's pallet. Father was crying softly and I reached for his hand. Illow stayed close but spoke not a word. Wiping the tears from his eyes, Father spoke of his sorrow for those left behind. "Should we have waited for them?" he asked Illow. "There is no answer to that question," she said gently, "we followed our hearts." "It is happening sooner than we thought," Father sighed. Illow nodded her head and said, "We must use the winter to develop our plan." Illow and Father walked away and I wondered what kind of plan they had in mind. I sat down by Thunar and noticed he had drifted off to sleep again. The space was warm and cozy and I dozed off too. I dreamed of another journey, a journey back to the Corpsety, to gather people from its deathly grip. The journey was full of danger, fear, and joy as we made our way back to the heart of the Wild. Tomorrow, I thought, I must remember to tell Father about my dream.

Part Two:
RETURNING

Deep in the heart of Life Community I blossomed. Moving from child to woman I grew into the wisdom that surrounds, nurtures, and guides.

ONE

Growing in Community

We would have starved that first winter but for a gift from the Great Mystery. Fortunately, a brown, shaggy giant chose to take its last breath just outside our door. It was frightening to think of meeting such a mammoth alive; but we were grateful for its final act of generosity. Father guessed it was at least twelve feet long and weighed as much as all of us put together! The animal had a great round head with short, curved horns and its skin was tough. Our cold, weak hands were sorely tried as we struggled to cut through the outer hide to get to the meat waiting inside. We drank the animal's blood and managed to eat enough of its meat to keep us from starving. Although we took our share, we left food for the creatures of the forest who suffered along with us during the long, cold, intractable winter. The Great Mystery had shared with us and we would share with others. This was the natural way of community.

Reduced to skin and bones, our bodies were weak, and we became mere shadows of our former selves. Our vitality returned slowly, but not before another winter was upon us. The buildings we had planned to build waited in our imaginations. All our energy went into gathering food and wood and tending the garden. Through it all, we were amazingly content. We had learned how to live well by nurturing and supporting each other. The difficult times molded our hearts and souls into strong, vibrant shapes. We were attuned to life in the Wild, and called our place "Life Community." The shadow of the Corpsety no longer ruled our lives.

Thunar's unexpected arrival had given notice that the Corpsety's condition was worsening, but returning was not an option during those early years. We had thrown ourselves into the Wild without understanding what it would demand of us. Vulnerable to our ignorance, we could not afford to focus on anything but survival. It was during a time of renewal, when green spread its wings over the land and birds offered their songs, that I dreamed once more of the journey back. I saw us traveling through the Wild toward a blackened Corpsety. People were clinging to us, begging not to be left behind. The journey was long and full of difficulties. I saw angry faces and a lot of bickering among people.

I woke with an uneasy feeling and drew solace from the sleeping faces of the people around me. This was my home and my people. I watched as they woke for the day with wild hair and clothes that were a mishmash of animal skins and remnants of clothing. Our appearance reflected our union with the Wild. Sitting around the fire in the morning we shared our food and dreams. It seemed natural to share dreams now, but I had not forgotten my distress while waiting for the group to honor my visions. Now that the stigma had been removed, sharing dreams became a usual part of our life. It was surprising how similar our dreams could be. I told them of my dream and a lively discussion followed. What could it mean? Others had had dreams of returning, but none as vivid as mine. Father ventured to say that our dreams might be telling us it's time to return. He suggested we call a meeting tonight to discuss the possibility. Father's words brightened Thunar's face and he leaned forward. Here were the words he had been waiting for since his arrival so long ago. Thunar had been patient because he understood our need to adapt to the Wild, but perhaps now his dream could be fulfilled.

We set off to do our work for the day, and I followed Father to ask what "returning" meant. "I don't know yet, but your dreams point to a Corpsety that is disintegrating and people who need us. Those we left behind have been weighing heavy on my mind lately. Perhaps it is time to decide if we can help them." He smiled at me while patting my head. "Remember to hold the vision for us, Mariah, so we can see the way." I smiled back at him. I no longer found my dream visions frightening and accepted them as my gift of service.

I spent the day with Illow and Roz in the forest. There were roots to dig, insects to catch, honey to carefully collect from bee hives, nuts and berries to gather, and eggs to sneak from birds' nests. We were careful to take only what we needed and leave the rest. The threat of another starvation winter was always on our mind, and we tended to our food sources carefully. If we took too much the beings of the forest could not survive, and neither would we. As we scoured the forest for food we talked about tonight's meeting. Roz and Illow were sure it would be a difficult one. "Why is that?" I asked. "Sending people to the Corpsety would be hazardous," Roz explained. "Everyone in our community is important, and the loss of even one person is a loss to all." "On the other hand," Illow reasoned, "we do need new people for our community to remain viable. And, we need more tools, clothes, shoes, and small things like combs, needles, and scissors." Illow was right. Although there was plenty of wood in the forest, putting enough away for the winter was a problem. Possessing only two hatchets limited the amount of wood we could cut. Our clothes were ragged and shoes were almost a thing of the past. We had not yet mastered the art of creating clothes, shoes, and tools, and the Corpsety was the place where we could find such things. Roz and Illow continued talking. Opening up the community will also bring problems, they agreed. I was curious and asked, "How many people are we talking about?" They guessed there might be thirty or more people. "That's a lot," I blurted out with a mouthful of berries. Laughing at the purple dribble running down my chin, Roz teased me: "Really, we have no way of knowing. Maybe there are hundreds." Yes, I thought, this decision would a hard one to make. People in the Corpsety needed us, and it seemed we needed them. Getting together would be the problem.

The day passed quickly as it always did when I was with Illow, and soon we were making our way to the meeting. Father asked Thunar to repeat the request from those left behind in the Corpsety. Thunar stood quietly but with resolve, and my heart warmed with his presence. We shared a special bond. I had nursed him back to life and he had become my first male friend. I noticed how his curly black hair moved ever so slightly as he rose. The passion in his dark eyes drew others in, and through a veil of shyness he spoke simply but powerfully. "The Corpsety is collapsing. There have been a series of epidemics causing shortages and chaos. Those who remain behind are desperate to leave and are relying on us to come for them." Thunar sat down and Father asked everyone to sit quietly and let Thunar's words move through them before we proceeded. Grounded in silence, we began to talk.

Lef reminded us of our vulnerability and our dependence on every man, woman, and child to survive. His words brought murmurs of agreement. Then a young woman spoke. "What Lef says is true, and it's also true that we need more people if we are to survive as a community." There was silence as we considered the truth of their words, and then everyone began talking at once. The now familiar buzz of voices filled the air. Only the wise ones were quiet as they listened and watched. Emotions began to rise and the buzz turned into a roar, causing my head to hurt. I looked at Father and Illow, but their faces were calm and composed. They seemed unfazed by the noise. Finally, Cean brought out the drum, and spontaneously people stood to shake. When our bare feet touched the earth tensions released, bodies softened, and our heads cleared. Darkness descended and we decided to regroup and continue in the morning. As I was walking toward the sleeping shelters Father stopped me and asked, "Would you start tomorrow's circle by repeating your dream?" Without skipping a beat I answered, "Yes, I'll be happy to." My dreams no longer separated me from the others.

That night the dream returned to me, but with a difference. The faces of the people and their fear were stark and compelling. I could feel their voices calling out for help. I slept fitfully and woke with a lump in my throat. I ran to tell Illow of my dream. She listened solemnly, and I noticed her eyes narrowed as I shared. "You must speak from your heart of the pain and suffering brought to you in this dream."

My feet were heavy as I walked to the meeting, and each step required a great effort. A mixture of fear, passion, and pain moved inside me. I knew I would have to speak, for only by speaking my truth could I release my feelings. People were settled into the circle by the time I arrived. We shared a few moments of quiet and then Father asked me to speak. I rose from my seat to tell of my dream, but words failed me. I stood in silence for what seemed like an eternity until the words found me again. "I have dreamed of those left behind, and the terror on their faces is imprinted on my soul. They reached out to me with long, thin arms, and cried through tortured lips for help. I felt their agony and saw us making a journey to bring them home to Life Community. There is much about the dream I do not understand, but it filled me with a deep desire to return before it's too late. My heart calls out for the journey to begin."

I sat down, worried that I had spoken too strongly and not as the wise ones would want. And yet, because I had spoken from my heart, I felt relieved. I was surprised to see Lef and Sert rising together. "After last evening's discussion," Lef explained, "our minds and hearts came to agree. It is time to make a sacrifice for those who are trapped." Tears began to flow around the circle as Sert reminded us of the horrors of the Corpsety. "How can I ever forget the polluted grayness, hunger, thirst, chronic illness, constant danger, and oppressive Corpses?" She invited us to imagine the lives of those still caught in the Corpsety's sick hands. We sat quietly, each with our own image of the malignant Corpsety, until Grund rose to speak to us of duty. "There are times when we are called to step outside of ourselves and help the cause of life. The Great Mystery has shown us the universal laws of connection and community with others. The evil spawned by the Corpses has permeated the Corpsety, causing great harm to everyone living there. We must act to help those who want to leave. I propose we send six people on a journey and lay out a plan as soon as possible."

The group discussed Grund's proposal and it was warily accepted. Responsibility for planning was given over to the elder wise ones. Father, Grund, Illow, and Roz would make this decision, while Cean, Lexy, Thunar, and I waited along with everyone else. I desperately longed to go, but knew I was too young to be considered.

For two days and nights, the wise ones convened. On the third day, they called everyone to a meeting. A course had been charted back to the Corpsety with a supply of water for most of the journey. The trip would still be dangerous, but the route would be known. Getting into the Corpsety would be the initial challenge. The wise ones suggested everyone contribute their remaining clothes so those who travelled would blend in with the Trashers. We had come to view the Trashers in a new light after leaving the Corpsety. In a way, the Trashers were outsiders like us. They had been banished from the Corpsety for one reason or another and therefore had the tiniest bit of freedom. Because they had travelled no further than the Trash pits, they were still subject to the ills of the Corpsety. But, like us, the Trashers had learned how to meet their needs beyond the reach of the Corpsety. The wise ones suggested striking up conversations with Trashers who looked sympathetic to find out how to enter the Corpsety. Their help would be central to our success. On the return home clean water would, once again, be our most pressing problem. Those leaving the Corpsety would need to bring bags of water and travel rations for the journey. The plan seemed solid and well thought out. Then a surprise dropped on my head with a force that bowled me over.

Grund announced the return journey would be one of learning and teaching. This was to be a journey of transition from the Corpsety's way of life to a life way based on the natural laws. This shift would not be quick or easy. Only the wise ones could bring about such a change, I thought, and even then it would be difficult. When Grund announced I would be part of the returning group along with Thunar, Grund, Cean, Lexy, and Roz, a shock pulsed through my body. Me go? Surely they had made a mistake, for Father must go. Grund explained how they had chosen a mix of old and young from the wise ones. Some wise ones were left behind just in case the travelers did not return. My heart was beating so hard it caused a ringing in my ears, and I ceased hearing what he said. He must have called for shaking because I saw everyone stand as Cean beat the drum. I shook and then sat quietly until I recovered from the shock. When I opened my eyes, Father was standing over me. "Come with me, Mariah, we must talk."

I followed him as he grabbed some food from the common area and headed toward the mountain path. It was steep but blanketed with afternoon sun and wild flowers. He found a place to sit where we could look out over the land. "It's a beautiful place, isn't it, Mariah?" "Yes, it's beautiful any way you look, up or down." Father nodded his head in agreement. "Mariah, I want to talk about the journey. You don't have to go, and it will be your decision to go or stay behind. No one will think less of you if you choose to stay. You are, after all, still very young. But, I want you to know why we chose you, and yes, I was one of those who selected you. Your power to see the future in your dreams is growing, and so are your insights into our way of life. I believe you are needed to help navigate the journey's dangers and teach the new ones. Though I am reluctant to let you go, I feel the gifts you have been given are called for on this journey. I need to know how you feel. If there is even the slightest sense that this is not for you I want you to say so, and that will be the end of it." He paused and took my hands in his as he looked deeply into my eyes and whispered, "You know you are dearer to me than my own life, Mariah, please tell me what is in your heart."

I answered him with an unflinching gaze and said, "I am honored to be asked and ready to go. When I heard Grund's announcement, I was surprised and then afraid because I could not imagine going without you. But, you are right, the dream calls me to the journey with an urgent voice. I trust that the Great Mystery will provide for us." Father stooped to hug me and we shared a wonderful moment of closeness. "Mariah, you are surely your mother's daughter," he whispered as tears rolled down his cheeks. "My heart will be with you every step of the journey." I wished I could stay in this place with his arms around me forever, but like everything in life, the moment passed. Father and I made our way back down the mountain path. Neither of us knew what the future would bring. We were confident in our alignment with the natural laws. And that was all we needed to know.

The next days were a blur of activity as we gathered supplies and prepared for the journey. Those who stayed behind would have their hands full building additional shelters and gathering larger stores of food in preparation for those who would join us. We would all be challenged with our tasks in the coming months. The night before we were to leave, I said good-bye to Wolf and gave her over to Illow's care. I noticed Illow was starting to stoop ever so slightly and move more slowly. Her face was growing thinner but her eyes still sparkled with intelligence and high spirits. "You will come into yourself on this journey," she told me. "This is your time to become a woman." She patted my hand as she talked, and I felt sad to be leaving her with so much work to do. "Don't worry about me, little one," she said sternly. "As long as I have breath I want to be of service to my community, and when breath leaves I will fly on the wind to the next place waiting for me." I marveled at her fortitude. She truly believed in death as a natural transition and nothing more. We said our good-byes with tears and laughter. This was Illow's way, and I was happy to be arounded by her love. During the night the wind lifted its voice to howl for us. Warm inside the sleeping shelter, I found peace listening to the song of the Wild.

TWO

Leave Taking

I woke to stillness. The wind had moved on and in its place was a blanket of cold. I collected my things and walked to the community center. Father and Illow were there packing our final provisions. My spirits were high and I was eager to begin the journey. The community gathered in a circle around us and chanted a blessing for our safety, success, and timely return. They opened the circle as we took our leave and continued to chant as we walked away from our beloved Life Community.

Grund set a brisk pace and memories came flooding back of our journey out of the Corpsety. Would we walk for days again until we reached exhaustion? Silently, I moved on absorbed in thoughts and feelings about leaving. We stopped to make camp for the night, and Grund spoke of the things we would teach the new ones. Connecting with the Wild, cooperation, and conservation—all would be critical to their survival. We hoped to model respect for each other and for community. There would, of course, be other things, but these would make up the core of our teachings.

Lexy questioned how we could be teachers when we barely knew these things ourselves. "How did you learn?" Roz asked.

Lexy was quiet but Thunar jumped in to answer, "When I came to Life Community, I watched others and copied them." Roz smiled at Thunar's eagerness and said, "That is one way to learn. First and foremost we will be role models for them. They will not have the luxury of easing themselves in over a long period of time as Thunar did."

"We will also need to give them direct teachings," Grund advised. "Remember how disconnected we were from the natural world and from each other when we first began? They will be the same, only more so. They will favor individuals over community, greed over sharing, competition over cooperation, jealousy over gratefulness, and violence over peace." I was quiet as I considered his words. We were faced with doing in a few months what had taken our small group years to accomplish. I couldn't help voicing my fears and asked, "Is it possible to do this?" Grund was quick to answer my question: "Anything is possible, Mariah, if we put our hearts and minds to the task and trust the Great Mystery to work through us." I was reminded of my dream vision and of the ancients. Perhaps the Great Mystery would send them to help us lead the way.

The days passed uneventfully as we found waterways, walked, and became more aware of each other's presence. I noticed Thunar and Lexy often sat together talking. I wasn't sure how I felt about this. I liked them both but sometimes felt excluded by their friendship. The fifth day of our journey started out well. We gathered roots and Cean caught a rabbit. Late in the afternoon thunderclouds moved in, the sky darkened, and we were caught in a storm. We were searching for a shelter from the storm's wrath when I heard Cean's call. I found him struggling with a wolf, and this time I was prepared. I picked up a stick and yelled, "Leave us alone, we mean you no harm." I continued swinging my stick as more wolves circled us. Their low growls caused the hair to rise on the back of my neck. Why were they attacking us? Oh, how I wished I had Wolf by my side. "Run," Cean shouted, but it was too late. I was inside the circle and our fate was sealed. Something buzzed past my ear, causing a wolf to yelp and run away. Another flew past and then another until the whole pack was on the run. Thunar had saved us with his slingshot. I knelt to care for Cean, who was hurt. One of the wolves had bitten him on the side and he was bleeding profusely. The others joined us, and we carried him to a resting place. Roz and I set off to look for healing plants.

I closed my eyes, as Illow had taught me, and called to the plants. I let myself be guided to plants with healing powers. We stopped Cean's bleeding with pressure, and I applied a poultice that would clean the wound and promote healing. I watched as Roz pulled out a small vial of honey to add to my poultice. "It will prevent infection," she told me. Cean was weak, so we half-dragged, half-walked him to a shelter where he could rest. Pulling out my dried meat, I remembered the rabbit Cean had caught earlier. The rabbit tied to his belt was gone and in its place was the wolf bite. That must be it, I thought, the wolves are competing with us for food. I made a mental note to remember that in nature there is competition, as well as cooperation. Thus far, I didn't much like the results I had seen from competition.

We were wet, cold, and shaken by our encounter with the Wild. Sitting around the fire we talked. "No one can tame the Wild," Grund reflected, "and it was foolish of the Corpsety to believe it could. Our only hope is to learn how to live with the Wild as our teacher. We will have to be good students in order to survive." In the morning a bright sun greeted us, but Cean was too weak to travel. He needed meat to recover. Leaving Cean by the fire, we set out to find food and returned with our pockets full of nuts, roots, and sprouts. Thunar and Lexy arrived later with arms full of success. Thunar had caught a fish and Lexy had downed a large bird with her slingshot. We would eat well tonight and for the next several days. We gave thanks to the Great Mystery and to the animals for their sacrifice.

Nutritious food and another night's sleep improved Cean's condition and we resumed our journey. Surprisingly, Cean harbored no ill will toward the wolves. When I told him why I thought they had attacked, he agreed, and told the others to be watchful about carrying meat. The days merged one into the other as our bodies settled into the routine of walking and making camp. I often travelled alongside Roz and was growing closer to her. I had not fully understood or appreciated her good humor and gentle fortitude before our journey. She found ways to make us laugh even on the most miserable of days.

We travelled quickly and made good time. The sky had been gray for a couple of days before I realized it signaled our closeness to the Corpsety. Grund predicted we were within a few days of it. That night we talked about our plan. Cean thought staying in the Trash pits until we found a place to enter would offer the most opportunity, but he didn't know how long this might take. He assumed the Trash pits were still dangerous. Hopefully, we would not spend much time there.

As we drew closer to the Corpsety, the sky turned darker and a sense of doom and gloom descended on us. The air was hard to breathe and the streams we passed were vile. I began to feel the old disconnection with the natural world creeping up on me. Sitting around the fire, we acknowledged the presence of disconnection, and Grund reminded us that this would be the norm for everyone in the Corpsety. "We will be entering the Corpsety any day now," he told us. A nervous excitement filled me, and I could feel it coming from Lexy and Thunar too. Roz shared some simple breathing techniques to help us relax and stay balanced. Then, Grund gently guided us to a state of quiet where he encouraged us to remember Life Community. "It lives in us," he declared, "and we carry it with us wherever we go." We reaffirmed our commitment to the journey and ended the evening with quiet swaying together. We were safe and secure in each other's arms and in the knowledge that we were united in purpose, united in process, and united in spirit. We would need this security in the days to come.

THREE

Return to the Corpsety

It was mid-morning when we entered the wasteland of the Trash pits. We didn't draw much attention with our dirty faces and ragged clothes. In fact, we fit right in with the Trashers. No one would talk to us, so we spent the day sifting through trash and in the evening found a not-too-smelly pile to sleep on. I was used to the fragrance of the forest, and the sickening sweet and sour trash smells made my stomach turn. The next day was much the same and I began to wonder if we needed to change our plan. On the third day, we busied ourselves digging through trash while Cean struck up a conversation with a Trasher who looked approachable. He was unusually tall with broad shoulders and bright blue eyes set in a face that was black as night. He didn't seem desperate, which was unusual for a Trasher. Cean told him he needed to find a way back into the Corpsety. Without hesitation the man offered his name—Nestor—and shared what he knew. Cean thanked him gruffly and walked away.

We moved on, not as a group, but within sight of each other. A thin, wiry man grabbed at me, and turning to look at him, I was taken aback by the deep suffering in his face. I looked him in the eye and said, "It's not me you need but food. Here is a scrap of biscuit I found. Take it and be well." Shocked, the man let go of my arm and shuffled away, while others watched. I would have to be more careful. Generosity was not among the things to be found in the Trash pits, and I didn't want to draw attention to myself. Even though I had lost sight of the others I could feel their eyes on me. I turned and saw they had encircled me. Roz nodded her head and I smiled at her. She passed her hand over her mouth, and I remembered that smiles would set us apart from others. I had to remind myself that I was in an alien land and needed to act accordingly to survive.

We spent another day in the Trash pit picking up a few things so we wouldn't look suspicious. As night fell, the noise of people sorting through trash died down and we decided to make our move to Nestor's point of entry. Slowly, we made our way to the place, but were dismayed to find it was treacherous. Without drawing attention to ourselves, we would have to navigate a steep wall surrounded by polluted water. We were discussing whether or not we could do this when Nestor showed up. "I thought you could use some help," he told Cean. This was strangely out of character for a Trasher, but we needed help and didn't have time to care about his motives. Cean motioned to us and told Nestor we were together. He shrugged his shoulders and stepped up to the wall. Cean and Nestor crossed the wall together without any problems. Roz and Lexy followed. Thunar was next. He took a few steps onto the wall and froze. I remembered he was afraid of heights, so

I scrambled up beside him and took his hand. "Follow me," I whispered. We had moved only a few steps when the Corpsety's guard light flashed on the wall. I pulled Thunar down and we lay motionless on the ledge while the light moved over us. As we slowly crawled to the other side, my hands moved through slime and I prayed to the Great Mystery we wouldn't slip. Grund was the last to go. I was afraid for him as he felt his way across the ledge in darkness, but he deftly managed it. We had made it into the Corpsety!

Thunar's face was white and he looked miserable. I squeezed his arm and reminded him that everyone is afraid of something. He gave me a grateful smile and I felt closer to him than I had in weeks. Grund gathered us together as we watched Nestor walk away. "Should we consider asking Nestor to help us?" he asked. "If we do," he cautioned, "we will be putting our trust in someone we know nothing about. He could turn us in to the police." Grund asked for our intuitions about Nestor. "There is something different about him, something special that I can't put my finger on," Cean reckoned. Lexy was uncertain of him but felt no ill will. Thunar was quiet, so I spoke. "I like him. I don't know why, but I do." Thunar was not certain, but thought Nestor looked vaguely familiar. If that were true he might be someone we could trust. Cean suggested we ask Nestor if he knew Thunar's father.

We caught up with Nestor, and with some hesitation, Thunar asked if he might know his father. Nestor stood silently staring at us and I noticed his body was completely rigid. I looked at Grund and Roz, who were watching Nestor closely. Should we run?

Suddenly, Nestor started crying great, torturous sobs and I feared he would collapse. We stood waiting quietly for the flow of his tears to subside. "You have come back for us," he managed to say. "We had given up hope. Come, I will take you to a house where you can stay." We followed him silently through the winding streets full of shacks and broken-down buildings until we arrived at a large, dilapidated house. "Wait here while I explain who you are," he whispered, and then disappeared inside. We stood waiting, looking at each other. It has begun already, I thought, the journey back is before us. Nestor reappeared and ushered us into the house where we were surrounded by joyful people. We sat on the floor while they offered us the long forgotten biscuits and canned meat. We ate their offerings gratefully. Even though they had given up hope for our return, the group continued meeting and a network of people had survived. When we asked how many people remained, they guessed there were between fifty and seventy. Thunar's father had died, and there were others who had given up or disappeared. They agreed to arrange for us to meet with their network. Before retiring to their pallets, each of them thanked us for returning and I noticed how familiar their faces seemed. Then it dawned on me: these were the faces of my dream, lined with suffering, despair, exhaustion, and tragedy. I prayed our presence would bring them the relief they had waited for.

Alone again, we arounded Thunar and shared our sorrow at hearing of his father's death. He quietly told us how he had long ago accepted it. His father had known his death was close when he sent Thunar on the journey to find us. We slept on the floor that night and woke to the noises of the Corpsety.

Over a familiar breakfast of biscuits and water, the house's inhabitants shared their assessment of the Corpsety. The epidemics had further alienated the Corpses from everyone else. They had withdrawn behind walls and tended to their business from afar. Without oversight, many of the factories were no longer producing much of anything. There were frequent food and water shortages, and the caravans were constantly under attack from daredevil Bandits. Without proper police protection the caravans were unable to transport provisions. Only a fortunate few held jobs that provided food and water. Most people were forced to scavenge in the Trash pits. Life had been bad in the Corpsety before, but now it was intolerable. People were just waiting to die. Whether they died from starvation, disease, or violence it didn't much matter. Life itself held no value.

Nestor spoke of Thunar's father and his unshakable belief that the Great Mystery would bring us back to lead them away from the Corpsety. Holding his vision, even after he died, had kept them alive all these years. A hopeful vision was one of the few connections to the Great Mystery available in the Corpsety, and they had clung to it tightly. Thunar reached out to hug Nestor and tears rolled down their cheeks. "I didn't know what had happened to you," Nestor told Thunar. "Now I understand. You were sent on a mission by your father who was looking after us even though he had one foot in the grave." Releasing Thunar from his strong arms, he thanked us for returning. We shared the story of Life Community and explained why it had taken us so long to come back.

We gave instructions and urged the group to start preparing for the journey immediately. They would need to gather water, food, blankets, clothing, and tools for the journey. Nestor would secure the items Life Community needed. The rest of the network would meet with us over the next few weeks so we could develop a plan for leaving.

The impoverished household could not afford to feed us, so we worked in the Trash pits to earn our keep. The Trash pits were full of stuff. Apparently the Corpses still had plenty to throw away. The sounds of shouting and fighting filled the air, reminding me of storms in the Wild, but this was a human storm created by the Corpsety. The Trash pits had not changed much since Father and I first saw them. The Trashers were filled to the brim with anger and despair, using what strength they had to compete with others. A young girl assaulted Roz as she sorted through trash. Roz looked her in the eye and asked, "What do you want?" The girl sputtered, "This is my space." She was a thin waif of a girl and dirtier than I thought a human being could be. Roz apologized and offered to move. The girl recoiled in surprise. She had expected a fight; no one in the Trash pits apologized. Feeling sad for the young girl, I let my thoughts wander as we moved away from her. She was no older than I was when I left the Corpsety. What must her life like? What had brought her to the Trash pits? What would happen to her?

Our time in the Trash pits left us tired, but our day was far from over. Tonight we would meet with others from the network. Slowly, we walked home and prepared for the meeting. Tonight's group arrived early. We sat with them to explain our plan. The group didn't seem very grateful for our return. They wanted to know how they would be protected and how far they would have to travel. Grund explained the trip would be long and hard, and that we could give them no assurances. Both protection and provisioning would be the work of each person. "Perhaps we will die on the journey," he said quietly. "There is no way to know. All we have to offer you is a chance to leave the Corpsety and journey toward Life Community. The rest is up to the Great Mystery."

The group was quiet except for some grumbling noises coming from the back of the room. Roz encouraged them to consider Grund's words carefully. "The journey is not for the faint hearted," she warned. Many of them shuffled out after she spoke, but a small group came over to talk. "We want to leave with you," they said, "but we need to know if the journey can be made with young children." I held my breath, wondering what the answer would be. "How many children are there?" Grund asked. They had five children ranging in age from newborn to three. "We are not opposed to bringing children along, providing you understand the risks," Grund told them. "Our children are dying here of starvation and black smoke," a woman replied. "We will take the risk." There had been a blanket of black smoke in my dream, and when I asked her about it her face clouded over. "At times the factories put out a thick, black smoke that engulfs the Corpsety. That's all we know except that it makes breathing difficult and creeps inside our buildings to smother our children." So, it was settled; this small group would come with us.

As we prepared for bed that night, I realized I was tired in a way I didn't experience at home. I was tense from constantly monitoring my surroundings, deadening my ears to the noise, and hardening my heart to the pain and suffering around me. Holding this tension took an incredible amount of energy, and I longed for the peace of Life Community. There we had challenges to be sure, but we were not drained of our energy. I drifted off to sleep remembering the small girl who had attacked Roz. I wondered if I could help her.

We continued working in the Trash pits by day and meeting with people at night. Some of the network decided to go with us while others fearfully held back. Everyone we met had sad, worn out faces and desperate stories. The Corpsety was sucking their lives away more quickly than I could have imagined. I remembered the long ago description of the Corpsety as a sinking lifeboat. Maybe for some a sinking lifeboat is better than the unknown. Not for me, I thought; I'd rather die swimming than stay anchored to the Corpsety. Tonight we would talk with our last group. We were growing tired. Our spirits were overwhelmed by the tragedy known as the Corpsety and quite simply it was time for us to leave.

None of us were prepared for this evening's meeting. As soon as we entered the room, I felt something different. These people were strange in some way I couldn't quite grasp. Their clothes were not ragged, but it was more than that. I looked at Grund and saw that his eyes had narrowed. Cean put his hand on my shoulder and whispered, "Mariah, these are not Jobbers or Trashers." What did he mean? I started to ask but the talking had begun and Grund was taking the lead. The group was restless, noisy, and not at all attentive to what Grund was saying. Finally, a man identifying himself as Nake announced, "We have already decided to travel with you. We want to know what special accommodations you can offer us." Grund asked what he meant by special. Nake flung his arms out and said, "You don't expect us to travel with Jobbers and Trashers, do you? We are Corpses who have lost our homes and want out of this wretched place." I flinched at his put-down of the Jobbers and Trashers who were our new friends.

Grund continued, "We will all travel together as equals, sharing work, food, and dangers along the way. Where we are going, hierarchy does not exist, and everyone has equal value." The room went silent. People were visibly shaken by Grund's calm declaration. Nake spoke again: "We can pay for your services and we demand our own accommodations." It was a tense moment and Roz stood to respond. "Your money will do you no good outside the Corpsety. Outside we are all equal and dependent on one another. You are welcome to join us, but only on the terms we have laid out. Stay in the Corpsety or come with us, but we will make no special accommodations." After Roz had spoken, we stood to leave, reminding them of the need to make their decision quickly.

We hurried back to our friend's house and asked about this group. "Yes," Nestor told us, "this is a difficult group. We included them because they sincerely want to leave the Corpsety. Did we do the right thing?" Grund affirmed their decision to include the Corpses. "It will be up to them to decide whether or not they will accept our terms." Before we retired for the night, the six of us formed a circle. Sitting on the hard floor, I searched the faces of my friends. They looked tired, and I supposed I did too. The Corpsety was wearing on us even after a short time. Grund spoke what we all were thinking: "The group we met tonight will be a challenge, but it is a necessary challenge. They are part of the Corpsety and we must be prepared to work with them. In future times more of them will want to join us." We nodded our heads in agreement, but the thought of working with Corpses made the task ahead of us seem grim. I took this opportunity to ask if we could we take one of the orphan children back with us. The group felt that an orphan child would have to carry her share of the load, follow our guidance, and be healthy. Otherwise, they had no objection. It was settled, then. Tomorrow, I would look for the girl and find out if she was an orphan. Surely she was, for I couldn't imagine a parent who would send their child unaccompanied to the Trash pits.

At long last, we set out for our last day in the Trash pits. Our remaining time would be spent organizing for the journey. Throughout the day I sorted trash and looked for the little girl. With a sinking heart I began gathering my things to leave when I caught sight of her. She was giving me a wide berth, so I motioned for her to come closer. She moved just a bit and looked at me warily. I moved closer while looking her over. She seemed fairly strong and healthy. Though she had layers of dirt and matted hair, her eyes were bright and clear. I asked about her parents. "Dead," she answered. I asked about her home and she replied, "Gone." This one didn't waste words. I offered her a biscuit, which she stuffed half of in her mouth and half in her pocket. I took a deep breath and asked if she would like to come with me on a journey far away from the Corpsety. Her eyes registered fear and she backed away while shouting over her shoulder, "Leaving the Corpsety is a death sentence." "That's not true," I shouted back, and my words stopped her in her tracks. Once again, I asked if she would like to come with me. Moving closer, she closed her eyes and spoke softly: "I have dreamed of a place in the Wild where there is clear, moving water. Is your place like this?" I was surprised to find a little one who could dream truth. "Yes," I told her, "and it has a great mound of land behind it and a forest with large, green trees below." Her eyes widened and she said, "That is the place of my dream!" "Little one," I whispered, "you have the power to dream rightly. I hope you will follow your dreams, for they will take you where you need to go." She hesitated and I feared she would refuse my offer. "I have a brother," she said, looking down at her feet. "I don't suppose he could come too?" My heart went out to her. How could I say no? Without even asking the age of her brother, I said they were both welcome to come with us. She flashed me a bright smile and told me her name was Flow. So she knew how to smile . . . that was a good sign. I watched as she ran to collect her brother and noticed how the name suited her. Her long brown hair and graceful movements gave the illusion of water flowing. After she had gone, the impact of my words hit me. What had I done? I didn't want to lose the goodwill of my friends. I found Roz and told her what I had done. "You did the right thing," Roz assured me. "We will manage." Darkness was falling by the time I saw Flow's figure walking toward us with her brother in tow. She brought their only possessions—two blankets and a small bag of clothes—

with her. And, she brought money to buy food and water. She was an enterprising girl.

I introduced Flow and her brother, Hak, to the others. We moved slowly through the Corpsety trying not to draw attention to ourselves. We were almost home when a policeman stopped us and demanded to know why we were travelling together. Didn't we know groups are forbidden? Before anyone could answer we were surrounded by policemen. I had never seen a policeman up close. Their tight, metallic uniforms had razor-sharp spikes protruding along their spines and the backs of their arms and legs. Their heads were protected by large, black helmets, which hid their eyes behind vertical slits. Only their mouths were exposed as they snarled at us. I was reminded of wolves. Their guns, like the wolves' teeth, were poised to harm us. I stood there frozen, shocked by their appearance, until I heard Flow speak loudly. "They are protecting me from some men who tried to hurt me." The lead policeman moved closer and asked, "How do we know you are telling the truth?" Flow raised her shirt and showed him large bruises and a deep cut. He turned his back without comment and shouted as he and his officers took their leave. "You're lucky we didn't dispose of you. See that it doesn't happen again." We hurried on our way in silence.

When we were safely in the house, I asked Flow about her injuries. "It's nothing," she told us, "just the result of my latest fight in the Trash pits." My instincts were right. Flow would not have lasted much longer in the Corpsety. I doctored her cut and told her she could rest easy now. Vilet, a tall, large-boned woman with dark hair and no children, took an immediate liking to Flow and Hak. She gathered them up in her arms, washed the dirt off their bodies, and made sleeping places for them. Her mothering helped settle Flow and Hak into their new life.

We ate a late dinner and talked about organizing meetings for those who would be journeying with us. A series of three meetings were set to accommodate everyone. Extra care would need to be taken in light of our recent encounter with the police. Grund wanted to know what had caused the Corpsety to act so violently against groups, and Nestor explained. "After the disease struck, desperate people formed groups and stormed stores and factories looking for food and water. They caused a lot of damage. The Corpsety is fearful of such uprisings and strictly forbids groups of any kind under penalty of death." The policeman's words still rang in my ears: "Lucky we didn't dispose of you." In the Corpsety, perhaps a quick death at the hands of the police was preferable to its imitation of life.

FOUR

Preparing the Way

There were too many of us to leave together. We would divide into three groups, and the six of us would lead them in pairs. Nestor had secured our supplies and we were ready to hold the final meetings. The knowledge that we would leave soon gave us cause for celebration. In high spirits we began shaking. Awkwardly, the others joined us and warmed to the movement. Everyone was happy and relaxed for a change. Our housemates were curious about the "shaking." "We believe it creates goodwill and relaxation," Roz told them. As they walked to their beds, I noticed little shakes and laughter following them.

Nervously, I waited for our first meeting at the house. Would they be prepared? Would they be difficult? The six of us sat in silence waiting for their arrival. One by one families and individuals filed in until the room was full. Roz welcomed everyone. Then, she shared our community guidelines:

1. Respectful relations with people and the natural environment
2. Equality
3. Cooperation and sharing

4. Group problem-solving and decision-making
5. Nonviolence in words and actions
6. Valuing differences
7. Valuing community
8. Wise resource use by taking only what you need.

Roz had just finished speaking when a man stood. He was of medium build with a balding head and eyes that were lively. Calling himself Stun, he directed his words to Grund. "How can we be expected to follow such guidelines?" Roz responded to his question, "We understand this will be a new way of living and that the task will not be easy. Our guidelines offer a way of life instead of the Corpsety's way of death. The guidelines are based on the natural laws of community, cooperation, connection, and conservation." Stun was not convinced. He growled out a challenge to Roz's authority as a woman and demanded to hear from Grund. Grund stood just long enough to say, "We are serious when we say all are equal here. Roz speaks for us."

The room began to buzz with people's voices. We sat and waited as they processed this new information together. Several people got up and left but most, including Stun, stayed. After the buzzing quieted, Stun spoke again: "Those of us who remain will go with you, though we doubt our ability to follow your guidelines. What will happen to us if we cannot comply? Will we be abandoned?" Roz smiled and gently spoke, "We do not abandon those who are learning the path of community and connection. We will make the journey and succeed or fail together. In Life Community we understand that we all rise up or all fall down together."

Roz asked everyone to stand and shake with us. Cean and Nestor had fashioned drums out of Trash pit scraps and they surprised us with drumming. I watched as the group's self-conscious stiffness warmed to the sound of the drum's rhythm. A joyful energy moved through our bodies and out into the room. When we sat down, Cean asked if the group had secured their supplies. "We are prepared," they told us. He gave directions as to where and when we would leave. Cean and I would lead this group together. People left in high spirits and I felt good about the outcome of our first meeting, even though the beginning had been rocky.

I complimented Roz on her calmness and noted that she had not received an apology. "No apology is needed. I know I am an equal, and no man can take that from me. Stun will learn and we will continue to remind him." I left the room to say goodnight to Flow and found her sprawled on the floor sound asleep beside Hak, Vilet, and Tunk, Vilet's partner. They had formed a family of sorts and I supposed that was good. Across the room I saw Thunar and Lexy sleeping next to each other, and I was pretty sure they were becoming a couple. I felt a little lonely. I could still be Thunar's friend, of course, but it would not be the same. Thunar's life was changing, and since his life touched mine, I would be changed too. How mysterious life is, I thought. We spin and turn and dance with those in our lives on the winds of change instead of solid ground.

The second group went smoothly. A woman who was young, strong, and passionate emerged as a leader. Stear was her name, and she had long blonde hair and cool gray eyes. Unlike Stun, she was excited about the guidelines and eager to begin using them. The group followed her lead and embraced the guidelines without question. Thunar and Roz would be their leaders.

After the second group left, the six of us talked. We wanted to be prepared for the third group. Grund would lead the discussion and we would stand beside him for support. Grund reminded us that these people had also been harmed by the Corpsety, but in a different way. "The Corpses believe they have more rights and deserve privileges not given to others. This is just another way the Corpsety corrupts people, while violating the natural law of connection," he explained. "Community cannot exist when some are set above others." I listened intently to Grund's words and hoped they would help me to be patient with the Corpses.

Sleep came fitfully that night. I dreamed of a great cloud of dark smoke that choked me and enveloped the Corpsety. I woke with a feeling of urgency and told Grund and Roz of my dream. "What do you think the dream is telling us to do, Mariah?" they asked. I closed my eyes and called the dream back to me. "We need to leave as soon as possible." "In fairness to the last group we cannot leave today," Grund reasoned, "but we could leave tomorrow." I was uneasy with the delay but understood why we needed to wait. We gathered our housemates around us and told them we would leave tomorrow at midday. They immediately set about letting the others know about the change in plans.

The house hummed with activity as we readied for the journey. Food, water, clothes, tools, and blankets were piled everywhere. Excitement coursed through the house, and so did emotions. I watched as people argued and shouted at each other, sometimes resorting to pushing and shoving. I pulled Flow aside and told her this was not the way to treat others. She looked at me solemnly and whispered in my ear, as if she were afraid the others would hear, "I know, my father taught me that." I gave her a hug and a smile. "Little one, it sounds as if your father was a wise man."

The last group arrived early and we sat in a circle with them. Grund began to present the guidelines, but before he could finish several men challenged him. "This is rubbish," someone spat out. A man with a drawn and worried face pointed out that the guidelines were "unnatural." At this point, Nake spoke up and the group listened attentively. "We are not looking for a utopian community. We want to leave the Corpsety, and we need your help. We do not believe in your guidelines, nor do we wish to follow them. We are Corpses, and we are not on the same level as Jobbers and certainly not Trashers. As I said before, we are willing to pay you well for your services, but you have no right to ask us to follow your ridiculous rules."

Grund stood slowly and firmly addressed the rowdy group: "We do not have much time. We will be leaving tomorrow due to a change of plans. You must decide whether or not you are willing to abide by our guidelines. There will be no exceptions; either you agree to follow them, or you do not go with us. As Roz pointed out earlier, your money is no good outside the Corpsety. If you want our help, you will have to work within our framework, not the Corpsety's. We have left the Corpsety and all that it represents behind us. We are not going back to the Corpsety's ways for anyone."

This was as strong a statement as I had ever heard Grund make. He encouraged the group to talk with each other while we waited outside. "What do you think they will do?" I asked. Grund paused for a moment and said, "Mariah, they are a divided group. It is hard to tell which side will win or if any of them will come." Lexy was disgusted and said, "Personally, I hope they don't come." "Why do you say that?" Roz asked. "I don't like them or their arrogant ways," Lexy replied. "Aha," Roz exclaimed, "there is something about them that is causing you to react. That's why you don't like them. The answer lies within you, Lexy." I wanted to hear more about this but Roz was interrupted by the Corpses calling us back.

I could feel a softer environment as we entered. Nake stood at the front of the room but he was now accompanied by a small, thin woman with gray hair and a strong voice. Her name was Moed. As usual Nake spoke first: "You give us no choice but to accept your terms. We agree to do what you ask, but it goes against everything we believe." When he had finished, Moed stepped in front of Nake, and in a strong, clear voice announced her position. "We also understand that this leave taking is a new chapter in our lives. Many of us agree that the old ways have not worked and are open to learning new ways of living. What Nake said is true, we have been arrogant parasites, and it will be hard for us to change. And, we will do our best to follow your lead." With that said, she sat down and Nake gave her a dark look. The division was clearly represented by these two, and yet, both wanted to go with us. How this would play out was anyone's guess.

Grund honored their decision and spoke of the difficulty we all have in following a new path. "The diversity you bring will make us stronger," he said as he welcomed them into the journey. We briefly discussed the details for tomorrow. Several members asked if books and other personal items could be brought. "You are welcome to bring whatever you can carry along with the necessary supplies," Grund replied. Before people started leaving, Cean brought out his drum and we stood to shake, inviting them to join us. Some began to move timidly while others looked on with disapproval. Those of us who moved our bodies found lightness while the abstainers remained dark and gloomy. It seemed that even the Corpses had a dark and a light side. They were not so different from the rest of us.

The meeting came to a close. When we were alone, I shared the disrespectful and sometimes violent behavior I had witnessed earlier in the house today. All agreed this needed to be addressed, but not until we had left the Corpsety. Inside the bowels of the beast it seemed an impossible task to make anything positive happen. Once we were outside, change could come.

FIVE

Leaving

I woke with a terrible, suffocating stink in my nose. I thought the house was on fire and jumped up to warn the others. To my surprise, I found my housemates undisturbed. The house was not on fire; it was the black smoke that brought death. They predicted it would get worse as the days went on. The stifling smell and darkness made preparing for the journey difficult. Finally, with packs loaded on our backs, Cean and I left to join our group.

The smoke allowed us to hide our numbers, and it made our task more difficult. Holding hands, we made our way out of the Corpsety, but we didn't go quietly, as planned. It was impossible not to cough, and the children were crying. Cean and I exchanged worried glances as fingers of fear crept up my back. After we had walked some distance, a gruff voice pushed its way through the fog, "Who goes there?" Cean quickly answered, "Just some of us Trashers going to the pits." "Stay off the streets today," the policeman commanded. Cean shouted into the fog, "Yes, sir," and we continued walking. We stuffed our mouths with rags to muffle our coughing and stifled the children's cries. Now, I understood their suffering. The blackness rolling out of the Corpsety was so vile, so full of illness, that it sucked the life from our lungs.

We stumbled and fell, but continued to hold hands as we made our way out of the Trash pits. The smoke was growing thicker by the minute and Cean had trouble locating our meeting place. He found what he thought was the right place, and the group sat down to wait, but no one arrived. Something was wrong. Cean and I recalculated our position and decided to move. Still holding hands, we walked to another place but found no one there. By now the smoke was so thick I couldn't see my hands or feet. We could not afford to wait any longer. The children were ominously quiet as the adults struggled to take each breath. Accompanied by black smoke and hope, we walked on until exhaustion forced us to stop. We ate biscuits, drank water, and fell into a fitful sleep on the hard ground.

With the stench of smoke still in our noses, we woke the next day. Without the sun to guide us, we could only hope we were walking in the right direction. Toward evening, we noticed the smoke was beginning to lift. We could see each other, and what a sight we were! Our clothes and bodies were covered with soot. We collapsed, exhausted on the ground, laughing at each other's appearance.

That night I dreamed we were walking in circles. Around and around we went until we moved to the right, which took us out of the endless loop. In the morning I shared my dream with Cean and the rest of the group. Flow had a dream to share, too. In her dream we were calling out as we walked. We changed our course and began calling out as we walked. Exhaustion filled our days as we walked on alone and forlorn. The group grew anxious and fearful. Cean called a meeting so people could speak. Nestor admitted he was worried: "I am afraid of being lost and of dying in the Wild." Some of the group began to talk about going back to the Corpsety. Others expressed anger and blamed the smoke for ruining our escape plan. A whirlwind of negative words and feelings swirled around us, but Cean and I remained unruffled. The group's energy rose to a fever pitch, and then quieted. Vilet and Tunk stood to speak and said, "We do not want to go back to the Corpsety, where a certain death awaits us. We knew that risk, danger, and possible death would be part of this journey. If we die trying to find a better life then so be it." I was impressed by the determination of the two women. They sat down and a murmur of praise went around the circle for their courage.

Cean stood before the group and said, "We must all agree on our next steps, for this is how we make decisions." I looked at the upturned faces and saw fear beginning to recede. Around the circle each person signaled agreement for continuing the journey. Nestor played his drum while our movements renewed the hope living in our hearts. That night I witnessed the magic of the circle as it moved through the group.

I woke to the sound of people shouting, "Here we are." I sat up and began shouting, too. Grabbing our things, we ran shouting in the direction of the voices, but found no one. What we did find was a dirty stream, which Cean and I recognized. We were on the right path! As darkness fell we heard another call. This time it was closer. Running wildly toward the voices, the two groups collided. Laughing, we rolled on the ground and embraced each other. Flow had dreamed truth. The wind had carried our voices to the others, prompting them to call out to us. Our happiness at finding each other was soon dampened. The third group was still missing.

We made camp together and laid out our food. It was plain to see the other group was not interested in mingling with us. Most of them were sitting apart, not sharing their food or company. Before going to bed Grund, Lexy, Cean, and I sat in a circle to discuss our next steps. We needed a plan to guide us as we searched for the third group. And, just as importantly, we needed to encourage community among the two groups. Grund praised Cean and me for our leadership in keeping the group together. His praise awakened my shyness, and I looked down at my feet, but he was right I had a growing sense of strength and confidence.

The next day began with a morning circle. Grund opened by asking us to share a few moments of quiet, and then he came right to the point. "Last night I observed some of you separating yourselves. I want to remind everyone that we are equals on this journey. When we say 'community' we mean a place where all are treated with respect. There are no divisions in our community." Grund paused and waited for the group to respond. Tunk stood to accuse the Corpses of shunning her. Her words opened the gates and a flood of accusations rushed out. The Corpses asserted their right to do anything they wanted and claimed superiority over the others. When it seemed people were about to come to blows, Grund stood and motioned for quiet. He said, "Do you see how nothing is getting resolved here? Your accusations and superiority only add to the bad feelings. I invite you to talk with one another and find a way to live together so we can continue our journey." Both groups froze at his words. They had been so intent on proving each other wrong they had lost touch with their purpose. I watched their faces, which had been flush with anger, turn white with fear. That their conflicts could jeopardize the journey had never occurred to them. There was an awkward silence and then talking.

Eventually, Nestor's great height and broad shoulders rose above the crowd and Moed, tiny though she was, joined him. "We have decided to set aside our differences in service to the journey," they told us. "Names like Corpse, Jobber, and Trasher are no longer useful. They belong to the Corpsety we left behind. Now we will go by our given names and nothing else. Over time we hope the old labels will be forgotten." Grund congratulated them on a job well done and continued to address the group.

He chose his next words carefully: "We need to develop a plan to find the other group." There was silence as he waited for responses. It was Nestor's low voice we heard first. "They left from the east and could still be heading in that direction. Should we change course in the hopes of finding them in the east?" Nake jumped up to suggest we move on and let them find us. "Would this honor our guidelines of connection and community?" Grund asked. Nake frowned but agreed with the others that it would not. Moed gestured to the east and suggested we travel in that direction. Nake argued that going east would cause us to lose precious time. "Now, what Nake says is true," Grund acknowledged. "I'd like for everyone to consider what you would want us to do if you were in the lost group." Around the circle, people agreed they would not want to be abandoned. Finally, it came to Nake, who spoke with his eyes cast down: "I can go along with everyone else but I still think it's a waste of our time." And so, the group made its first serious decision. We would travel east in search of our fellow travelers, and we would do it together.

The group's consensus laid a brick in the foundation of their new lives. Nestor brought out his drum and many joined him in shaking and moving. It was fun to have more than one drummer. Nestor danced around as he drummed wildly while Cean stood quietly and kept to a certain rhythm. I enjoyed the diversity they brought to the group. Negative feelings were hard to hold onto as our bodies cast them to the wind. With a lighter load, we continued our journey.

We walked for days without any sign from the other group, and I began to worry about water. We had planned to be beyond the polluted water by now, but we were far from that goal. Grund had already asked people to ration their water. "Soon," Grund told me, "we will have to reconsider our decision." I was sad to hear his words. I did not want to desert Roz and Thunar, but I understood his reasoning. Love alone could not be the basis for a decision. More days went by without a sign of the lost group. We called out as we walked, but our hope had fallen as low as our tired and battered feet. Flow was walking out beyond the rest of us when, unexpectedly, I caught sight of her hair streaming in the wind as she ran, yelling, "Here we are, here we are." Our legs followed her call and soon we found ourselves in the arms of the lost and found. After a frenzy of hugging, crying, and laughing, we sat down to talk. Several of the young children in the lost group had succumbed to the smoke. They were forced to stop and tend to the sick children. It was a miracle they had stopped, for this allowed us to find them. Surely, this was the Great Mystery holding us close.

SIX

Finding Our Way

That night around the fire, we were happy together. The divisions were beginning to fade as people got to know one another. I watched my new friends and realized how important they were becoming. Friendship is mysterious, I thought. Just when I was certain my heart was filled to the brim with loved ones, it opened to receive others. Maybe hearts are meant to be filled and refilled until they grow large. This too was a mystery.

In the morning we started out as a single group. We numbered more than fifty. The deer, rabbits, and squirrels we passed looked warily at us. They were being invaded by a strange, new herd that stood upright while dragging their possessions behind them. Our smoke-blackened bodies produced a raucous noise that filled the air before and after we appeared. Surely, I thought, we must be frightful creatures in their eyes. Walking long into the evening, we fell to the ground in a stupor that night and were up at dawn the next day. We walked at a grueling pace because of our need to find water.

The six of us had paired off so we could watch over different sections of the group. We hadn't walked far when Lexy called out for help. People were yelling, screaming, hitting, and kicking each other in her area. Grund's stern voice called out, "Stop," and the fighting subsided. Roz called a circle meeting right then and there. She asked for those who were fighting to come forward. "Violence of any kind is a disease," she told them, "which must be carefully addressed and healed. We believe community cannot co-exist with violence because it destroys connections between people and between the Great Mystery and oneself." Someone managed to say, "Don't you want to know why we were fighting?" "First, we must address the violence," Roz responded. "After that we can talk." The perpetrators sat silently, looking sullen.

"Now, we ask each of you who committed violence to work with us to restore the broken harmony. Are you willing to do this?" she asked firmly. Reluctantly the violators mumbled their agreement.

Roz motioned for those who had been attacked to come forward and explain what had happened. Eagerly Nake rushed forward to speak, and I couldn't help noticing how his balding head was so often out in front of us. "They accused us of hoarding water and not sharing it," he shouted. Others supported Nake, saying they had been unjustly attacked. "Are you hoarding water?" Roz asked. "Absolutely not," he responded. "Then why were you accused?" He was silent and she asked again, "Why were you accused?" "Perhaps they are jealous because we have done a better job of saving water," Nake said smugly. Vilet shyly asked if she could speak. She had overheard women talking about bringing extra water, and Flow had seen the same women hiding extra bags of water inside their clothes. Roz asked if this was true and Nake denied it. Then, she asked the attackers, "What did it feel like to believe others had extra water they weren't sharing?" The attackers expressed anger and also sadness because the others didn't care if they were thirsty.

Upon hearing their words, some of Nake's supporters began to falter, and soon we had the truth. The wealthy Corpse had purchased extra water. They decided not to share it, in order to ensure their survival. Looking guilty, Nake complained, "Don't we have a right to look out for our own welfare?" Much to Nake's surprise Roz responded positively. "Yes Nake, you not only have the right but the sacred responsibility to look out for your welfare." A smirk came over Nake's face as he drew himself to his full height and puffed his chest out. Roz continued, "Tell me, Nake, if your small group survives and the rest of us perish from lack of water will you have looked out for your welfare?" Nake was mute as the smirk faded from his lips. "How long do you think your group would last alone in the Wild?" Roz continued. Nake collapsed under the weight of her words. He looked as if all the air had been sucked out of his body. He stood there looking small and bewildered. Roz was quiet for a moment and then she spoke: "We have learned it is better to share so that everyone is nurtured and cared for. In this way, we protect the diversity of thinking, acting, and being that resides in each person. Without such diversity we would not live long in the Wild, for its challenges are vast and unknown. We need each other in order to survive and thrive. Taking care of others *is* taking care of our individual welfare."

After Roz finished speaking, people rose and brought their

extra water to the circle, placing it in the center without being asked. "Shared water is holy water," Grund announced. Pouring out a few drops on the ground, he offered it up to the Great Mystery in prayer. After a time of quiet, he asked, "How many people have a day's supply of water left?" About half the group raised their hands. "If we share this water and conserve, I think we can expect to keep going for a few more days. Hopefully by that time we will have reached a safe water supply." Around the circle everyone looked relieved. Roz requested one more thing before we ended our circle. "To lie about something as serious as life-sustaining water is an act of violence. I would like for those who lied about the extra water they carried to work with us to restore harmony." "Do we have a choice?" Nake asked. The others in his group shouted for him to sit down and take his medicine. Nake sat down. He had been roundly chastised by his own group. He would go along with the others. "You have made a wise decision," Grund announced as we gathered our things and continued the journey.

Cean and I were given several of those who had been violent to work with. One of them was named Quake, and he didn't seem happy to be with us. Cean asked about his background, but he didn't have much to say except that he had worked in the Trash pits for a long time. Cean observed how hard that must have been and Quake nodded but didn't say more. In this way, we began the process of nurturing and arounding him with our presence and goodwill. We would stay with Quake and the others until they could let go of their violent ways.

On and on we walked, stopping only briefly to eat or rest.

One evening I was exhausted and tripped over a rocky patch, but Quake caught me before I fell. I gratefully thanked him and for the first time I saw the shadow of a smile pass over his face. The night was cool and Cean and I drew close together to stay warm. We encouraged Quake to move closer and share our warmth, but he was reluctant. "I have never slept close to anyone," he explained. Cean and I shared how we slept in the company of others at home. Quake looked puzzled. "Will you tell me more about this in the morning?" We nodded our heads. At least our gentle influence was beginning to break through his guardedness.

With bleary eyes, we met another gray day and walked toward the chance of finding water. The black smoke was gone and I longed to dip into a stream and be rid of its residue. Quake walked beside us as we explained what life was like in Life Community. We spoke of our respect for elders and healers. I shared how much fun it was too search for food, build shelters, and prepare meals together. When Cean described how group meetings helped us grow, Quake wanted to know about the meetings. "Do you always agree on things?" he asked. "Well," Cean said as he scratched his head, "sometimes it takes a long time but, yes, in the end we all agree." Quake shook his head and replied, "This seems unnatural to me. The way of life is to fight and argue." "You are right," Cean agreed, "fighting is one way to respond to life, but it is not the only way. We find that listening and speaking our truth in a spirit of respect and cooperation works much better than arguing and fighting. Think about this, Quake. When you fight with someone what is the outcome?" "Sometimes I get what I want and sometimes

I don't." Cean pressed him further: "And what happens to your relationship?" "We don't have one." "Oh yes you do," Cean countered. "You have a negative relationship based on using—power over." Once again, Cean pushed him to reflect: "How do you think this will affect your future relationship?" Quake shrugged his shoulders in confusion and then spoke in a whisper, "You are not like me. You see and understand things in strange ways. I'll never be good enough to belong to your community." I saw the same wary look in his eyes that I had witnessed before. I put my arm around him. "You are good enough, Quake. You cannot be expected to act differently just yet. We are here to see that you have the opportunity to learn another way." He quickly turned away from me but not before I saw the tears in his eyes.

Teaching made the time fly by and soon it was evening. With no water in sight, Grund called another meeting. A strong current of unhappiness flowed through the group as we sat eating dry biscuits that stuck in our throats. "How many people have water left?" Grund asked. Only a few people lifted their hands. He asked for ideas about our next step and Nake launched an all-out attack on Grund. "You're the leader; you are supposed to know what to do next. You got us out here in the Wild without water and now you are asking us what to do. Are you crazy or just plain stupid?" I noticed Grund's protruding ears turned a little red, but he remained calm though Nake's onslaught. "Treating me with disrespect will do us no good, Nake. To answer your question, yes, I am asking you and the others what you want to do now. What is your solution, Nake?" Nake glowered at Grund: "I want someone else to be our leader. I want someone who knows how to find water to take us there." In the midst of their conversation, Flow raised her hand tentatively and Grund acknowledged her.

"I have an idea," she said in a small voice. All eyes turned to her and I moved closer to lend support. I knew what it felt like to stand before a group of hostile adults. "Why don't those with water go exploring tomorrow? They could take empty bags with them." Glowing with maternal pride, Vilet suggested we follow Flow's plan and send the strongest and fastest people. Grund asked for other ideas but no one came forward. There was considerable grumbling about following the advice of a child and I put my arm around Flow's shoulder for support. Still, no one could come up with a better solution and, in the end, Flow's suggestion was accepted.

Grund invited everyone to stop and consider what had just happened. "We have no leader in this group but our collective selves. Together we are wiser. Tonight it was a child's inspiration that led us. When we share and build on each other's ideas, we create leadership that exceeds what any one of us could provide. I realize this is a new idea for those of you who are accustomed to the Corpsety making your decisions. And, I ask you to consider the difference. In the Corpsety there is needless suffering and death based on leadership of the few. In Life Community we seek to promote life and prevent unnecessary suffering through leadership of the many. Leadership is something we create together."

Grund thanked everyone for staying in the circle and coming to a decision. He signaled for Nestor to bring out his drum for shaking. Even though we were tired, our bodies responded to the rhythms of the drum and we were lulled into quietude. The others drifted off to their sleeping places while Grund asked for those of us from Life Community to stay. He reckoned Cean, Lexy, and I would be the best ones to accompany three of the young people to look for water. We agreed. He pulled out the map and advised us to carefully take note of our surroundings so we could find our way back. We were grateful to Grund for his work with the group tonight and arounded him in a giant hug. He smiled and opened his arms wide as if to embrace the whole group and said, "They are learning, and so are we. The Great Mystery is working though us. What more can we ask?"

With the beat of the drum still in my body, I slept soundly and woke early. I was ready to be of service. Cean had the map and would lead the way while Lexy and I took note of the environment. Not far from camp the ground turned rocky and steep. I hoped this was a sign we were close to water, but we were not so lucky. It took another two days before the sound of moving water pulled us to it. As if beckoning to us, the stream opened its arms and we gladly surrendered to its embrace. Once again the Wild had granted us life and we gloried in its cool wetness. With water spilling out of our bags, we began walking. We needed to reach the others as quickly as possible. Our camp was simple that night, without a fire or protection except for a single night watchman.

I had just drifted off to sleep when Cean awakened me. Through the fog of sleep I heard him say, "Stand tall and pick up rocks. Wolves are surrounding us." I helped wake the others while Cean lit a torch that revealed the now familiar yellow eyes. Soundlessly they edged closer to us. We began shouting and Cean waved the torch at the wolves. They retreated a short distance but did not leave. Suddenly, a large wolf lunged toward us, but Lexy was poised to strike. She hit it with a well-thrown rock and the stunned wolf retreated. Unmoved, the rest of the wolves continued to circle us. Yelling loudly, we picked up rocks and began throwing them with wild intensity. We were quite fierce and the wolves eventually scattered. It was dark and we couldn't be sure how far away they had moved. Lexy, Cean, and I held the torch and kept watch for the rest of the night. We set out again at daylight hoping to reach the camp by nightfall. Shouts of joy greeted us when we returned to the group late that night. Life-sustaining water had arrived.

In the morning we held a ceremony of thanks and told the story of the circling wolves. The group was frightened and announced they would kill any wolves they encountered. We listened to their fears. Then, Roz spoke of Life Community where all beings—human, animal, and plant—live together in harmony. "We kill animals and gather plants when we need to eat or defend ourselves," she explained, "and afterwards we honor their spirits. The majority of the time we live in harmony with animals and they with us. In this way, the natural balance is maintained and all are free to enjoy the Wild's abundance." Her voice deepened as she continued. "We are not better than the wolves or any other beings. We have our place and they have theirs. It would be wrong for us to kill them out of fear. It is better for us to deal with our own fears." Around the fire, I saw the wary look return. To the others, perhaps we were as frightening as wolves. After all, we were asking them to cross the line between human and animal, and live openly in communion with the Wild. In their eyes this was blasphemous.

Today the sun appeared from underneath the gray pall. It was a golden ball hanging in the sky. People were mesmerized and stared at it so long they began to see black spots. We travelled to the stream to refill our water bags and wash the Corpsety's stain from our bodies. It was here that a few people announced they were taking their water bags and heading back to the Corpsety. Grund and Thunar spoke to them about the dangers but they were resolute. They wanted nothing to do with the kind of uncertainty we faced. And so, we let them go. Thunar offered directions and extra food for the journey, which they gladly accepted. Everyone watched as they walked away, some with sadness and others with envy, but all watched. I wondered how they would fare alone in the Wild. I saw Thunar in deep conversation with Grund and moved closer to hear what they were saying. Thunar was trying to understand if there was something he had failed to do to help the two who had been in his group. Grund listened while Thunar talked and then asked, "Was there something you neglected to tell them?" Thunar could come up with no answer. "Then," Grund counseled, "you have done the best you could and that is all we ask of anyone." I was surprised to hear Thunar doubting himself, but it was also reassuring. Perhaps my doubts had a purpose if they helped me to reflect and make changes.

At nightfall another surprise awaited the group. They were awed by the sight of yet another orb and twinkling points of light. Around the fire we talked of that which is unknown to those living in the Corpsety. One by one the group members voiced their gratitude for the opportunity to witness beauty. The Wild had begun to weave its web of connection around them.

In the days that followed we saw trees, and soon we were in the forest. The magic of the forest captivated everyone including Nake. Hunting was possible now and Thunar and Lexy killed a young deer that we cooked over the fire. This was the first time many of the group members had tasted fresh meat. The Corpsety's soft canned meat had not prepared them for the tearing and chewing real meat called for. I did my best not to laugh as they tore it with their hands and let it hang out of their mouths as they chewed. I'm sure I must have been a funny sight the first time I ate meat. We also found grubs to roast and shoots and nuts to eat. These foods were strange to the new ones and initially some refused it, but hunger had a way of cutting through their squeamishness.

After our meal we sat around the fire and Cean began singing a song of thanksgiving. When the song ended Moed asked its meaning. "Our song offers gratitude to the deer, insects, and plants who offered themselves to us," Cean replied. "It also tells the other beings of the forest we mean them no harm and will take only what we need to survive." Moed was skeptical and said, "Are you joking? Everyone knows insects, animals, and plants can't understand words." "Are you sure of that?" Cean countered. "We sang from our hearts, which is a universal language." Cean's response did not convince Moed, so Roz added, "We can choose to ignore our connections to nature and all the beings of the world, or we can choose to honor them. Honoring them gives us a sense of balance and connection that is nurturing and healing. The Corpsety fosters disconnection and teaches that the natural world exists only for our exploitation. In Life Community we opened our hearts to the Wild and discovered just how wrong the Corpsety is." Moed and the others looked confused and we left them to their confusion. This was all part of the learning.

SEVEN

Learning the Ropes

Each day it seemed I woke to the sounds of arguing. Once I saw Nake raise his arm as if to strike his wife only to lower it when he noticed he was being watched. Clearly the group was struggling with conflict. Our environment was being flooded with constant bickering and an undertow of violence. I found myself becoming tense and watchful, just as I had in the Corpsety. I shared my feelings with Roz and she agreed. "We are all being affected by the negative currents," she said. The wise ones decided to call a circle meeting to speak of it.

"How do you respectfully approach each other when you have a conflict?" Roz asked the group. They avoided looking at her and gave no response. She asked again but was met with silence. "Ah," Roz said, "not knowing must be causing you a lot of grief." This got a response. A few heads nodded and some even mumbled affirmations, so she continued. "In the Corpsety there was no reason to be respectful. You went about your business unconcerned about others because you had no relationship with them, no incentive to cooperate. Oh, perhaps you had a family or a few friends, but mostly you did not interact with others. Am I right?" Everyone's head nodded this time. "Here, in the Wild, we are dependent on each other for protection, leadership, food, and community. Treating others with respect is the first and most important skill you need to learn in order to live in Life Community. Respect asks us to value others, even when we disagree. With respect we speak gently, listen carefully, and offer a kind response. Seeking to understand, we let go of judgment and invite curiosity. Once we understand where another person is coming from, we offer our perspective. Only after these things have been done is it possible to resolve conflict."

"In Life Community we have learned that the natural law of cooperation cannot exist where unresolved conflict is present. Notice I didn't say where conflict is present, but rather *unresolved* conflict. The natural laws do not require the absence of conflict. Conflict is like an arrow pointing to differing needs. If we let the arrow pierce us we will be hurt. But, when we follow the arrow's trajectory back to its source, we discover the answer to working together. Since we cannot survive without cooperating, there is a powerful incentive to learn how to resolve conflict." Roz paused and invited someone with a conflict to come forward.

Vilet rose and, with a voice choked with emotion, shared her conflict. "Others are talking about me and spreading rumors that I'm not a good mother to Flow and Hak. I've never had children of my own so I worry that I'm doing something wrong. No one will speak directly to me about this and I'm feeling worried and angry. I would like help instead of hurtful whispering behind my back." I admired Vilet for being so honest and vulnerable. Grund moved closer and named what was happening to her as "gossip," a particularly injurious form of emotional violence. "Violence isn't always physical," he said. "Words and negative actions can be as harmful as a fist."

He asked for those who had spread rumors about Vilet to come forward and share their side of the story. Grund stood silently waiting while we waited with him. Eventually, a soft-spoken woman came forward to say she was afraid she had started the rumors. She had not meant to hurt Vilet when she told others about offering Vilet advice and being rebuffed. After that the rumors had taken on a life of their own and she didn't know how to stop them. "How do you feel now?" Grund asked. She hesitated and took her time answering, "Well, I guess I still feel Vilet thinks she is better than me and doesn't value my opinion." "Is there more?" Grund asked gently. "I'm ashamed that I've caused so much trouble," she said quietly, "and I'd like to apologize." Now, it was Vilet's turn to talk. "I'm so sorry I gave you the impression I didn't care," she said with tears in her eyes. "I do care and I never meant to brush you off. I know so little about raising a child that I need all the help I can get." The two women hugged and expressed their relief.

Grund nodded at the two women and asked the group, "Can you see how misunderstandings and gossip hurt others?" Some, but not all, of them nodded in agreement. "Can you see how respect, listening, and honest sharing can bring about resolution?" Vilet's partner Tunk responded to Grund's questions. Tunk was a happy person who hardly ever had a quarrel with anyone. She had a big, loving heart and I was surprised to hear her speak. "I can see how it works, but I still don't know how to do it," she said. "You will learn," Grund told her. "It is our job to teach you."

"Gossip is part of the Corpsety's world," Grund explained, "where judgment, unresolved conflict, and violence are the norm. Gossip eats at the roots of connection and causes relationships to fail. In Life Community, we attend to seemingly small issues, like gossip, because they reflect the value system of the Corpsety. The Corpsety has corrupted our human value system by turning us away from the natural laws of connection, cooperation, conservation, and community. It is often in small ways that we must be vigilant about upholding human values, while giving up the Corpsety's values of competition, greed, violence, and conflict. Learning how to be together in a different way is what Life Community is all about. It's as simple and as difficult as that."

After Roz and Grund had spoken, a loud buzzing filled the air as people talked. When the group quieted Grund asked each person to answer a question: "Can you agree to abide by our guidelines?" Around the circle each person promised to do their best to follow them. He thanked the group for their willingness and assured them we were not asking for perfection, only commitment.

The fog of distrust and judgment began to fade as we travelled, and people often gathered around us to listen to our Life Community stories. Cean and I told of finding our place, building our buildings, discovering foods, making difficult decisions, discovering the Wild, and, finally, learning to live together. They showered us with questions, and although we listened, we encouraged them to find their own answers. We did not want to become the experts they had followed in the Corpsety.

One evening as we looked for a place to camp storm clouds rolled in, and it quickly became dark. We began to set up camp outside the forest. A few people wanted to camp in the forest for protection. We gave them our reasons for staying outside, but they argued with us. They were certain they had a better solution and headed for the forest, despite our warnings. They would have to learn their own lessons since it was not our way to force them to stay with us. Soon it was raining and the wind was rising. We huddled together with blankets over our heads, shivering with cold and fear. Thunder and lightning crashed around us and we hugged the ground to escape the storm's wrath. The fierce wind howled through the forest, and I was concerned for those who had chosen to stay there.

Hours later we stood to shake the rain off as the storm transformed itself into a drizzle. Quake was the first to see the others coming toward us. We ran to meet them and were shocked to see their wild eyes, torn clothes, and bloodied hands. I knew at once they had experienced the wrath of the Wild. They told us large animals had attacked them during the storm, and though they called for help, their voices went unheeded. We lit our torches and set out to find the rest of the group. Just inside the forest we found them. The sight we witnessed was far worse than the fallen tree I had imagined. There were mangled dead bodies scattered on the ground while those who survived were walking around in a stupor. Nake had been wounded trying to save his wife and child. The survivors followed us back to camp without complaint. In the morning Roz, Lexy, and I would gather herbs and roots to make compresses. We comforted them as best we could and slept fitfully through this dreadful night. In the morning, we covered the dead bodies with blankets until the fire grew hot, and then we sent them on their way with our blessings.

Quake and Thunar found a cave where the injured could be tended. I feared they would not survive their wounds, but surprisingly only one person died. We stayed in the cave for several days until the injured began to recover. They returned to life with an overwhelming desire to kill the animals which had attacked them. They wanted revenge. Nake was particularly angry at us for not coming to their aid. Grund called a meeting so they could speak what was in their hearts. We hoped this would bring healing to their injured souls.

Everyone listened as the survivors told their terrible stories and shared their anger and fear. When they had finished, Moed was the first to respond. She spoke of her sorrow for lost friends and the pain of injured friends. She reminded Nake that they had been warned but chose to stay in the forest. After Moed finished, Vilet rose to speak. She said, "The forest is home to the animals and we are intruders. What happened was horrendous and I am deeply sorry for your pain and suffering. That does not mean the animals deserve to die." Her words did not impress the injured. With his face screwed up into a grimace, one of the injured cried out, "How can we live with such animals? They care nothing for us." Another appeared as if she were in a trance but spoke nonetheless. "You were not there, so you do not know how horrible the animals were, tearing off arms and legs without any remorse. And the sounds they made, the sounds are still in my ears, I don't think I will ever be rid of them." A child who witnessed the mauling raised his arms and began growling and grunting as if to attack us. "You see," his mother said as she tried to quiet him, "he cannot forget the horror either." Obsessed with their losses, they believed the only solution to their pain was to seek revenge. Cean rose to speak. He stood tall with his mane of russet hair, broad shoulders, and tears streaming down his face. His presence brought a measure of calm to the group.

"In Life Community we are sad when someone dies," he acknowledged, "because we miss their presence. And, we know that death and change are part of the natural order that we cannot escape. When we experience a death, we honor the life of a person and then we let them go. Death is a passing over into a place we do not know, a place inhabited by the Great Mystery. We go on with our lives because we must. That is what life asks us to do. Revenge is not a helpful response to loss because it prevents us from letting go."

Nake stood with a face full of rage and sorrow. He could hardly speak but managed to sputter, "That's easy for you to say. You have not lost your wife and daughter." Cean moved closer to Nake and knelt down in front of him. He spoke gently, "You are right, Nake, I have not lost a wife or daughter, but I have lost dear friends who meant a great deal to me. I will have to live with my loss just as you will have to live with yours. Please, let us comfort each other rather than blame and isolate ourselves. We need each other's company now more than ever." Nake closed his eyes and fell into Cean's arms, sobbing. We sat and cried with him, letting our tears and moans create a cacophony of grief. I reflected on the fickle nature of life. It could be full of passion, beauty, and movement one minute and stone cold the next. There is no comfort to be found in holding on to life, I thought, we can only embrace it moment by moment.

When the sun rose the next day, we set off once more for our journey. I noticed Quake was not beside us as usual and sought him out. I found him pulling a sled fashioned out of branches for one of the injured children. I was awed by the transformation I saw in him. His violence and belligerence had melted away under the warmth of friendship. Now he was happy being of service to others. "Have you noticed a change in yourself?" I asked. He smiled a sheepish grin and answered, "Oh, yes. I've noticed." "You've done good work, Quake, and I don't think you need to walk with us anymore," I responded. His face quickly fell and I saw his brow furrow as he mumbled, "But I want to walk with you." "Oh, Quake, I didn't mean you couldn't; I just meant you don't have to anymore." I put my arm around his shoulders and invited him to be my friend. With tears in his eyes, he thanked me without turning away. Quake had finally found his place in the world.

The group moved at a snail's pace. People were tired of the journey, and we were slowed by the infirmities of the injured. Those of us from Life Community sat down to assess our situation and Grund asked for our opinion of the group. We agreed they had made good progress. The violence was diminishing and we saw more cooperation and sharing. And, there were still areas of weakness.

EIGHT

Waiting to Get In

Grund reckoned we were within a few days of home. He asked what we thought about setting up camp outside Life Community while the group continued to work on the weak areas. He was not sure they were ready to enter. This seemed like a good idea to us, but we wondered how the group would take the news. They were sure to be unhappy and possibly even resistant to our plan. I was excited to be returning, but then again, I would not really be home. Along with the group, we would be entering a liminal state that was somewhere between home and not home. I wondered how we would navigate this strange place.

We traveled until we arrived at a place with water and shelter. Even though it was midday we set up camp and Grund called a meeting. People were curious about why we had stopped, and a buzz of voices greeted me as I moved into the circle. Grund, Lexy, Roz, Thunar, Cean, and I stood together as Grund announced we were near to Life Community, but would not enter until we felt the group was ready. Although he was still unsteady on his feet, Nake stood and challenged our right to make this decision. "We are ready," he shouted, "and who are you to tell us what to do? You said we are all equal, and this isn't equal treatment." Others joined with him while shaking their fists at us. Roz responded to his complaints with a firm but quiet resolve. "You are correct, Nake, we are all equal, and we do make consensus decisions. But, this is a special situation. We have been given the task of helping you learn the community guidelines. When you enter Life Community, you must be able to adjust to a different kind of life. We continue to see areas where more work is needed. The fists you raise today are good examples of this." She asked each person to honestly consider if they were ready to enter into a community where our guidelines are the norm.

Around the circle people acknowledged they were not yet ready to enter a place where they would be held to such high standards. They also admitted to their fear of failure. Nestor summed it up for many people when he spoke: "I know what you want me to do and I want to do it, but I've been doing things the opposite way for so long that I doubt my ability to change. I don't want to turn people in Life Community against me. I want to join them as an equal." Nake, and those who sided with him, did not back down. They demanded to make their own decision and do as they liked. Grund asked for a vote on the issue and it went in favor of waiting. Before Grund could speak, Nake shouted that they would not abide by the vote. Grund rose slowly and acknowledged Nake. "We don't expect you to abide by it. We expect you to sit with everyone and work out a solution we can all live with." Nake had presented the group with a perfect problem-solving opportunity, and

Grund was not about to let it slip away. He asked the group to begin talking about possible solutions. Hesitantly, the group engaged each other in a dialogue which continued throughout the afternoon without agreement. Restlessness overcame the group as evening fell and Grund called for shaking. I noticed everyone, even Nake, was shaking with us. We sat quietly afterward and people began to drift away. We would reconvene tomorrow morning, but for now we could eat and relax. I was walking away when the sound of Grund's voice called me back. We needed to discuss our next steps. Roz, Thunar, and Lexy would return to Life Community to get supplies and let them know about our plan. I was disappointed not to be going home, but I didn't want to miss the meeting tomorrow either. The others would give my love to Father and Illow. I would see them soon enough.

People talked into the night around the fire and seemed to genuinely want to find a good resolution. I noticed Nake and his group keeping their own company, so I went over to talk with them. They were unhappy because the others wouldn't go along with them. "What will happen if we leave the discussion?" Nake asked. I told him they would be on their own. This got their attention. "Have you considered what you really need?" I asked. "I mean, what is behind your desire to enter right away?" Nake responded that they needed to be in charge of their own lives and make their own decisions. "And yet," I said softly, "you don't want to be left outside of Life Community. How do you reconcile these two things?" Nake was confused and said, "I want to do both." "If you can't do both, which do you choose?" I asked. The small group was silent. I could see I had struck a nerve, so I continued. "Life Community is based on community principles, not on the rights of the individual. While individuals are free to express their uniqueness, decisions and guidelines are made by the community and upheld by individuals. Otherwise there is no community." Nake's face screwed up into a grimace as he said, "So, we are not free to do as we choose." "If your choices fit within the community's values and guidelines you are free to do as you please, and you are always free to leave," I responded. They continued talking heatedly and I took my leave. I wasn't sure if I had helped or made the situation worse.

The next day we woke to find that Nake's small group had left in the night. I worried that I had caused them to leave and told Grund about our conversation. "They made their own decision, Mariah," he said sadly. "It was not your doing. Perhaps the guidelines are too difficult for some to abide by." Grund started the group by calling for shaking and then quiet sitting so we could send our goodwill to the people who had left. Everyone was touched by their absence and it cast a cloud over the group. It was late in the evening before the group made the decision to stay outside Life Community for two weeks and then reassess.

Roz and the others returned with well wishes, food, and water. Life Community understood our decision and gave us their blessing to stay outside as long as we needed. With sadness in our voices we told them of those who had left in the night. Roz responded much the same as Grund had, saying, "Life Community may not be for everyone, and we must accept that." Still, it was sad to think of them wandering alone, and I was worried that Nake was still in shock from his losses.

We resumed the teachings, encouraging people to apply the values and guidelines to their daily lives. We challenged them to move out into the natural environment and sit with the plant and animal world. We delighted in watching them grow and discover the treasures life held. Our confidence grew until we felt our small group understood how to live the values and guidelines of Life Community.

At the end of two weeks, a meeting was called, and people seemed nervous as they gathered around the circle. Before the meeting could start we were shocked to see Nake and his small group of followers in the distance. We stood with gaping mouths as they approached and quickly made a space for them in the center of the circle. They were thin and walked slowly. Nake spoke weakly, "We ask to be let back into the community. We were wrong." Grund asked what had changed their minds. Another man continued, "We started quarrelling almost as soon as we left about which way to go, what to do, and how to get food." Nake spoke again: "You were right about needing a community and how the individual can't do it alone." Then, he collapsed on the ground and Roz moved to help him. Grund announced that he would like to extend our time for two more weeks so the small group could catch up with the others. There were rumblings and someone shouted out, "They've been dragging their feet all along. How long do we have to wait for them?" Grund stood and surveyed the group with eyes that commanded attention. "We will wait as long as it takes. It's clear everyone has not yet learned the primary lesson of community:

we all rise up or all fall down together. It is our responsibility and our honor to help those who are struggling to find their way. This is both the strength and the power of community. The proper response would be to greet them with respect and a desire to be supportive. So, what shall we do now?" he asked.

People were embarrassed by Grund's stern words. It didn't take long for the group to reach consensus. They agreed to reassess in another two weeks and dispersed in a subdued mood. Cean and I made it a point to tell Nake how much we appreciated his honesty and the courage it took to return. Cean reminded Nake how the natural law of connection teaches us that until all are ready none are ready. I thought Cean's words were especially wise, and the intensity of his blue eyes caught my attention. Here was a man to be reckoned with, I thought.

NINE

Home and Back Again

The next day Cean, Grund, and I set out to visit Life Community. Wolf ran out to greet us and I was happy to see her yellow eyes. I had worried Wolf might forget me, but she greeted me with yelps of joy. Father and Illow met us at the entrance and I noticed Illow was walking slowly. Her sunken face made her eyes large and bright. She seemed tired. I wondered how much longer she would be with us. Father clasped me in a warm hug and didn't want to let me go. "Mariah, you have changed," he said, as he pulled away. "You've become a woman." I noticed a tear rolling down his cheek and moved to wipe it away. "Father, I will always be your little girl," I teased. He smiled and patted my head, but he was right, I had changed. We walked to the community center to greet everyone and were arounded by their love and friendship. More than ever, I understood why the new ones needed to wait. It would be a tragedy for them to disrupt the harmony we had worked so hard to build. I told Father and Illow it would be at least two more weeks before we brought the new ones into the community. Illow nodded her head and said, "It will be no easy task for them or for us. You are right to take your time."

A community celebration was quickly put together and we were showered with food, singing, and dancing. Dance was one of my favorite activities. As our bodies pressed one against the other a warm connection held us. We became one with the beat of the drum and with each other. I felt close to the Great Mystery when I danced with my friends because our dance was an affirmation of life.

That night, another dream held me close. The Great Mystery appeared to me as a golden light telling me everything we have is a gift and nothing we do is original. Ideas, thoughts, words, and discoveries are the Great Mystery's way of sharing with us. Individuals may channel knowledge, but it does not belong to them. The natural order of things is to let knowledge flow freely, for gifts from the Great Mystery belong to all. We may use, share, and return gifts, but we must never place limits on them through ownership. Gifts are meant to pass from individual to collective and back again to the Great Mystery in an unending cycle.

I awoke with a feeling of confusion. The golden light had warmed and soothed me, but what did the words mean? I needed some help and sought out Father and Illow. They were in the community center sharing a cup of fragrant water. I shared my dream and then my feelings of confusion. Father was silent but Illow spoke solemnly: "Mariah, I think your dream reminds us that what we have created, Life Community, is not of our making but is a gift from the Great Mystery. Perhaps it is no mistake that this comes at a time when we are bringing new people in. We will be tried and tested when the new ones arrive fresh from the Corpsety's grasp. Your dream reminds us of the gift of community and of our responsibility to share it." Father nodded his head in agreement and added that the dream ought to be shared with others in preparation for the arrival of the new ones.

Father left to arrange a meeting while Illow and I walked. I was worried about her and asked how she had fared while we were away. She looked at me, her thin face alight with enthusiasm. "I am well, little one, and I am slowing down. I notice my energy has decreased, but my joy in living is still strong and will keep me going for a while longer. It is kind of you to ask," she said softly, as she put her frail, blue-veined hand in mine. We walked silently into the forest and spent the afternoon gathering, visiting, and enjoying each other's company. I tried to put Illow's words "a while longer" out of my mind.

Returning from the forest, I caught sight of our home rising up against the mountain surrounded by the flowing stream. Its beauty brought tears to my eyes and I told Illow I hoped it would never change. Illow stopped in her tracks and an odd look came over her face. Had I said something to offend her? "Mariah, you must remember that life is always changing and nothing stays the same. All of life is in a constant state of movement and even communities must change." Her words caused me sadness. "Is there nothing to hold onto?" I sighed. Tenderly, Illow put her thin arm around my shoulders. "What are you sad about, little one?" I shared what had happened between Lexy and Thunar and what I suspected was happening between Roz and Father. I told her of my fears about being left alone. "We do not know the future, Mariah, but life can be good without a partner." I had forgotten that Illow had never been partnered and started to sputter an apology when she stopped me. "I have found comfort in my relationship with the Great Mystery and have desired no other." This relationship allowed me to see how the cycle of life is without end. How life seeks to grow, even after death, as our bodies supply nourishment for other living things. How our spirits continue to grow and learn through death and eventually into rebirth. And, it has blessed me with the gift of spiritual healing. As a healer, I have been given the honor of sharing in the birth of the life cycle over and over again. I have experienced great joy by participating fully in life and in the life of the spirit. Her words of wisdom settled over me and I was comforted. She had given an important teaching and I did not want to forget it. "Thank you, Illow," I whispered as we entered into the center of Life Community.

Spirits were high around the circle and I was happy to be arounded by the energy of people looking forward to a meeting. Father began the circle by announcing I had a dream to share. I stood and looked at the faces of my friends who were waiting to hear what I might say. It was good to be home. I shared my dream, but no one seemed to understand its meaning. Illow shared her sense that the dream pointed to the community we had created and how we would soon be asked to share it with others. "I believe it is a sign that we will be sorely tried and tested as we hold fast to the natural laws and the will of the Great Mystery," she told them. There was silence as the group absorbed Illow's words. Then, with a solemn nodding of heads, they accepted the responsibility and the challenge that stood before them. The community they had created did not belong to them—it was to be shared with others.

The next day Grund, Cean, and I returned to a camp in turmoil. Two of the children had eaten poisonous nuts. To my horror I found that one of the children was Flow's brother, Hak. The children had brought nuts back to camp with them and when they became ill, Roz was called. She immediately identified the nuts as poisonous but did not know how to counteract their effects. I went to work trying to help Roz find an antidote, but the best we could do for the children was to give them herbs to make them vomit. Hak vomited a little, but the other child could not. We made the children as comfortable as we could and sang soothing songs while stroking their little arms and faces. Both children were feverish and delirious. Roz and I stayed with them through the night, and toward dawn one child took his last breath. Only Hak remained.

We waited with him for two days until he became responsive. His eyes were sunken and ringed with dark circles. His face was ashen and he looked like a ghost. When Hak finally opened his eyes they held an odd blank look, but it seemed he would survive. Flow cried and threw her arms around him, but he was indifferent to her. He had been harmed in some way by the poison. Vilet took Flow to get some rest while Roz and I cared for Hak. We would need to find someone in the community to sit with him until he made a full recovery.

A funeral bonfire was built for the dead child's ceremony. He had brought joy to his parents and his presence had changed their lives. Flow spoke for Hak, telling of their friendship. In silence the small body was placed on the fire, while we sang songs and sent our prayers with him. We thanked the Great Mystery for his life as we gave him back to the spirit world. The fire consumed his young body as we held each other in a circle, swaying and weeping together.

Illow called a meeting to ask who would volunteer to stay with Hak as he recovered, and much to my surprise Nake volunteered. Perhaps caring for Hak would help Nake move through his grief over the loss of his child and wife. Roz asked everyone to teach the children not to eat anything unless it had been approved by an adult. "The Wild is a dangerous place," she explained. "We must teach and protect the children until they can fend for themselves."

Under Nake and Roz's care Hak gained strength and became more responsive, but he had lost the ability to speak. Flow was happy he was alive, and they seemed to be able to communicate without words. Nake's sore heart softened as he cared for Hak, and he became his friend and mentor.

The teachings continued. Once again we saw growth in the group's ability to embody the guiding principles. Our last task would be to mark the transition from the Corpsety to Life Community. We wanted to honor letting go of the old corrupt ways as a heroic task, for we knew living life backwards makes it difficult to turn around. A rite of passage needed to be created so the group could leave the past behind and go forward toward life and the natural order of things.

TEN

Turned Toward Life (The Ceremonies)

We settled on a three-part rite of passage for the group's final transition. First, there would be a circle of leave-taking where people would make peace with their past and say good-bye to the wounds they suffered in the Corpsety. Next, they would enter into a circle of renewal. Here, individual stories would be told and growth honored. Finally, a circle of reclamation would allow people to call back the fragments of their spirits lost to the Corpsety's values of greed, violence, "power-over," and judgment. This final step would help them to become whole people again.

At each step, we anticipated there would be an outpouring of pain and grief. We knew a "safe container" would be a crucial part of the process. The container would be created by the group's willingness to listen and bear witness, without turning away, as each person spoke of their pain and suffering. The witnessing of the group would be crucial, for tragedy must be faced fully in order to bring forth healing. Once the circles were completed, we would form a procession and walk to Life Community.

We were preparing for the circles when Nake and Moed interrupted us. They wanted to talk privately. "A group of men have been killing small animals for sport," Moed shared. "It started with some Corpses but quickly spread to include others." Both Nake and Moed felt this was drawing the group closer to the Corpsety's death cycle. We were stunned. Clearly everyone was not ready. We affirmed their wisdom in coming to us and shared a moment of grateful silence. We would call the group together tomorrow, but not for the purpose we had planned.

Grund, Roz, Cean, Thunar, Lexy, and I were somber as we entered into the circle the next day. This time Cean took the lead. He began with strong words: "It has been brought to our attention that some of you have been killing for sport. This is in direct violation of our guidelines. We need to know who was involved in the killing and who knew about it. I'm asking you to come forward now." Moed and Nake stood to say they knew about it, but no one else came forward. We sat in stillness. Cean broke silence briefly to say, "We will wait in the circle until all those involved come forward." The evening passed and darkness descended. Children began to get restless and their mothers took them off to bed. Soon others wandered off to find their sleeping places. Cean, Grund, Roz, Lexy, Thunar, and I continued to sit in the circle, and so did Nake and Moed. Those who had abandoned the process woke the next morning to see us still sitting in the circle. Reluctantly, they rejoined us. We continued to sit in silence. The sun was overhead by the time a solitary man stood hesitantly and with a bowed head admitted to his acts.

Four more joined him and two others confessed they knew but had kept silent. We thanked them for acknowledging their acts and affirmed our commitment to help.

Cean asked the rest of the group what effect knowing about the killings had on them. People spoke of sadness over the loss of life, and anger at friends who let go of their connection to life. Hearts were heavy with the knowledge of the men's acts. Cean allowed time for the words spoken by the group to enter into the transgressors' hearts. Then, he gave instructions to the guilty men. They were to go alone into the Wild without food, water, or blankets for three days. In the Wild they would look for some animal, insect, tree, plant, or other natural being that captured their attention and spend the remaining time listening to what it had to say. If they encountered one another they were to leave without speaking. At the end of three days the men would return and share their experiences. They were to leave immediately.

Moed and Nake requested to go along with the group. They felt they had waited too long to tell what they knew, and thus, had contributed to the killings. And so, nine people solemnly set out for the Wild, and we sent our silent blessings with them. We watched as they disappeared and quietly returned to our work. Logs were moved into the circle for sitting and extra wood was gathered for the ceremonial fires. We built a threshold of rocks and branches for each person to pass through as they symbolically left the old ways behind and entered into Life Community. By the end of three days, we were ready for the group to return.

They came late to the camp after we had lit the evening

fires. We offered them food and water and gathered around to listen to their stories. Even by firelight, I could see they had been transformed. They told of fears about going into the Wild. Some feared getting lost and did get lost and found again. They were fearful of being attacked by animals, though no one was. The biggest fear, the one which haunted them the most, was being alone with their thoughts. With only their senses to guide them, they explored the Wild and its mysteries. Their ears became sensitized to the sounds of the natural world and, in time, they began to listen with their hearts. Gradually, they eased into the Wild's healing presence and opened to receive its messages.

Always ready to be first, Nake stood to share his experience. "Doing nothing, when harm is being done, harms you because it breaks your connection with the natural laws of life." he said. A small tree in the forest had taught him this. The others had stories to share too, and after they finished, all nine stood and gave us a vow. They promised to remember their connection to the natural world and to the community which they now belonged. When they asked for our forgiveness, we extended our arms and joined in a circle of joy. We were all together now...one in heart, one in mind, and one in spirit. Grund announced we would begin the closing ceremonies tomorrow. Excitement and gratefulness flushed the faces of the group and, that night, all was well.

A delicious golden light enveloped us as we began the ceremony of leave-taking. Each person was asked to consider the wounds they suffered while living in the Corpsety and share them with the group. Their voices painted a bleak picture. The

Corpsety's blackness filled people with despair, dependence, loneliness, greed, judgment, aggression, and most of all fear. Under its spell they had become unwilling monsters. Trust, friendship, community, and sharing were disregarded and no one, not Corpses, Trashers, or Jobbers, could see beyond their own noses. Everyone listened and witnessed the hideous portrait of life in the Corpsety.

By evening all had spoken of their suffering and the mood was dark. A large fire burned brightly in the middle of the circle. Grund asked each person to find an object and imagine putting their wounds in it. Next, he instructed them to throw the object into the fire and shout farewell as they watched their wounds turn into smoke and ashes. Cean drummed as people stepped forward and shouted good riddance to their wounds. The burden of suffering lifted with the rising smoke, and we began to shake and dance. With firelight coloring our faces, we moved away from the tragedy of the Corpsety, and into the arms of community.

We broke the circle just long enough to collect food for our meal. We ate together with a renewed appetite-not only for food but for each other. I reflected on how close we had grown to one another. None of us are all that different, I thought, we share the same fears, wounds, sufferings, and desires. In the Corpsety our sameness is obscured by isolation and hierarchy. In Life Community we experience unity because we are known to each other as equals. I gave thanks to the Great Mystery for bringing me to this group and to the wisdom of ceremony.

The next day began again with the rising sun as we gathered to begin our circle of renewal. Cean and I would lead this ceremony, and we wanted to create just the right environment. Cean asked people to think about their life story and look for areas of growth and change. "Sharing our stories fosters deeper connections," I told them. People reflected in silence for a long time. Cean put his hand on my shoulder as we waited, and I felt a shiver go through my body.

Nestor began the ceremony by sharing that he had only known his mother, who worked in the caravans. It was from her he inherited his blackness. She had died when he was young and he was forced to labor in the caravans where he was beaten regularly. Alone in the world, he survived because he was strong and worked hard. He had no thoughts in life of anything but eating, sleeping, and surviving. One day he happened to meet a man with clear grey eyes and a gentle way about him. Nestor was drawn to him and risked striking up a conversation. They talked briefly, and the man invited Nestor to his home. Nestor accepted his invitation and never returned to the caravans. Instead, he joined those who were living in a crumbling house and began working in the Trash pits. He learned from this man, Thunar's father, how to be a real person. "I became fully human," Nestor told us, "When I learned how to care about others." He expressed profound gratefulness to the Great Mystery, and to us, for giving him the opportunity to leave the Corpsety. Nestor sat down while we rose to call out our affirmation of his story and his presence.

The sharing of stories took a long time. By the fourth day we were nearing the end and there was only one person left to tell their story. Nake had waited until last.

Nake stood and hung his head. "In the past I was a

despicable person but I didn't know it, didn't have a clue," he said. "I thought I deserved everything I had as a Corpse… good food, clean water, education, and plenty of money to buy anything I wanted. I ruled over other people, dictating what they should do, and forcing them to meet my needs. I had no concern for anyone but my family. I knew people were starving and living in filth, but I didn't care because I believed it was their own stupid fault. I didn't stop to think how I had been born into the elite Corpses. Perhaps I didn't want to face the fact that the poor had been born into their place as well. All I cared for was my own greediness and lust for power. Even though the Corpsety was collapsing, I managed to hold onto my vision of the world and my place in it. I still didn't relate the wrongness of the Corpsety to my vision of the world. All I knew was how I needed to get out of the crumbling Corpsety. When I met you people I was pretty full of myself and didn't know what I was getting into. I thank the Great Mystery I did get in and you didn't kick me out, though you probably wanted too! I was a slow learner and I made more than my fair share of mistakes, but eventually I saw how my "better than" attitude wasn't getting me any place. That was the turning point for me. Oh, I was still focused on myself, but I started to see the world differently. I have come to see that the problems of the Corpsety, and the reason for its collapse, are the same as my problems. The Corpsety and I were ignorant of the natural laws. I finally realized that if I didn't want to collapse under the weight of change, I would have to learn how to live by the natural laws. I feel good now that I am starting to live differently. You have rescued me from the jaws of a death I didn't even recognize. Because I was rich and powerful I thought I had nothing to fear from the Corpsety, but I was wrong. The Corpsety robbed me of the true value in life and replaced it with money and things. I can never hope to repay you, but I can try each day to show my gratitude, and that is what I plan to do." Before Nake could sit down, everyone stood and gave him a standing ovation.

We gathered for our evening meal and talked. People were happy with the ceremonies and Cean and I were relieved to hear this. We would begin the final ritual tomorrow, and then we could all go home at last. It was time.

The day arrived gray and cloudy for our last ceremony, but Roz and Thunar hardly noticed because our shining faces lit the circle. Roz explained how this was to be a ceremony of reclamation. "In this circle," she told us, we will call back the parts of our spirit lost in the Corpsety. Calling these parts back is essential to becoming whole again." After Roz spoke, no one moved a muscle to come forward. We sat quietly waiting until Quake's large body broke the stillness.

He stood tall with the look of a fierce warrior, but spoke in a soft voice. "I lost my sense of decency and respect for other living beings when I killed. Now, I would like to call back that part of myself that cares for the earth, cares for others, and cares for myself." He began to cry great wrenching sobs and Roz asked if he would like for us to call out with him. Still sobbing, he nodded his head. Softly, he began calling, and we joined him in a harmony of voices that called his spirit home.

After Quake finished we continued around the circle. Some asked us to "call out" with them and others did not. Either way the experience was deeply moving. Toward the middle of the day Stun stepped forward to share. I noticed the intelligence in his eyes was unclouded by fear today. Stun pointed out how negativity and judgment tied him to the Corpsety. Now, he asked us to join him as he called back his hopeful nature and goodwill toward others. We joined Stun and our voices rang out like bells calling for the return of hope and goodwill. On and on we went around the circle until the curtain of night fell down. Moed was the last to speak. "In the Corpsety," she began, "I was never still or quiet. I learned early on how to divert myself so I would not think or feel. Now, I want to call back those parts of myself that can dream and feel deeply. I want to call mystery and beauty back into my life." She stood there in her smallness and I noticed the sadness on her face. She asked us to join her, and though we raised our voices for Moed, beauty and mystery descended on everyone. When our calling came to an end we fell into each other's arms and swayed together. Held in the circle of life, the Great Mystery's gift, we were filled to the brim and moved slowly toward our sleeping places. Tomorrow we would begin a new life together.

Before I left the circle, I looked deeply into the eyes of each wise one. We were not the same people who began the journey many months ago. I felt a deeper connection and respect for my friends. Our journey back to the Corpsety had not been easy. It had been full of challenges and difficulties, but we had done it together. There is nothing quite as sweet as joining with others to do a difficult task, sharing the burden of responsibility, and seeing it through to the end. Together, we create a tie that binds us for life and perhaps beyond. This, I thought, is the spirit of true connection.

We woke to a bright blue, cloudless sky that shouted for us to come and join it. The group moved toward the arbor we had built. Roz, Thunar, Lexy, and I burned sweet-smelling herbs while Grund explained what the final ceremony would look like. Each person would pass through the arbor as we chanted, "You have turned toward life and are returning to wholeness." Cean asked everyone to choose something to leave outside the arbor which represented all they were leaving behind. We sang and blessed each person, including the children, as they passed through the sweet, smoke-filled arbor. After the others had gone, Grund motioned for us to pass through. I left behind a small toy I had carried with me from my home in the Corpsety. It seemed like a good time to let go of my childhood since it was a remnant of the Corpsety. We held the space for Grund to pass through and the ceremony ended. We were turned toward life now. The arbor and the things we left behind were burned. There would be no going back.

Part Three:

TURNING AROUND

The only way out is in.

ONE

Bringing the Natural Laws Down to Earth

We welcomed the new ones into the innermost sanctuary of everyday life. With infinite patience we guided them in the ways of community. We prepared meals and ate together, played, danced, and sang together, and gathered food and wood together. In all that we did we shared our lives with open abandon. It was mid-summer when they arrived at Life Community. Everyone was busy since it was a time of harvesting, gathering, and hunting. Our days were full to the brim. But when fall arrived and work slowed, the bickering began. Gradually a tension invaded Life Community, filling even the corners with dis-ease. Under the cover of darkness, Moed sought out the wise ones. "The new ones are fighting and in a turmoil of conflict," she reported. "They are trying to hide their problems because they fear being kicked out of the community." Father called a meeting to discuss how Life Community could help them resolve their conflicts, but he was met with sullen resistance. "We have no problems," the new ones protested, "We are doing well here. Moed is just trying to cause trouble." We reviewed the guidelines and how to work together cooperatively, but this did little to resolve the problem.

It was deep into winter when the crisis erupted. Days of being cooped up together with snow reaching the top of our shelters finally caused an explosion. I never knew who started it, but someone threw a pot and after that chaos broke loose. Men, women, and children began fighting, tearing at each other's clothes, and causing injury. Those of us from Life Community stood briefly with our mouths open and then rushed in to try to stop the fighting. Some of us were injured. When the frenzy passed, the community center was in a shambles and so were we. We tended to the injured and contemplated what to do next. The new ones had not adopted our values and were struggling in ways that we had not. Something was holding them back.

The shadow of the Corpsety, where death masquerades as life, reaches far and wide. It arrived at Life Community with those we had rescued from its grip. Deep inside, they held shadow seeds of greed, violence, and domination, which took root in Life Community. We had done our best to guide those we rescued toward life-affirming values and the natural laws of connection, cooperation, community, and conservation; and we had failed. Instead of everyone rising up, we had all fallen into an abyss. The psyches of the rescued ones were entangled with the roots of destruction and, caught in this trap, Life Community values were beyond their reach. What we did not know, what we could not know, was how to dislodge the stranglehold of such malevolent roots.

We named these roots "ruinous" because they caused

people to be destructive of self, others, and the natural world. No matter how much the rescued ones wanted to follow our example, entanglements continued to sabotage their efforts. Unknowingly, they had brought the Corpsety's disease with them. And now, we were charged with finding a cure. Could the roots of the Corpsety be unwound? Would we learn our way back into the graces of Life Community? The answers are hidden in yet another story. Dear friends, I invite you to listen to the story of our final journey.

✦ ✦ ✦

The community relied heavily on the wise ones for help through this time, but it challenged us perhaps most of all. Though we were young, Cean, Lexy, Thunar, and I were now part of the wise ones, and the task before us seemed daunting. We had done everything in our power, and still there was chaos and dissent. After many discussions and community circles, we were unable to come up with lasting solutions to our problems. Finally, the wise ones acknowledged they had reached an impasse and Illow suggested we go to the forest, even though snow was still on the ground. There we could seclude ourselves and commune with nature, the Great Mystery, and each other. Hoping for a miracle, we said our farewells to the community and set out for the unknown.

With heavy hearts we were drawn deep into the Wild, into a forest we did not know. Trees with barren branches rustled as we moved past. The snow-blanketed forest seemed cold and unyielding. Travelling in silence, we walked until we found a place of our own. Once there, we made snow shelters for sleeping and spent the days collecting wood and meditating. We needed to settle and let go of the frustrations that were weighing us down. Solitude and silent listening would return us to balance and to the Great Mystery. As our minds cleared, our hearts would open once again. Only then could our dreams and insights return. Each of us retreated into a place of quietude of our own making. Days went by with nary a word being spoken. Wrapped in silence, we warmed to our inner wisdom.

Soon, we began to share our dreams, and a measure of hope grew from the rubble of our failure. Teaching the natural laws and community values had been a start in the right direction, but they had not been enough. The rescued ones needed something more, something that would replace the corruption they clung to. What they needed was beyond our understanding. And so we turned the solution over to the Great Mystery, and waited.

Day after day we sat at the fire sharing our dreams, wondering about tomorrow, and trying to hold onto our faith. Walking was one of the things we did to occupy our time and release our fears. Wandering deep into the unknown forest one day I heard a voice as low and clear as thunder. It was a powerful voice, soft yet insistent. I looked over my shoulder to see who this voice belonged to but saw nothing. Automatically, I turned in a circle and was confounded by the absence of a body. Then, this miracle of a voice said to me, "Learn the vital skill of feelings." I shook my head to clear my mind but the voice continued. "Listen to what I am telling you!" I was dumbfounded, but obeyed a command I dared not ignore. Words dropped from the sky explaining how the gift of feelings can be positive and negative. I opened myself to receive the words, and then, as mysteriously as it had come the voice was silent. I walked back to our camp pondering what had happened and eager to tell the others of my experience. Illow was there when I arrived, looking serene and peaceful. I opened my mouth to speak excitedly, but she shushed me and motioned to sit down. One by one the others arrived and sat down quietly in a circle. Illow broke the silence by singing a song of thanksgiving.

Oh Great Mystery I hear you calling; Oh Great Mystery I hear your song; Thank you for filling me with wisdom; Thank you for filling me with wisdom. Oh Great Mystery I see your beauty; Oh Great Mystery I see your wonder; Thank you for bringing me home; Thank you for bringing me home. Oh Great Mystery I feel your presence; Oh Great Mystery I feel your blessing; Thank you for arounding me with love; Thank you for arounding me with love.

I listened as her low voice filled the space above and around our circle, holding us fast to the earth. When she finished my excitement disappeared, and I was filled with peace. "I have had a wondrous encounter," Illow shared, "And I wonder if I am the only one?" Like a clock striking the hours, each of us rang out our encounter. After all had spoken, we gave thanks to the Great Mystery from which all things come. And thus, our prayers were answered.

The Great Mystery had given us teachings, exactly eight teachings in all, which provided a compass for the journey yet to be taken. We named these teachings "vital skills," for they affirmed the vitality of life and love. Here was the missing piece, the alchemy we needed to transform our situation.

We did not leave immediately but worked together to develop a plan for teaching. We lingered in the forest until we were confident in our ability to communicate the skills that would save Life Community from disaster. The night before we left, I slept soundly and dreamed we were visited by a swarm of bees which buzzed around our heads and gave us terrible headaches. People became angry and fearful, but yelling and slapping at the bees only made matters worse. The buzzing got louder and louder, and just when we thought we would all go mad, a great wind blew the bees away. Quiet descended on us, and our hearts were filled with peace. We bowed to the ground and thanked the Great Mystery, which had sent the wind to rescue us. In the morning, I shared my dream with the others and together we puzzled over its meaning as we walked. The snow was beginning to melt and in its place was slush mixed with soil. Soon, it would be spring.

TWO

The Wind Speaks

We returned to a community in tatters. In the Wild, we had no sense of time, but the others had counted the days. They feared we had abandoned them and greeted us with anger and recriminations. "Why did you go away for so long?" "Don't you care about us?" "Don't you know we can't manage without you?" They gathered around the circle as Illow spoke of our encounter with the Great Mystery and of the teachings we were given. She proposed we begin the teachings right away, because the community was teetering on the brink of disaster. Her words were not welcomed. People were talking loudly with excited voices. A high-pitched drone filled the air and I was reminded of my dream. The group came close to quieting several times but the noise was tenacious. We were caught in its shrill vibrations until Grund asked each person to say a few words about our proposal.

The rescued ones were hesitant and suspicious. "You told us we would fit into the community after the last teachings," Nake said angrily. "Why should we believe these teachings are going to make any difference?" Lef was not angry, but he was wary.

He said, "I'm tired and worn out from all the arguing. We were doing just fine before the new ones came. Maybe they can't fit in and need to start their own group." Vilet shared while softly crying, "I don't know if I have any energy left in me to learn something new."

We listened carefully as each person spoke, taking in their words, feelings, and energy. The group was far from consensus and we were not going to force our will on them. Illow asked everyone to shake and spend the rest of the day in quiet reflection. We would reconvene in the morning and continue talking. We stood to move together, but the shaking was subdued and the relief I usually saw on people's faces was absent. They were suffering from an inability to connect.

After the circle broke, the wise ones met to talk. "What will we do if the group cannot reach consensus?" I asked. Thoughtfully, Grund answered, "We will continue to meet. I don't know what the end result will be, that is in the hands of the Great Mystery." Then Illow spoke of my dream: "I sense a great swarm of negativity among the group. I wonder if this could the buzzing that is driving us toward madness from Mariah's dream? If this is so, we must wait for the wind to come and bring peace to our hearts." She suggested we focus on staying in our hearts to create an environment that encourages heartfelt communicating.

When I returned to the community center, I was surprised to hear the sound of silence. People were actually taking time for quiet reflection. Everyone retired to their beds with hardly a word being spoken. The next day we gathered, and Illow began with a meditation centering on our hearts and opened the circle with these words: "We are honored that you are here today and we invite you to speak from your heart, for in the heart lies wisdom." Lef stood to offer an unusual request. "Those of us who are still undecided about the new teachings would like to retreat to the forest. We want to see if we can receive insights just as you did." Illow stood quietly and directed her words to everyone. "You have made a wise decision, my friends, and we honor your request. Take all the time you need to receive your wisdom. We will wait for your return." They prepared to leave while the wise ones met.

Illow felt their decision showed willingness to model after us, which was encouraging. Now, it was our turn to trust the Great Mystery to help them learn what they needed to learn. The days and weeks passed slowly. We carried on with our usual chores, preparing for spring. We cooked meals and continued to try to have fun and enjoy ourselves. But, time grew heavy on our hands as we waited for their return. One afternoon, a strong wind swept through the forest, bowing trees and forcing us into our shelters. The wind was fierce but brought no storm, which was unusual. That evening those who had gone into the forest returned to us, shaken but serene.

We formed a circle around them as they shared their experiences. Lef spoke first: "In the solitude of the forest our minds cleared, and we were able to reach into the depths of our hearts. It was not until today, though, that we truly understood our path. A fierce wind blew through the forest, and we feared for our lives. As the wind tossed us about, we joined hands around the large tree and held on for dear life. We survived because we were united. The tree held us in its embrace, and we were spared." When Lef finished, Stear continued: "We have relearned the value of connection with the natural world and with each other. Now, we know what to do when our heads are buzzing with confusion. The path of wisdom points us toward connection with nature and the Great Mystery. In order to connect we must practice entering the silence and cultivating an open heart." Vilet, Stun, and Nake stood to speak together and said, "If we are to survive the storms of life, we must connect with wisdom. And, we must hold onto each other as we did in the forest. This is the way to save ourselves. We want to continue with the teachings, and we hope you will forgive our stubborn ignorance."

We gave thanks for their safe return and for the wisdom they had shared. "Mistakes are nothing to be ashamed of," Roz reminded them, "for that is how we humans learn." Everyone started shaking to the beat of the drum, and as our breath quickened, I caught the slightest glimpse of joy on people's faces. The wind had brought the lesson home, and the meaning of my dream had been revealed.

THREE

The Old Ways Come Back to Life

Early the next day, we resumed our customary work of collecting food and taking care of the community. I was sweeping when I heard Illow's voice calling us. It was time to make a decision about the teachings. Everyone gathered in a circle and spoke from the heart. "We have been hiding our conflicts, and we know that was wrong," the new ones admitted. "There can be no resolution to that which is hidden. We are willing to do whatever it takes to rid ourselves of the poison of the Corpsety." They stood and opened their hands to the rest of us. "Will you help us?" Hesitantly, Life Community members stood to speak. "We have suffered with you and struggled with our feelings of resentment. And, we realize we need you in order to make Life Community stronger. We will join with you and agree to continue the journey together." Everyone joined hands and we became one again.

The teachings would be our lifeline to rebuilding what had been lost. Illow started us off with the vital skill of self-valuing. We waited eagerly for her teaching, and I was looking forward to discovering along with the others. Illow's bright eyes shone as she told us how valuing one's self is the foundation, the crucial piece, upon which all else is built. A person must love and nurture his or her body, mind, and spirit before they can extend love to others. In the Corpsety, people have no opportunity to learn about themselves. They cannot imagine how to affirm and love a self they do not know. Those of us who grew up in the Corpsety must learn how to love ourselves, "And here is how we begin."

First, we look for the good in ourselves and come to know who we really are and what we truly need. She cautioned us to watch out for negative thinking, which distorts our view of life and self. There will always be both positive and negative in our lives, she reminded us. The Corpsety encourages the negative. In Life Community we encourage the positive, hoping to strike a balance between the two. In her gentle way, she challenged us to observe how judging ourselves and others leads to conflict and unhappiness. Illow asked us to face our mistakes without judgment and see them as learning opportunities. "While there may be things we want to change about ourselves," she counseled, "acceptance of our imperfections is also part of the process of self-affirmation."

Then, she spoke of equality. "Thinking we are better than others or less than others creates imbalance in ourselves and in our lives. In order to be free we must truly believe we are equal." She directed us to make a practice of giving gratitude for who we are, what we do, and the gifts we have been given. "Each one of you is irreplaceable," she said as her eyes swept over the group. "We need you to strengthen our community and brighten the world. In order to do this, you must embrace the value given to you by the Great Mystery." With these words, she concluded her teaching and sat down.

Now came the hard part. We were expected to take what Illow shared and apply it to our daily lives. There were no divisions between the old and new members of the community. We all participated as equals, and I was no exception. I often found myself getting tangled in the web of judging. It took me some time to learn how to watch my thinking and turn it around. We shared our struggles with each other in groups after the evening meal. It was in small ways that each of us made changes, but these grew large as we shared them collectively. Looking at negativity with new eyes, we could see how it cast a shadow over our lives. Our minds took on a lightness of being when negativity and judgment were absent. The burdens of self-doubt, guilt, frustration, and pain also lifted. There was magic in our sharing. We were able to laugh at our negativity and at ourselves. Together we healed. Our laughter lifted the bad feelings from our hearts and floated them into the clouds.

Self-acceptance was much easier once we had shifted the negative energy. We made games out of naming the good things about ourselves and challenged each other to look harder. After weeks of supporting each other we began to embody the teachings. Nestor eloquently described where he had arrived: "I used to go through life without ever really looking at myself and without any thought that I could change. Now, I can see who I am and who I can become if I want to make the effort. It's like I have a new me to play with." Now that we were aware of our inner shadow, we could move beyond it.

Joyfully we prepared our morning meal together and began each day by sharing the things we were grateful for. It seemed like a simple and easy assignment, so I was not prepared for its powerful influence. Day after day and week after week, we shared our gratitude. It was surprisingly easy to find things to be grateful for once our attention was focused. A sunny day, rain, children, a good dream, soft breezes, the shade of trees, a kindly touch, delicious fruit, dancing, talking around the circle at night . . . any of these could foster gratitude. Optimism and kindness were flowing around and between us, softening our edges and opening our hearts. Gratitude had bestowed its blessings and we felt good about life again. We were ready to move on to the next teaching. But, first we needed to gather wood.

Pulling logs and cutting wood into small pieces was hard work. We spent long days together travelling between the forest and home. The work was exhausting, but it was energizing to work together joyfully. The woods smelled of moss, and I took in the scent with pleasure as I worked next to Father. He shared with me how the teachings had helped him. He had despaired of finding a solution to our problems and felt responsible for not knowing what to do. The weight of so much responsibility was heavy on his shoulders and didn't fully lift until he learned how to value himself for what he was, not what he could or couldn't do. "Mariah," he said, "the teachings are truly miraculous!" I listened to him solemnly and then remarked, "Isn't it strange that we continue to grow and change no matter what our age?" "Yes, even us old ones can sprout new leaves," he teased. Our time gathering wood ended and we turned our attention to Father, who would teach the next vital skill.

"Many problems and conflicts grow out of times when we feel attacked but don't know how to protect ourselves," Father began. "Boundaries protect us from others and they protect others from us. Even though boundaries are invisible, they are powerful in their ability to protect. It's boundaries that help us act wisely. How do you know when you are being attacked?" he asked. "When someone hits us," Nake shouted out. "Right, Nake," Father responded, "that is one kind of attack, but there are others. Can anyone name them?" Vilet quietly named gossip and criticizing as attacks. Stear came up with threats, name calling, and stealing. "These are good examples of attacks," Father agreed. "Now, how do you protect yourself from them?" Only Nake responded. "I'd usually say by fighting or using power over, but I know those are wrong. I guess I don't know the answer to your question." "Are there any ideas?" Father called out.

Hearing none, he asked, "Do you want to learn how to protect yourself from attacks?" Mischievously, we shook our fists at him. Grinning, he shook his head and asked us to close our eyes while he led us through a meditation. When we had quieted, he directed us to imagine a boundary that would protect us from physical attacks. This boundary could extend far out beyond our body. Then, he suggested we imagine a closer boundary that would protect us from the words, feelings, and actions of others, while keeping us from harming others. He encouraged us to sit quietly while the images had a chance to soak in. Then, he told us to open our eyes and share what had appeared. The boundary images were wildly imaginative and no two were alike. One person saw a burning bush, another saw a favorite piece of clothing, yet another saw a rainbow, and for me it was a nice soft cloud. Father assured us that these mental pictures would be powerful allies. "Boundaries," he explained, "will provide you with the freedom to decide how you want to act. And, don't forget your valuable self—it's your job to protect it." Father's teaching was brief but powerful. It was in our hands now, where boundaries belong.

Quake had an especially difficult time with boundaries. He complained that he had no self-control and lashed out reactively no matter how hard he tried to stop himself. Father gave him suggestions and opportunities to practice, but it didn't help much. I practiced using my boundaries with Nake. Though I had never said anything, he often irritated me. This was new territory for most of us and we were hesitant at first. Oddly enough, it was Nake who helped us break the ice. He had a habit of telling others what to do, and in one day he received several boundary reminders. This had an impact on him and on me. Nake announced he was glad we had called him out. Now, he could see his mistakes and make changes. This was a great insight for me. Not only did boundaries protect me; I could see how they helped others as well. Practicing boundaries fostered respect and cooperation for all of us except Quake. He became more and more frustrated as others gained a skill he couldn't master. Father advised him to relax and keep practicing. "Eventually it will happen," he counseled. Finally, one day during a practice session, Quake burst into laughter and yelled at the top of his voice. "I get it, I finally get it! I can stop your words from coming in. My shield has worked." He danced around the circle, holding Father precariously in his arms, as we laughed and rejoiced. Quake's success mirrored ours and his breakthrough signaled our readiness to move on. Now, it was my turn to lead.

I was to teach the vital skill of feelings. In preparation, I reminded myself that feelings are like a foreign language most people have never learned. The group gathered around me in anticipation, and I suspected mine would not be a popular topic. I started by sharing a basic list of feelings (anger, fear, pain, guilt, shame, joy/happiness, love, loneliness) that all people experience. I asked the group to share what they knew about feelings. Most disliked, didn't trust, or overlooked their feelings. It was, after all, feelings that caused them discomfort. They wanted nothing to do with negative feelings and believed they were best ignored or avoided. I asked if these techniques actually worked, and most of the group members' eyes wandered to their feet (a sure sign of avoidance). The rest squirmed in their seats, until someone blurted out, "Not really." "Would you like to learn something that actually works?" I asked. Playfully, they fell to their knees and begged for me to release them. Laughing, I began. "In this case, the only way out is in. If you learn how to befriend your feelings you can live 'with them' instead of 'in spite of them.'" I smiled again as a loud, collective groan went around the circle. "OK, OK," I shouted over their moans. "I know this seems impossible, but just give me a chance." The playful exchange with the group bolstered my confidence and I continued. We often misunderstand our feelings because we don't know how to use them wisely. Feelings actually contain information that helps us make good decisions. In the Corpsety, we were overwhelmed with negative feelings, but away from its influence we can reclaim all our feelings.

Together we edged slowly toward getting to know our feelings. We tuned into our bodies and noticed how the energy of a feeling moves in us. Then, we sought out the intelligence hidden within feelings. At this point, I gave everyone an assignment. They were to go back to their regular lives, and when a feeling arose, they would take note of what was happening in that moment. Equipped with this knowledge, they were to take the next step and try to discover what message the feeling was trying to convey. Day after day people struggled with this assignment and failed. They were not making progress, and I worried that somehow I had failed in my teaching.

I sought out Illow, hoping she could tell me what I should do. Instead of giving me advice, she asked me to consider what my worry was telling me. I should have known she would direct me back to myself. How quickly I had forgotten what I was trying to teach others. I tuned in to my body and let my mind reflect on what had happened. The message came clear and loud. My fear was telling me something was missing. I spent more time reflecting and came up with an answer. I had given the assignment too early. The group needed to learn how to "free up" their emotional energy before they could receive messages. Here was the error my fear was pointing out.

I gathered everyone together and asked, "How many of you are still using your old habits of blocking or pushing your feelings down?" Sheepishly, people admitted they had not been able to let the old habits go and kept their heads down, as if waiting to be scolded. Gently, I suggested, "This may be what is blocking your efforts. As long as you hold onto your old habits, nothing will change. The old habit energy needs to be cleared." "But how can we do that?" Stear asked. I replied, "Here is where shaking can help us. Shaking loosens emotional energy so it can flow out of our bodies once it has served its purpose." Without waiting for the drums, we began to shake and cry and shout together. Moved by our own inner rhythms, we threw inhibitions to the wind and wildly let our feelings work their way out of our bodies. When we were completely spent, we collapsed on the ground together in a heap and lay there quietly breathing. We continued shaking and collapsing like this for three days, in the blazing sun and under the watchful eye of the moon.

Our collective shaking opened people, and insights began to flow. Stun discovered how he had stuffed fear and pain, which were telling him to leave the Corpsety. Now that he was free he could let go of these old feelings. Nake shared his guilt at being a Corpse and how it was trying to tell him to live in a different way. The most amazing breakthrough came from Nestor, who was quiet and good natured. None of us guessed he was carrying around a large bundle of shame from his work in the caravans. He had been forced to kill and withhold food from people who were starving. In order to survive, he had pushed his feelings of shame so deep that he was unable to feel anything. After leaving the Corpsety, he had waited for the numb sensation to subside, but it remained firmly rooted. He knew his suppressed feelings were sabotaging him, but he could not let them go. He asked for our help and we formed a circle around him and called for his shame to move out into the world, so he could be free. Cean drummed as the shaking pulsed over, around, and through us. We heard Nestor's sobs—quiet at first and then louder and louder—as the energy of his pent-up feelings took their leave. We continued giving our support and held the container for him. Nestor fell to the ground, and we tumbled down with him. After a while, Nestor roused and stood with tears in his eyes. "I am crying tears of happiness," he shouted. "I must be unfrozen!"

In the weeks that followed, I watched as people shared their feelings, and I couldn't help smiling. Something deep had shifted in each of us and our feelings were no longer our enemies. We had run the gauntlet and claimed their power for ourselves.

The cold season was fading but food was still scarce. Everyone, except young children, disappeared into the forest in search of food. We were used to the cold, but the new arrivals were not. They complained bitterly about being away from the community fires. We had given them furs for warmth, but that didn't relieve their distress. Each day we went out to search for food, I heard the same grumbling. Finally, Lef snapped at them: "Why don't you quit whining? We are all cold, but we are not complaining." The new ones were quiet after that. We gathered for several weeks to get enough food to fend off hunger. The wind was beginning to warm and the sun was shining as just a hint of green hovered over the trees. It was time for our next teaching.

Grund stepped up to lead the vital skill of communicating.

He surprised us by asking, "How good are you at listening?" His question caught me off guard. We had come to learn about talking. Cautiously, Sert answered, "We all have ears, so I guess that makes us listeners." "Well," Grund continued, "hearing is not the same as listening. Listening is a critical skill that is important to good communications. A good listener sets aside her thoughts, perceptions, and assumptions, which isn't easy to do. We all have our own perceptions about things, and we make assumptions that may be right or wrong. By setting these aside, we are able to listen more accurately. Listening without interjecting our experience creates the space for us to focus on the other person's message. Our sincere attention is one of the greatest gifts we can offer others. After we have listened well, we speak honestly and from the heart. Honesty protects us from the trap of lying, which obscures truth and fosters confusion and conflict. Speaking from the heart assures that we will speak with integrity. Good communicating is also about sharing talking space," Grund told us. "Taking up too much talking space is greedy and does not lead to understanding. How do you feel when one person does all the talking?" he asked the group. A chorus of voices answered him: "I get angry." "I hate it." "I want to leave." "I get resentful." "I start daydreaming." Then Nake said, "I notice when I talk people often look bored and don't meet my eyes. I feel disconnected from them and, yes, I know I talk too much." We all laughed with Nake as he had spoken honestly from his heart. "Thank you, Nake, for reminding us how crucial sharing is to building relationships and to communicating," Grund said approvingly.

Communication doesn't end there, either. Once again he

gave us a question. "How many of you like to get feedback?" Facing a sea of frowning faces, he asked, "Why not?" "I don't like to be criticized," Vilet whispered, and heads nodded around the circle. "Honest feedback is another gift we can give each other," Grund counseled. "It helps us see ourselves through another's eyes. Helpful feedback is given in a gentle, respectful way so it can be received. As Vilet pointed out, harsh criticism is not helpful, because it creates resistance and shame." Finally, he cautioned against using words that hurt others. Calling names, judging, criticizing, and gossip feed the fires of conflict. Talking negatively "about" someone causes suspicion and distrust. It is better to speak directly to the person so you can find understanding and resolution. Grund encouraged us to think of communicating as "sacred speech." Speaking respectfully and honestly from our hearts, about what's important, takes us into the realm of the spirit where all things are possible. On this note, he ended his teaching.

The next days were strangely quiet. It was as if everyone was afraid to talk. Finally, at an evening meal, Flow had had enough. "Why is everyone so quiet?" she said in a loud voice. Her innocent question broke the ice, and laughing at ourselves, we started talking again. But, our conversations were different. They deepened as we listened and shared from our hearts. Lexy and I were able to clear up a misunderstanding I hadn't even known existed.

"I feel that you have been avoiding me because of my relationship with Thunar," Lexy revealed. "Oh Lexy, I am not avoiding you or upset in the least," I responded. "I just didn't want to intrude on you and Thunar." She gave a sigh of relief and smiled. "Please don't stay away. We both love you, and Thunar misses your company. I would especially like for you to be my friend," she said shyly. We hugged and I affirmed our friendship and how glad I was she had talked to me. I couldn't help wondering how long she had been harboring these thoughts.

Some of the new ones tentatively approached Lef. They told him how his words had silenced and shamed them when they were having a hard time adjusting to the cold. They had not intended to upset anyone. Lef was quiet. I was standing nearby and couldn't help hearing their conversation. I wondered how Lef would react, for he had a short fuse. He looked the group up and down, and then offered an apology. "I guess I was not very respectful, was I? I have forgotten how cold I was my first winter in the Wild. I sincerely apologize and promise to be more careful about my words in the future." The small group wandered away with Lef in tow, leaving guffaws and laughter in their wake.

Our days were filled with conversation now, real talk, not mindless chatter. We were learning about each other and having a good time too. Cean thought this seemed like a good time to continue with the vital skill of resolving conflict. The words "resolving conflict" had barely left Cean's mouth when I sensed a current of fear winding its way around the circle. Before Cean could say anything more, a rowdy group of new ones yelled out that conflict was to be avoided at all costs. "How do you do that?" Cean asked. "That's what we are waiting for you to tell us," they countered. "I cannot teach you how to avoid conflict, but I can give you skills to resolve it," Cean explained. "We know how to use boundaries, talk to each other, and take care of ourselves," Nestor responded. "What else is there?" "You're right, Nestor, we need all of those skills. And, there is more we need to know," Cean replied.

Now that he had the group's attention, Cean launched into his teaching: "When a conflict arises, we use the skills we already have to be respectful, listen, and share our view of the problem. As you know, these alone are not enough. Here is the missing piece of the puzzle. We look for a resolution that takes the needs of both people into consideration. Working together, we come up with a solution. But, finding a resolution is only part of the process. The other part is to build a positive relationship. If the solution fails, the relationship remains, and another solution can be negotiated."

Cean asked us to bring our unresolved conflicts to the next group. We would use these scenarios to practice finding resolutions. The scenarios quickly became real, and I noticed how easily people lapsed into emotional outbursts and aggressive behavior. I suspected they weren't using boundaries or managing the energy of their feelings.

I mentioned my suspicions to Cean during lunch and saw a look of relief come over his face. "I knew something was wrong," he sighed. Cupping my chin in his hand, he looked into my eyes. For a moment I was caught in the blue of his gaze, but I came back when l heard him say, "You have saved the day, Mariah. How can I thank you?" I smiled shyly and mumbled, "I'm happy to help."

The group began another role-play that afternoon. After a particularly heated exchange, Cean asked those involved to share what they were feeling. They reported feeling angry and frustrated. "Did you reflect on the message of your feelings?" he inquired. With reddened faces, they admitted they had not. "Were you using your boundaries?" he continued. It seemed they had forgotten about them too. "So, tell me what happened when you forgot to use boundaries and listen to your feelings." The onlookers decided it was time to get involved and shouted out, "You became reactive and argumentative." "Well said," Cean laughed. "The real challenge of conflict is to learn how to use every skill we have—at the same time. Right now this may seem impossible, but it can be done and it's a valuable skill."

With Cean's guidance, we learned how to face conflict with conscious awareness. He encouraged us to bring our bodies, minds, and spirits into alignment and move beyond our barriers. After weeks of strenuous practice, we were able to reach past our blocks and claim the essence of conflict resolution. Late one afternoon, Quake and Nestor stood toe to toe and resolved a difficult conflict without reacting or being disrespectful. These two had come to love each other as brothers. And, as brothers sometimes do, they competed to see which was the strongest. Over time competitiveness had strained their relationship, but neither Quake nor Nestor could give it up. They were giants among men, but neither was stronger than the other.

Using their skills of speaking from the heart and listening without judgment, they discovered the root of the problem. What started out in fun had turned into something neither of them could control. Friendship was what they needed and wanted, not rivalry. The resolution to their conflict was simple.

They agreed to let go of competition so love and friendship could flourish. We watched as they embraced each other and then thought of our own accomplishments. We no longer had to fear a disagreement, for we knew how to move beyond it. Cean had taken us into the valley of conflict, and we had managed to come out on the other side without fighting.

We took a much-needed break after Cean's teaching to work, play, and integrate our learning. Wolf and I visited the mountains where we sat watching clouds and birds fly by. The mountain air was cold and the wind took my breath away, but it felt good to be alone. I remembered the discussions about private spaces we had had when we first arrived. I marveled at the elegant system Father had created. He had given us the space we needed to be alone—together. At mealtimes we divided into small groups and prepared meals. I loved to chop food and listen to the others talk. In the evenings, we danced, allowing our bodies to come together as we basked in closeness. We worked and played at a leisurely pace until we were ready to return to the teachings. When we returned, Roz was ready for us.

Our next lesson would be on the vital skill of building relationships. Some of the group members had already started grumbling. "Why do we need to learn about relationships? We already know how to get along," they complained. Oh my, I thought, Roz would have her work cut out for her. She began by asking us to identify what makes a relationship good. Nake thought he knew and answered smugly, "Being respectful, not attacking or criticizing, listening, and speaking honestly from the heart." "These are basic skills," she agreed, "but what is it that makes a relationship close and nurturing?" Her question was met with a profound silence, and even I longed to know the answer. Roz smiled as she looked out over the group. "So, there are some things you don't know about relationships," she said. The grumblers sat mute with their eyes downcast.

"Let me ask the question in a different way," she continued. "What is it we all want in a close relationship?" This question we could answer. We wanted to be accepted, to be loved and nurtured, to be valued, and to be forgiven when we made mistakes. "Yes," Roz agreed, "this is what we want. Now, how do we get there?" After another time of silence, she answered her own question. "First, we get to know each other intimately by listening and talking honestly. We disclose what we know about our self and listen as the other person shares. Next, we spend time together sharing experiences, sharing feelings, and observing each other's actions. This fosters trust, which is integral to a close relationship. Trust allows us to be vulnerable yet safe with someone. Over time we come to expect the positive things we give, such as kindness, respect, honesty, trust, and nurturing, will be returned to us. It is through this giving and receiving of generosity and compassion that we ripen and grow."

Until now, I had not realized the true gift of deep relationship which Grandmother, Father, Illow, Roz, and Grund had so generously given me. Roz asked us to talk about the gifts we receive from close relationships. Thunar shared how his father had given him the courage and strength to leave the Corpsety. Tunk spoke of relationship as a source of security in the midst of chaos. Father shared how Grund helped him see himself more clearly. Only a few came forward, and I wondered about the experiences of those who held back.

Roz spoke solemnly, "Your own words have painted a vivid portrait of the warmth, value, and sacredness of deep relationship. I hope this knowing will move you to take the lessons from today into the relationships you have and deepen them. Cultivating nurturing, cooperative, and compassionate relationships strengthens our community. Children learn from us how to form relationships, and we want to give them the best we have to offer. We are spiritual beings," she reminded us, "and deeply intimate relationships lift us up and feed our souls." With that, Roz closed the session. I spent the rest of the day marveling over the gift of relationship. I hoped everyone would have at least one close relationship. Life would be awfully hard without it.

FOUR

Planting Seeds

We took another break as we tended our gardens and planted seeds saved from previous years. The garden was growing larger along with our community. Illow and I went deep into the forest each day looking for medicinal herbs and healing plants. I noticed Illow was thinner and frailer. Her eyes no longer held their sparkle and she walked delicately on feet that didn't seem to want to move anymore. I was concerned about her, but when I inquired all she would say is, "I won't live forever, little one, I won't live forever." We spent a wonderful day listening to the trees, inhaling the scents of the forest, and immersing ourselves in its deep green peacefulness. As we walked, I told Illow of the things I had learned on the return journey to the Corpsety. She listened and affirmed I had come into my womanhood. We walked in silence until Illow began to speak softly. "I have a feeling that I may be moving toward my death. I have had unusual dreams where I float upward toward a bright light and soothing warmth. And, I find myself wanting to be alone more often." It was hard for me to hear this, but I listened. "Does it frighten you to hear me talk this way?" she asked. "No, I'm not scared, but I don't like to think of losing you," I replied. "Ah, little one, don't you know that I will always be with you? We are joined in a way that only spirit can fathom," she said. I smiled wistfully and we continued walking, laughing at the squirrels who scolded us along the way. That evening we held a community dance to celebrate the planting of our garden. As we danced around the fire, I looked at the group's shining faces. The new ones had made things difficult, yet they brought gifts of energy, new ideas, and diversity to our community. The cost to us in terms of time and effort would be paid back a hundred fold, for a community is only as strong as the diversity it holds.

The celebration ended on a high note. Tomorrow we would be ready for another round of learning. Lexy would take the lead, and what a great teacher she was. With red hair flying, she ordered us to rise up and go to the community center and then return to the circle. We followed her instructions, but just as we sat down she told us to get up and do the same thing again. Grumbling, we got up and walked to the community center and back, only to be told to return again. Some started to openly challenge her but she remained firm, giving a steely look to those who questioned her. She sent us back three more times before we were finally allowed to sit. Once we were settled, she asked us to shout out what we were feeling in our bodies right now. Frustrated, angry, tired, confused, tense, and anxious were the words that came out of our mouths. "This," Lexy proclaimed, "is how life sometimes treats us. It's unfair, uncomfortable, aggravating, disorienting, and our body responds accordingly. We call this response 'stress.' How many of you think stress is an important part of your life?" A few of us raised our hands, but most did not. Lexy shook her mane of red hair vigorously, capturing our attention.

"I'm here to tell you that stress is just as fearsome as any bear, wolf, or storm you will encounter. Stress can kill you as easily as a bear; the only difference is it's a slower death. Stress is deadly. It makes it harder to know what is going on around us, which can mean the difference between life and death in the Wild. Remember," she reminded us, "I asked you to notice what was happening in your body. Stress lodges itself in our bodies and hides, causing illness and even death. Life is hard out in the Wild, and it can bring a lot of stress and uncertainty. If you are to survive and thrive, you will need to learn how to reduce your response to stress."

"We know what to do when we encounter a bear or a storm to protect ourselves. Now, we need to learn how to relax and let go of our attachment to stress," Lexy said. "I'm not attached to stress," Nake countered. Lexy challenged him, "What happens when you are confronted by something or someone?" Nake thought he would be smart. "I handle it," he responded. "Good, and do you completely forget about it afterwards?" she asked. "Well no," Nake admitted, "I still think about it sometimes." "So, you keep the stress going with your thoughts," Lexy announced. Nake sat down with a confused look on his face. He hadn't thought of that. "Our bodies hold stress," she explained, "and, our minds often add to it. Dwelling on stressful incidents keeps us attached and causes 'stress overload.' Relaxation skills help us release stress from our bodies and our minds." She directed us to focus on our bodies and notice if there was any stress lurking there. Focusing in on my body, I noticed tightness in my jaw. Stear reported her shoulders were almost up to her ears. Stun admitted his mind was racing in a million directions. Moed realized her stomach was tight and she was holding her breath. "These are all signs of stress," Lexy continued. "Let's see if we can begin to quiet and relax." She directed us to sit on the ground with our backs straight, legs crossed, and eyes closed and begin breathing deeply into our stomachs. Timelessness descended on me and I had no idea how long we sat there. "Open your eyes," Lexy said quietly, "and notice how you feel." Nake shouted out, "That felt good," and so did others. Lexy smiled and said, "This is just one of the many ways to relax. Would you like to learn more?" Nestor stood and stretched his arms like a bear. He chased us until we collapsed in a fit of laughter at Lexy's feet, begging her to save us from the "stress bear."

We spent a great deal of time with Lexy, deepening our experience and learning what she had been given to teach. We formed pictures in our minds that brought us to a place of peace, safety, and calmness. This was an all-around favorite. We called it our enchanted place. The last thing she offered was for us to draw shapes in the dirt. The children shouted with joy and fell to the ground immediately. The rest of us were less enthusiastic. It was only Lexy's persistence that won us over. At first we held back, then awkwardly a few of us stooped to draw and found it to be fun and relaxing. We called for the others to join us. Eventually, everyone was on the ground making shapes and laughing at our dirty hands. "Laughter is also a potent relaxer," Lexy explained, and she invited us to "play in the dirt" more often. She suggested we make colors from berries and paint our pottery, baskets, hides, and even rocks. "Anything is fair game." "And, don't forget," she reminded us, "to keep singing, dancing, and shaking, because they also release stress." By the end of our time with Lexy, we were all feeling mellow and it was noticeable. Father's face was soft and glowing as he sat with Roz. They would soon be a pair, I thought, and I was happy for them. Lexy's voice brought my attention back to the group. "Your practice is to use these skills when you notice you are stressed. We will meet at the end of several weeks to share experiences." I left with a sense of calm and a resolve to keep peacefulness alive in my life.

We collected berries to dry and saved the ones that were not good to eat for coloring. It was fun to see the red, blue, black, and purple colors mixed in small bowls. We started experimenting with coloring the plants we used to make baskets and then put color into the clay we molded into shapes. We laughed and made a mess of things, but the colors enlivened our lives. The weeks passed quickly. When we returned to the teachings, Lexy began by asking us to stand. People started groaning, thinking she was going to make us go back and forth between the circle and the community center. In fact, the groans were so loud, we all started laughing. After the laughter died down, she asked us to notice what our bodies were telling us at this very moment. I stopped to listen and realized I was relaxed and feeling good. The laughter had loosened and warmed my body. "Laughter may well be the most potent form of relaxation," she reminded us. She asked for our experiences over the past weeks. Moed had learned that her body actually did communicate, but she couldn't hear it unless she slowed down and listened. Stun felt, for the first time in his life, that he was truly "in" his body. As the group shared, it was clear that we had learned how to exert more control over the state of our bodies and minds. We recognized relaxation for the powerful force it is. A force we could tap into whenever we needed. Lexy closed with a reminder that daily practice was the only way to keep Nestor the "stress bear" away.

Soon it would be a full moon. We would sing, dance, and celebrate under its bright presence and take time off to tend our garden under the moon's watchful eye. After the moon began to wane, Thunar would teach the vital skill of accepting death. He was nervous about doing a good job. Lexy and I listened while he went over what he would say. We both felt it was good, but he shook his head and I couldn't help noticing how his black curls bounced up and down. "It's missing something, I just know it is," he groaned. We had nothing more to share, and so we left him to his thoughts. As we were walking away, Lexy announced that she and Thunar would be joining together in partnership.

Her words were not unexpected and I was genuinely happy for them. Her wildness combined with Thunar's passion and brilliance would make a good match. When I told her of my happiness she gave me a sidelong look, and her words caught me off guard. "What about your future plans?" "Honestly, I don't have any, although I do hope to find a partner some day," I told her. She put her arm in mine. "You will find someone, Mariah, you are too beautiful not to be partnered." I could feel the warmth moving up my neck as I said, "I've never thought of myself as beautiful." Lexy was never one to let the opportunity to tease pass by. "Next time you go to the water, look at your reflection, and then tell me you are not beautiful," she said with a twinkle in her eyes. I gave her a big hug and we laughed as we made our way back to the common area. What a blessing it was to have friends. I looked up at the almost full moon and thanked the Great Mystery for bringing me to Life Community.

We celebrated the moon's fullness with three days of singing, dancing, and planting in the moonlight. Daily chores didn't stop, but the anticipation of the nighttime celebrations lightened our days. We cooked large meals of meat, vegetables, and berries and sat around the fire telling stories until the moon was high above us. Once again the moon had gifted us. When we were filled to the brim with moon glow, it was time for the next teaching. I rose early to wish Thunar good luck but found he was not in the sleeping shelter. I wandered around until I found Lexy. She told me he had spent the night in the forest. Lexy and I sat down waiting for the others. Thunar was the last to arrive. He looked bedraggled with leaves and sticks in his hair and moss hanging from his clothes. But, his eyes were alight with passion.

In a firm but gentle voice, he asked, "Who of you will die tomorrow?" We were confused and didn't know what to say. He continued, "How about the next day?" Receiving no answer, he tried again: "How about next week?" Still, there was no response from the group. "We live," he announced, "with two invisible figures walking beside us. On the one side is life, and on the other side is death. Because we know and like life, we acknowledge its presence, while we ignore death. Ignoring leads to not knowing, and not knowing death, we come to fear it. Life and death are partners of a sort and are inseparable. They accompany us always, and when we fear death our lives are diminished. If we want to have full, meaningful lives, we need to give death its rightful place at our side. We will all die," he said, and then directed us to say out loud: "I will die." We sort of mumbled the words, but Thunar wasn't satisfied. "Say it louder," he commanded, "say it as if you mean it." We tried our best, but he shouted, "Louder," over and over again until we were shouting with him, "I will die, I will die, I will die." When we quieted he directed us to say, "Tomorrow I will die." No one wanted to say this and Thunar asked, "Why not?" Nake announced he wouldn't say it, because it wasn't true. "How do you know it isn't true?" Nake replied that he was in good health so he had no reason to believe he wouldn't be alive tomorrow. "What you say is true," Thunar acknowledged. "But tell me, isn't it equally true that you could die tomorrow? For example, lightning could strike, an illness could descend, or a tree could fall on you." Nake took his time to respond, and we waited in silence as he stroked his bald head. "I guess I see your point," he said, "but I don't like it. You are right. I really don't know."

Thunar turned to all of us. "Perhaps we don't like it, but what can we do?" He was still getting no response, but it didn't seem to dampen his spirits. He continued with vigor. "We can learn to befriend death and accept that we will die. If we let ourselves feel the presence of death, we can speak of it and teach our children about it. It is possible to live in the shadow of death with joyful appreciation for today. Once we accept death, it becomes our ally, reminding us of what is important. We must also accept the reality that life is about constant change, and each day we experience 'little deaths.' Acknowledging change opens the door for us to accept the inevitability of our own transformation, from life to death." Thunar finished his teaching by giving us an especially difficult exercise. For the next three days, we were to practice silence while carrying on an internal dialogue with death. He directed us to imagine our own passing and then ask death how it serves us. With our homework weighing heavy on our hearts, we walked to the common room to eat our meal in silence.

FIVE

Death Comes Knocking

I went up on the mountain to contemplate my death. This was the most peaceful place I knew. I wasn't fearful; in fact, I welcomed the discussion. I had felt death's breath on my neck many times as it pulled me closer. Had I somehow "cheated" death during those times, those split seconds, when I missed a fall by a hair's breadth or surprised a mother bear? Even leaving the Corpsety seemed like a reprieve from the grasp of death. Now, I had permission to talk with death and ask about those times. Darkness fell and I took my dialogue to sleep with me. I dreamed of death. Death was not a fearsome figure, but it was solemn and unsmiling. It opened its arms wide as if inviting me to join it. I had just begun walking toward death when someone crossed in front of me. Death closed its arms around the person and I was pushed back. I wanted to see who the person was, and I wanted to go with them. They moved on ahead of me toward a light I could see in the distance. I woke with a start. Father had come up the mountain and was shaking me awake. "Mariah," he whispered, "Illow has taken ill and is asking for us to join her." I jumped up and followed him down the mountain.

Father and Roz brought Illow to the sick house after she became ill sometime in the night. They helped her get comfortable and then called the wise ones together. We gathered around the bed which swallowed her small, shrunken body. We were ready to do anything she asked of us. She smiled feebly. "I've been weakening for some time and I feel my time to pass is near. I want you to know how grateful I am to have had your presence in my life and to have undertaken this journey with you. In the Corpsety, I was alone, but with you I have had the great good fortune to live, work, and play arounded by loving, nurturing friends. There can be no greater gift than this in one's life. I am not afraid to pass over to the other side. I believe the glimpse of spirit I have witnessed in the Wild, and in Life Community, has prepared me for what is to come. I know all of you cannot stay, but please visit when you can, as your presence is very dear to me. I would like for Mariah, her father, Roz, and Grund to accompany me as I make the journey from this life to the other." The four of us would stay with her day and night, bringing food and drink and keeping her comfortable. This was our custom.

Illow closed her eyes to rest while Grund, Roz, Father, and I settled in around her. I had not been with someone who was dying since Grandmother's death, and it brought memories of that time back to me. Father and Grund had gone to get food when Illow woke again. She motioned for Roz and me to come closer. "I need to talk to you both," she said. "Roz, you are gifted in midwifery and should stay with this, and I'd like you to help Mariah collect medicinal herbs. She is a gifted healer and will need a good assistant. Mariah, you can help Roz. I believe if you work together you will be a powerful team." "Roz is far better than me," I protested. Roz disagreed, "I have seen your healing gift, Mariah, and it is powerful. I would be honored to be your assistant and to have you help me." Illow pulled me closer to her and looked me straight in the eyes. Her eyes could still throw sparks, and she had my complete attention. "Little one, never deny your gifts which come from the Great Mystery. They have been given for you to share with others. They come through you, but they do not belong to you. They do not define you or make you better than others. They simply are." I fell into her arms, sobbing, and asked, "What will I do without you, Illow?" She reminded me that I was coming into my own wisdom, which would take me the rest of the way through life. "I will still be with you, Mariah," she whispered. She reminded me of the dream she had so long ago. "I know who will be watching over you. It's your grandmother, mother, and me." I was surprised. I didn't even know my mother, so it was odd to think of her watching over me. I looked at her and laughed, "You can still surprise me, dear Illow." My mood lightened, and Illow winked in acknowledgement of our connection.

Father and Grund returned with food for us and broth for Illow. While they ate, I fed Illow the broth, but she had little appetite. She drew me aside and whispered that there was more to the dream than she had shared. She had seen me with a man. "So, little one, I think you will not be alone after all." Then she closed her eyes and slept. We spent the next few days like this, sitting around the bed, comforting Illow, and telling stories of the past and present. We reminded her of the wisdom, courage, and gifts she brought to the community. Roz massaged her feet. We laughed as we remembered the time Illow tested a nut we were sure was a poisonous buckeye. Though she insisted it was not dangerous, we waited, fearing she would fall ill and die. The next day she woke, fit as ever. Illow laughed with us and shared that she could see the difference, though we could not. Suddenly, she sank back into the bed. With a gasp she was gone, the shadow of laughter still on her face. How quickly a beloved spirit leaves the world, I thought. We made a circle around the bed and gave our blessings for her safe passage. Then, we went outside to tell the community of Illow's passing.

Roz and I washed Illow's body and dressed her in clean clothes, and the four of us sat with her that night. In the morning, a fire was prepared, and the community gathered to talk about Illow's life. There were many stories to tell, for Illow had had a long, rich life. Father remembered her as Grandmother's friend. Others remembered how she had loved to sing and dance, and laugh. Grund remembered her as a beautiful young woman who preferred to live alone. We told the buckeye story, and there were many other stories shared that day. Evening drew near and the fire grew hotter. We lifted the pallet holding Illow and set it on the fire. As her body descended into flames, we began calling out blessings and prayers. We gave thanks for her beloved presence in our lives and the gifts she had shared. We were setting her free to continue the journey. I sat and watched as the sparks rose up into the night sky. The fire burned late into the night, and the wise ones stayed until the fire and Illow's body were no more. We had lost a wise one and I had lost my dearest friend.

I promised myself I would hold her in my heart. That way, she would always be with me.

Illow's death had given our assignment on death more meaning. I realized my dream had been about Illow. Death had come for Illow, and she had crossed in front of me to go. It was, I supposed, her turn. For no one can cheat death, no one. My conversations with death had taught me a great deal. Death is not waiting to "steal something" from me; on the contrary, it is walking by my side to remind me that I will die. If I am fully present to live in each moment, death can take nothing from me. And when the moment of passing arrives, I will be able to say, "I am ready to leave life and see what death has to offer. I have known life, and now I must know death." I could not yet call death my "friend," but the discovery of our relationship was oddly comforting.

The next day we gathered with Thunar to share our conversations with death. The group spoke openly of Illow's passing. Illow had faced death as she had faced life, without fear and with curiosity. Her example had had a powerful influence on the group. When we shared our conversations with death, I could sense that something had shifted. Acceptance of the inevitably of death and awareness of life's preciousness had grown, while fear and dread captured less of our hearts. We had gained a measure of peace. Perhaps this was Illow's last gift to us. I like to think it was, along with Thunar's night in the forest. Together they had brought us closer to death and to the Great Mystery.

My work partner was gone now, and I felt the loss as I readied myself to look for plants. I moved toward the collecting baskets and Roz joined me. I was happy to have her company. We talked as we moved into the forest. "Have you thought about choosing someone to share your skills with?" she asked. "No," I exclaimed, "have you?" "Yes, I've been thinking of it and wanted to ask what you think of Oel." This was a discussion she would usually have had with Illow. I supposed we would have to rely on each other's guidance now. "I think Oel is an excellent choice. She is quiet but very observant and kind." Two people came to my mind as possible students. "What do you think of Se or Flow?" I asked. Roz thought they were good choices. "Why don't you take both of them under your wing?" she suggested. I hesitated. Was I good enough to guide others? Illow's words returned to remind me: "Don't hide your gifts from the Great Mystery, Mariah, they are to be shared." I smiled and told Roz I would ask them. Illow was still with me.

SIX

Into the Blue

Thunar's teaching on death had completed the basic teachings.
Now, we needed time for our heads, hearts, and bodies to
absorb all that had been given to us. And, there was much work
to be done.

Roz, Grund, and I disappeared into the forest looking for
roots and plants. Illow had left instructions for remedies, some
with missing ingredients we hoped to find. It was good to be
finished with the teachings so I could relax in the company
of friends. As we walked deeper and deeper into the forest, it
worked its magic on us and our bodies quieted and softened.
Grund found the bark of a tree that would help with pain, but
Roz and I were still empty handed. We were in a part of the
forest that was strange to us and we made our way slowly. At
night we camped on the forest floor and during the day we
looked for treasures. Roz tripped on a stump and fell hard
against a tree. She yelled for us to come to her, and I feared
she was injured. We arrived to find her shaken but unhurt.
Roz wanted us to see the mushrooms she had found. Illow
had spoken of this mushroom with reverent awe. It held the

qualities of healing and insight. Her ancestors counted it as the highest medicinal of all. It was small and purple with black spikes on the stem. Carefully, we gathered several, and marked the spot so we could return. We had found enough for one trip and were headed back home when we ran into Father.

His hair, which was usually braided, was wild, and his face was drawn and pale. "You must return at once," he told us. "A sickness has struck the community and two children have already died." I was uneasy. How could a disease kill so quickly? While we hurried back, Father described the illness to us. "It came on a few days after you left. At first, we weren't concerned. Some people had diarrhea, which was not all that unusual. But, by the end of the day those with the sickness were much worse. Their eyes were sunken and their skin was a bluish color. One child died that night, another died in the morning, and more people are becoming ill." Grund skewed up his face, and his ears protruded from his head more than usual. "What you describe seems familiar to me," he mused, "but I can't quite put my finger on it."

It took us a day and a half to return to a deserted community. I had never seen it so quiet. No work was being done and everyone was either inside hiding or ministering to those who were ill. Roz and I hurried to the sick shelter, while Father and Grund stayed behind to talk. At the shelter we found a ghastly sight. People were lying on the floor in pools of their own vomit and feces. Some cried out for water, but most were lethargic, staring at us from sunken eyes. Their skin was a strange blue color unlike anything I had seen before. Dead bodies tended to be gray and then greenish. Sick people were usually pale or red. What could be causing this unnatural color? Roz and I were overwhelmed by the sight and smells. Oh, how I wished Illow were here with us. We stepped outside to catch our breath and talk. "This is surely a water illness," Roz announced. "There is water coming out of their bodies at an alarming rate; we must find a way to stop its flow." Illow had told me about a combination of herbs, honey, and water that could cure diarrhea. We decided to try her remedy. Roz and I supplied herbs to disinfect the area and remove the stench so that others could cleanse the room. We worked tirelessly to administer our precious store of remedies. Lexy, Cean, Thunar, Father, and Grund arrived to help, and by the end of the day the sick shelter was tolerable. People were clean now, but their conditions continued to deteriorate. Death was relentless in its desire to take people to the other side that day. By nightfall more people had died, and panic prevailed. In the midst of this terrible crisis a fight broke out. Several of the original community members were accusing the new ones of bringing the "blue death" from the Corpsety.

Late that night, Grund called a meeting. Everyone circled the fire and I could see their haggard, pinched faces. The new ones were huddled on one side, and the original community members were glaring at them from the other side. We were at a critical juncture. Grund addressed the group: "I want everyone to remember the teachings. Blaming hurts our ability to— " and then he was cut off. Lef had interrupted Grund: "I have seen this illness before. I tell you in the Corpsety people turned blue when they drank polluted water. The new ones have brought the illness with them!" Grund called for quiet, and his voice still had the ring of authority, even though he was exhausted. "Please try to understand," he pleaded, "we must work together if we are to find a way out of this disaster. Dividing ourselves thwarts our ability to act." "Has anyone noticed something unusual about our water system?" Father asked. Se came forward. She had seen some of the women using the water canals instead of the compost pits to relieve themselves. At the time she had not thought much about it. But, when Father asked about water, she had remembered.

Grund's face clouded over briefly and I saw a hint of anger pass over him. He asked for Father to continue and withdrew himself from leading. Father asked the women who had used the canals to come forward. "We need to know what happened," he said softly. A small group of former Corpse women approached with downcast eyes. "Yes," they told us, "it's true we used the canals." They had used the waste pits initially, but hated the smell. Several days ago the women had started using the canals. In the Corpsety, they reasoned, water had taken their wastes away, so why couldn't it do the same here? For modesty's sake, the women had used the canals only when others were not around. With no hint of anger, Father motioned for the women to sit down.

"This is the source of our illness," Father announced. "Human and animal wastes pollute water and cause illness. This is why we built the waste pits. This is why we run our water through canals to cleanse it." The women began crying and begging for forgiveness. "We didn't know," they wailed, "we didn't know." Grund rose to speak again. "Now that we know what the problem is, we will use the remaining tablets to purify the water we drink. Then, we must clean the canals so they will work again. We will begin this work at daylight tomorrow."

Roz and I returned to the sick shelter and began administering our remedy with purified water. No one else came down with the illness and we lost no more people to the "blue death." Se's keen observation had saved us. I had no doubt we would all have succumbed to the disease without her. Once again, I was reminded that we can never know where the voice of wisdom will come from.

We built a fire to honor and release those who had died. After we had sent them on their way to the spirit world, we stayed in a circle. Something was left undone. Roz spoke gently to the group, "We need to see about healing ourselves." She asked the women who had polluted the water to come forward. They were weeping with heads bowed in shame. She asked them to share their feelings with the group. They gave voice to the guilt, shame, sadness, and fear that was consuming them. "Now," Roz asked the group, "can you forgive the women for their mistake?" They had not intentionally brought death to others, and Roz believed they deserved to be forgiven. Around the circle some agreed, but those who had lost family members were not willing to forgive.

"How can we just let them off without any punishment?" they shouted. Stear rose to say, "What was done was done. It's not our role to judge the women. They will have to live with the knowledge of those who died because of their acts." "That's easy for you to say," family members shouted, "you didn't lose anyone. Those women caused our relatives to die."

Roz intervened, "I hear you and understand how you have been wronged. Your request deserves to be honored. Would you be willing to wait until the wise ones can come up with a solution?" Roz had spoken with a heartfelt intensity and the family members took comfort in her words. They agreed to wait. Roz closed the circle with a prayer: "May I be forgiven, May you be forgiven, May all beings be forgiven. May the light of the Great Mystery hold us in its arms, and lead us rightly. Amen."

We were beyond exhaustion and it took several days to recover from the strain of sudden illness and death. During this time of rest, the wise ones met to talk. "It seems we have overlooked important teachings," Father lamented. "The new ones need a guide to Life Community, something that will help them understand the 'why' of things." We knew why we built a canal system, but the new ones did not. They were still under the influence of the Corpsety. Once again, we were tasked with creating a series of teachings. "What will we teach?" Thunar asked. Father, Grund, and Roz identified work, fun, councils, violence and healing, leadership, connection, and community life as topics. Each of us would take a topic to teach. Sometimes it seemed as if the teachings would never end.

SEVEN

Life Community Revisited

We talked with those who had lost family members. We wanted to honor their losses with a "healing circle" followed by a resolution to their grievances. And, we asked that they wait until we came to the teachings on violence and healing. Uneasily, they agreed to wait to address their grievances. And so we began our teachings about life in Life Community. This time our focus would be on helping everyone to understand how we lived, so there would be no more costly mistakes like the one we had just weathered. I was to be the first teacher but the wise ones would lend their support. We were all in this together.

Work was my topic, and I explained the tasks each person was expected to learn: how to fish, hunt, gather food, build and maintain fires, collect firewood, perform guard duty, compost wastes, and participate in community-building projects. These basic survival tasks were to be shared by all because they sustained life. "In Life Community," I continued, "physical labor is valued because it has many benefits. It improves our health, encourages intellectual growth, fosters spirituality, and creates wholeness. Beyond these tasks we encourage you to explore your passion and interests. Life

Community needs people of all kinds to help with birthing, teaching, gardening, creating pots and baskets, maintaining the water purification system, cooking and preserving food, building and maintaining shelters, making clothing, healing, and collecting herbs. And, we need artists who create with color, music, dance, singing, and stories. We encourage you to follow your heart when selecting work. Beyond basic survival tasks, no one is forced into labor they dislike. We have found that satisfied people meet the needs of community joyfully—spreading joy throughout the community. This is what Life Community thrives on." I ended the session by opening the circle for discussion.

Stun wanted to know what would happen if someone couldn't do physical work. Roz answered his question carefully. "We all help whatever our ability. Here we have no competition or judgment, so all efforts are deemed valuable. Even children do what they can. Our focus is on the energy of the whole rather than an individual's abilities." Generally, the group seemed to be satisfied with the way we handled work and gave the signal they were ready to move on.

Grund stood to talk about councils. He said, "We use councils to make decisions, find resolutions, problem solve, and address community issues. Anyone with an issue can convene a council meeting. In the council circle we speak from our hearts and listen with openness. This allows us to find our deepest truths together. Speaking and listening from the heart creates a sacred circle, a group energy field, which wraps us in a blanket of empathy for ourselves and others. In this place it is easy to see how each person holds a piece of the truth. When the artificial boundaries between us begin to dissolve, we can see more clearly. The wise ones have a special responsibility in regard to council circles. Community members are free to stay or leave a council meeting, but wise ones must stay with the process until decisions or resolutions are crafted."

Hands shot up when Grund asked for questions, and Nake was first in line. "How do you get to be a wise one?" he asked. I was glad Grund would answer this and not me. I waited to hear what he would say, but it was Cean who kindly answered Nake's question. "A wise one has a cluster of traits that foster wisdom. She or he is curious, welcoming, deeply spiritual, trustworthy, forgiving, self-disciplined, creative, humble, compassionate, and connected to the unseen mystery of life. A wise one is able to move to the darker places, the shadows, in search of wisdom. They know deep in their bones that unity is the underlying reality. Wise ones are able to care for the soul of the community. Anyone can become a wise one who is willing to undertake a mentorship." For the moment, at least, Cean's response seemed to satisfy Nake. Moed asked if Grund could share more about the group blanket thing. Grund grinned and scratched his head. "It's hard to describe, but once you are in it you know." He likened it to being in love. "Love takes us to a higher place and a different way of being. The group field, that blanket of warmth, closeness, and excitement that surrounds you, is the same. Being in a sacred circle transports us to a place where we experience magic together." Moed shook her head and said, "I guess I will have to wait until the magic comes." "It will come," Grund smiled, "it will come." After Grund's teaching, I continued to think about councils. Although they were often troublesome, I had experienced the magic of being deeply connected. In the Corpsety, sacred circles were rare because people were closed, fearful, and unaware. It would take time for the new ones to experience the magic of the council, but it would happen.

That evening Roz and Father sought me out to tell me they would be asking for a "joining ceremony." They wanted my blessing. Father stood back a little and seemed hesitant. I looked at Roz's warm brown eyes and thick brown hair. She had never looked more beautiful. Father, with his graying braid and solid frame, still seemed powerful and handsome to me. Tears of joy rolled down my cheeks as I told them how happy I was, and how deeply I loved them both. I joyfully accepted an invitation to be part of their ceremony. Quietly, Father moved over to my side, holding something in his hand. He explained that it was a hair comb from my mother. The comb was the only thing he had left of her. Now, he thought, it was fitting that I should have it. I took the comb in my hand and tried to imagine my mother wearing it. Then, he pulled out a letter. "This is from your mother," he whispered. "She wrote it just before she died and asked me to give it to you when you were grown." The shock must have registered on my face, for Father leaned over to steady me. I thanked them again for including me in their new life together and thanked Father for his gifts. My mind was befuddled, and I hardly noticed when they left. A letter from my mother; whatever could it say? I laid the letter down carefully and looked away from it. Turning toward the light, I looked more closely at the comb. It had a beautiful mixture of dark red, black, brown, and gray colors. I held it tightly in my hand as I opened the letter.

Dear Mariah,

By now you will be a woman, perhaps not much older than I am now. I don't have much time left in this world and I want to leave you with something of myself. I want you to know how much I love you and how deeply I wanted to be with you. But, that was not to be. Your father is a good man. He will have given you the best childhood one can have in the Corpsety. There is not much I can give you except this. I have dreamed of a place, a place of beauty beyond all belief, a place where people are free of the Corpsety. I see you in this place, Mariah, and generations of your children too. You must be strong and follow your heart, for only then will the dream be realized. Only you have the power to make this dream come true. I cannot tell you how I know this, but my dream is true. My eyes are fading, dear child, and thus I must go. Look for me in the heavens and know that I will always be with you.

With All My Love, your mother

Tears streamed down my face as I touched the paper to my lips. This was as close as I would ever come to my mother. It was she who had given me the power to dream truth. She had prophesied our journey. If she had lived, what else could she have told me? I would never know. Tomorrow, I would share the letter with Father. That night I dreamed of Illow, Grandmother, and my mother as they hovered above me watching. My mother's face was fuzzy but familiar. When I woke, I wondered if it was a dream, or if they were truly watching me. Oh well, I thought, it doesn't really matter. Either way I felt good.

I shared the letter with Father and it brought tears to his eyes. "Mariah, she surely did dream truth. I had no idea what was in the letter." We shared a long hug and then he praised me for doing exactly what she had asked me to do. "Maybe she was directing me," I suggested. "Well I'll be," Father laughed, "maybe she was!"

Today, Father would begin the community teachings by speaking of violence and healing circles. He was well aware of the immediacy of this teaching. Any form of violence, physical, verbal, and emotional, is treated as an illness, he reminded us. Violence occurs when someone exerts "power-over" others. Any attempt to use power-over is an indication that something is out of balance in a person. When violence erupts in Life Community, someone from the community is given the task of accompanying the offender until learning, change, and justice are served. "Remember how you did this on the journey from the Corpsety to Life Community?" he asked. "We do the same for all kinds of violence, including self-harm, harming of community members, and unnecessary harm done to animals and the natural environment. We seek justice that restores the balance between the aggressor, his or her own self, those harmed, and the community." He paused, and then explained, "We believe everyone in the community is harmed when violence occurs. We use 'healing circles' to help us find our way to a just resolution and forgiveness. Forgiveness is an integral part of the process. It must be asked for and received before healing can occur and balance can be restored. Even when we kill an animal or take from plants, we ask for forgiveness. Acknowledging our violent behavior in front of others removes the temptation to become self-righteous and arrogant and forget our place in the whole of life. Healing circles allow us to confront violence and open a space for those who have been harmed to talk about their experience. A healing circle is a safe and supportive place where all are respected, even those who commit violence. In the circle, people speak of their feelings and the harm done to them while the aggressor listens. After all have spoken, then, and only then, the aggressor is asked to share her or his story. The aggressor is expected to reflect on what led him to commit violence, and how she was harmed by the act. When the sharing is finished, the aggressor asks for forgiveness from everyone touched by the violence. In a healing circle, there is no room for judgment, and we do not judge the aggressor. We listen with compassion, just as we listen to those who have been harmed. Finally, people begin to speak of what they need in order to heal. Now, a resolution is possible. Carrying the understanding of the healing circle in their hearts, the community is now ready to enter into a council and find justice." Father paused here for questions.

There was a long time of quiet until Nestor rose to his full height. His presence filled the circle as he spoke. "The Corpsety is rotten to the core with violence. I have been sick with violence myself, and here in Life Community I hope for a cure. We must be careful, though, not to carry the rot with us. I support your healing circles." He sat down. In stark contrast, the slight figure of Moed stood to address the group. "What happens if someone refuses to participate in a healing circle?" she asked. "That depends on who it is," I responded. "If the aggressor refuses to participate, the wise ones will talk with him or her about what refusing means—being asked to leave the community. On the other hand, if it is someone who has been harmed, we support and nurture the person until they are ready to share their story." People were puzzled by this new process but, like Nestor, they were ready and willing to learn how to heal violence. Father suggested we prepare to undertake a healing circle with the women who caused the "blue death" and the families of those who died.

The wise ones met with the families while the community scrambled to put together a circle within a circle. The families were unsure what they were supposed to do. Roz counseled them to speak of their feelings about what had happened and their suffering. In addition, she asked the families to consider what they might need in order to heal. She reminded them that the whole community would be sitting in a circle around them so they would be supported. One woman was not sure she wanted to revisit the pain again. "You can say as much or as little as you want," Roz said gently. We moved toward the circle and the families took their place in the middle. They told how their lives had been changed and of the loss and pain they continued to experience. Finally, they spoke of their anger at the women. No one interrupted and many cried as they spoke. The family members ended their part and it was time for the offending women to move to the inner circle.

The women walked slowly and sat silently. Their voices were strained and they did not look at us as they spoke. One by one each woman shared how a moment of daring to defy the community norms had changed her life. They were no longer happy and felt like pariahs in the community. They could see no relief from their suffering. Day and night it followed them like a dark cloud. Many community members cried with them as they spoke, and I even saw some of the family members crying.

Now, it was time for the community to speak. With tears in their eyes, people spoke of sorrow for both groups. They spoke of not feeling whole. They spoke of divisions that felt uncomfortable and unbalanced. They spoke of finding a resolution to end the suffering.

We asked the families what they needed in order to heal and they stood to speak. "This process has brought us healing," they announced. "We needed to be listened to and have our suffering acknowledged. Now, we understand the suffering of the women and how they, too, were harmed. We forgive them for their mistake. Most of all, we need to return to connection. We are not served by holding onto grief and anger, and the women are not served by holding onto shame. We want a return to community." Now, it was the women's turn to speak. "We deeply appreciate your forgiveness and honor your suffering. In order to release ourselves from the shame we carry, we need to be of service to the community. We ask to be allowed to clean the waste pits for a year to remind ourselves of our mistake and the great harm it caused." Although we were surprised by the request, we agreed to their terms. After all was said and done, everyone joined hands and swayed together in peaceful resolution. Later, we cooked a festive meal and sat around the fire singing and enjoying each other's company. The circle was no longer broken. Life Community was whole again.

We gave ourselves a few days off and then regrouped again

for more teachings. Roz directed our attention to leadership. She said, "In the Corpsety leadership is self-serving, but that is not the path we take. We believe true leadership is serving and working with others. In the Corpsety leadership is based on being better than others and exerting power over them. Life Community requires leaders to serve the community. We have found that leadership is better served when it is a shared responsibility. If leadership is held too long it stagnates and attachment creeps in. By sharing leadership we create a continual source of fresh energy and ideas. Our goal is to support everyone in developing the capacity to lead. In Life Community you will be called upon to lead in many small and large ways, for leadership has many faces. When your task is finished, you will return to your regular responsibilities. Moving back and forth between leading and following helps us maintain humility and balance. And, it discourages holding onto leadership." Roz paused and Nake's face pushed through the crowd. He wanted to get his question in first. "How can you say the wise ones have no more power than anyone else when they are always leading things?" "That's a good question, Nake," Roz responded. "Wise ones have no more power than anyone else. However, they have the responsibility to teach and stay with the council process. Perhaps it seems their role is greater now because of the teachings, but this is not the norm. Wise ones are sources of wisdom, but they do not have the final say. Decision-making is the function of the community." Nake considered her response quietly without protest. Several of the new members gave voice to an uneasiness about trusting everyone to be a leader. They didn't have much faith in their peers or in themselves. Roz asked them to remember how leadership emerged on the journey. "It came from many sources, including children," she reminded them. "It will be the same here. No one moves from being told what to do, to assuming their own power overnight. Give yourself time and you will find the confidence to lead. I am certain of this," she announced as she ended the teaching.

Cean interrupted my thoughts and I was happy to see his familiar face. "Mariah," he asked, "do you have time to go to the forest with me?" I was on my way to organize the celebration marking the end of the teachings. "I don't have time right now," I told him. I could see the disappointment in his eyes as he turned away, but he didn't say anything. "I could go tomorrow," I called out, but he had swiftly moved beyond the reach of my voice. What had he wanted? Should I have changed my plans? As he walked away, I was reminded of Father. Cean was gentle and like Father he had a commanding, solid presence. What would it feel like to kiss him? I wondered. I could sense Illow smiling down on me. Did she have a hand in this? I moved quickly to busy my hands and stop my racing thoughts.

Another day of teaching arrived. Rain forced us inside, where we were cramped for space. With elbows and knees overlapping we were about to begin a teaching on connection and community. Perhaps the close quarters would make the teaching more real. Cean began by retelling the story of the forest.

"Look at the trees arounding us. Trees live together in a community called a forest. No matter how strong or large or beautiful a tree might be it can never compete with a forest.

You see, the forest is a place of refuge where trees grow together nurturing, supporting, and protecting each other from the vagaries of wind, rain, and sun. Wrathful winds do little damage to a forest because of the support trees offer one another. Torrential rains that might uproot a single tree find it harder to move a tree in the forest. When the sun's heat bears down and there are no clouds of relief, the trees share water and are saved. You see, the forest is a sanctuary, a place where trees can grow and thrive. Any tree deprived of its forest is less than it could be and is vulnerable to the whims of nature."

He continued, "As it is with trees so it is with people. The ancients knew we are more when we are together and less when we stand alone. Like the forest, our community supports one another. We are protected by our collective presence and we are less vulnerable to the whims of nature. Together we grow in wisdom, because the collective mind we share informs and enriches us. We grow in health because we receive nurturance and do not have to stand alone when the winds of change blow hard against us. Though our ancestors are gone now their life ways continue through the Life Community we have created."

"In Life Community you are encouraged and supported to become fully yourself.

We expect you to choose work you are passionate about and to develop your interests. We encourage you to explore and discover the world around you. You are free to do as you please as long as you follow our values of respectful relations, equality, cooperation, sharing, group decision-making, and nonviolence. We ask that you hold these values so the community, our forest, can survive. This is a small concession to make when you understand that alone none of us could survive for long in the Wild." Cean stopped speaking and spontaneously we stood and joined hands. His wise words moved us to sway to the rhythm of our hearts. "We are the tree and we are the forest," we chanted, "we are one together." Cean sat down and I noticed how the sun brightened his hair to copper.

Sitting snugly against one another we readied for the next round of teachings. Lexy explained why we use the word Life Community instead of "city." She said, "For us, community speaks to the reality that we are a unified whole working together for the good of all. We are in essence one body in an ocean of wildness. A city is simply an inhabited place where people live as disconnected individuals. We do not intend for Life Community to ever grow into a city, because cities become Corpsetys, and Corpsetys become agents of death. Our goal is to remain small enough to maintain our connections so we can provide the following: a sense of order in which everyone is engaged; leadership that is not corrupt; equality and fairness; a slow pace of life with time for contemplation and reflection; close relationships which nurture us from birth to death; education for everyone; peaceful relations; and balance between play, work, learning, and solitude. In Life Community," she continued, "we cultivate a nurturing environment with interactions based on compassion, acceptance, and shared learning." There were no questions and so we moved on.

Now, it was Thunar's turn to come forward and explain how our days are divided. One part of the day involves gathering food, hunting, fishing, and gathering wood, he explained. The second part is spent doing our chosen work. The third part is spent joyfully in "play." "And finally," he finished, "we spend time together sharing food and each other's company." Thunar opened the group for discussion, and Nestor spoke for several men who were questioning the "play" part of the day. "We don't know anything about play," he explained. "Are we still expected to do it?" Thunar laughed. "You will find that play can be the best part of the day once you get the hang of it. It will be our pleasure to show you the many ways to play."

The rain continued, and after a soggy lunch, Lexy continued to share about community life. "Children are cared for and nurtured by all community members," she explained. "Young children remain close to their parents and naturally move away as they grow older. All of us create a healthy environment by offering loving, nurturing relationships that help children grow and thrive. Community gatherings, councils, and healing circles are open to children from infancy. Their presence reminds us of our responsibility to future generations."

"Our living spaces are shared. We sleep communally because it brings us warmth in the cold, provides protection from the Wild, and assures that no one has to sleep alone. We eat, learn, and play together in our community center. Our councils and ceremonies are held in the community circle, which is the heart of Life Community. We have created separate shelters for those who are ill, dying, or birthing. In addition, there are two shelters for solitude. While we believe connection fosters wholeness, we also understand people sometimes need time away from the demands of community life. We have tried to provide for both," she said.

Finally, Lexy talked about the importance of ritual. She said, "The death ritual is but one example of how we celebrate life. When a baby is born or a person recovers from an illness, we celebrate. When two people partner, their new life together is celebrated. We hold rituals that connect us with the changing seasons, the earth, our abundance, and our community. We celebrate in our hearts and together with song, dance, drumming, and prayer. It is ritual that helps us shift and move from the ordinary into the sacred and then back again. This is how we stay connected to the Great Mystery."

It was late in the day by the time the teachings and the rain ended. Breathless from running, I caught up with Cean and told him how sorry I was yesterday had not worked out. His smile drew me in and I noticed how his blue eyes sparkled with the upturn of his lips. We ate our meal together and laughed as we shared a small slice of happiness.

The wind blew hard in the night and dreams swirled around me. I saw large numbers of people leaving a smoking Corpsety and wandering in the Wild. Small groups of men were riding horses and terrorizing others. People carried great boxes of things, which slowed their progress and made them easy targets. I woke in a fog and sought out Father and Roz. I shared my dream and Father looked at me solemnly. "Mariah, I believe you have dreamed of the Corpsety's collapse. If this is so, we will need to prepare for what is to come. After the last teaching, we will hold a circle to speak of this. The end of the Corpsety will force people out into the Wild, and some of them will surely reach us." I went to the next teaching with heaviness in my heart. How could anyone prepare for such a thing?

EIGHT

The Hero's Story

Now, we came to the last and most important teaching. "It's
time to speak of heroes," Grund announced. "Tell me about
the stories you heard growing up in the Corpsety." A sense of
excitement stirred the air as people reflected on their stories.
Everyone listened with rapt attention as common themes
emerged: There is a male hero who is wronged by an evil person
or monster. This evil force is trying to gain control of the hero's
world, and destroy everything good. In order for justice and
good to prevail, the hero and his followers must fight. Through
violence the evil force is defeated. Once again the hero and his
world are saved from ruination. Grund repeated the themes and
asked if he had gotten them right. Enthusiastically, the group
nodded their heads. "How do these stories make you feel?"
he asked. "Good," they responded. "Why?" Grund wanted to
know. "Because, the hero prevails and the world is saved." He
questioned their logic. "Was the world really saved?" "Yes,"
they shouted, "good was restored and the hero won." The group
did not waver in their belief in the heroic story that had been
handed to them so long ago.

Grund continued with his questioning. "If the world was saved, then why is the phrase 'once again' always part of the story?" Moed was quick to answer, "The hero has to keep fighting because evil continues to come back in one form or another." "Why do you think this is?" Grund asked. Moed opened her mouth to speak, but Nake rushed to answer. "Because humans are violent and evil and we have to keep fighting these tendencies in ourselves," he explained confidently. Gently, Grund persisted. "Surely it has been proven that people can be violent and evil. Violent tendencies are *part* of being human, but they are not the whole story. Humans also have traits of courage, kindness, sharing, and nurturing as part of our heritage. In fact, the hero often personifies these positive traits. Perhaps we learned how to favor the violent part of ourselves in the Corpsety, where violence and evil rule. Those of us living in Life Community do not believe evil can be overcome by violence." He asked us to suspend our belief in the hero's story and consider a new story.

"Suppose," Grund offered, "the natural law of the universe is nonviolence. If this is so, the hero sets himself up for defeat as soon as he resorts to violence. The hero may win a battle but he loses the war, because violence begets violence. Using violence guarantees the battle will never be over. The heroine, for the new heroic role is not limited to men, must find ways to stand up to violence by working with the natural laws of the universe. Those who are violent and aggressive put themselves outside of the universal law of connection, and outside the cycle of life. They remain trapped in the cycle of death and destruction, and so does the hero who responds to aggression with violence. Violence creates imbalance, and balance cannot be restored by more violence. It can, however, be restored through courageous nonviolence."

He continued, "Humans have a powerful resistance to killing other humans. Our thinking, feeling, and instinct all tell us it is wrong, deeply wrong, to kill others. Even when we kill animals for food we ask for forgiveness, because we have put ourselves outside the cycle of life. We make an offering to the animal's spirit and give gratitude for its sacrifice, so that we may live. All this we do in order to be accepted back into the cycle of life. When we kill another human we place ourselves outside of the cycle of life. Outside is a dangerous and lonely place to be. You don't know who to trust or where to turn for help. Each time you kill someone, you move farther and farther away from life. Your heart and spirit are weakened. Hope, compassion, and love fade away. Your ability to connect with others and with the Great Mystery is broken."

"In the old hero's story the evil person or monster is always less-than human in some way. They may be animal-like, evil, mean, or mentally deranged, but in some way they are less valuable than the hero. The hero is justified in killing this less-than creature because of its unacceptable nature. This idea, this way of thinking, goes against the natural law of connection. We are connected even to the violent things in life. How we choose to act within these connections makes all the difference."

"We need a new heroic story. A story that reflects our understanding that peace is superior to violence. A story that recognizes a peaceful community is not passive. A peaceful community actively maintains peace through solidarity, and the embodiment of nonviolence. We need a hero who understands the human desire to exercise power-over, and the equally strong desire to hold power-over in check. We need a story that acknowledges diverse responses to conflict and builds on women's ability to respond to violence with nonviolence. We need a story that honors the values of connection and community as the most basic survival skill of our species. And finally, we need a story committed to solidarity and a firm resolution against violence. The old hero's story was a lie. If you fight evil with violence there is no happy ending, no heroic honor. All you get is more violence. This has been true for thousands of years of human history."

"While the aggressor may seem to be free of fear, this is only an illusion. Fear drives violence. A man who inspires fear cannot be free of it. It's time to create a truthful story, a story that resists evil, not on violent terms but according to the natural laws. We need a heroine who has the courage to face fear, and go beyond it. This is a challenge we must meet if we are to move away from violence. We ask you to join us in our commitment to nonviolence, and to standing up to violence wherever it occurs." A deep rumbling moved through the circle, and I heard some gasps of disbelief. "Before you consider what we are proposing," Grund continued, "let me explain how we plan to accomplish our goals."

"First, we must understand the hearts and minds of those who are violent. Violent people are fearful people. We need to find out what it is they are afraid of. Violent people have been corrupted by their greed and desire for power-over. We must look deep within ourselves to understand how corruption distorts thinking. And finally, we must learn how to respond to those who would control us with threats like: I'll steal from you; I'll hurt you; I'll hurt your family and friends; I'll kill you; and I'll kill your family and friends."

"People who are violent are still human. They need affiliation, affirmation, and love. It is fear that has separated them from their need for connection. Disconnected and fearful, such people live in a perpetual state of vigilance, which causes great stress. Seeing others only through the lens of threat and alienation limits their options and leaves them vulnerable." Here, Grund stopped his teaching. The rumbling had turned into a roar. Nake's face had turned reddish purple and I feared he would explode before he could speak. With a voice that sounded like broken glass, he asked, "Do you mean to tell me we are to let violent people attack us without defending ourselves?" Before Grund could respond, the floodgates opened, and the group was awash in fear.

Grund remained calm and quiet. He listened as Stun, Quake, and Stear voiced their fears about being vulnerable without protection. Grund waited until all had spoken before responding. "When an aggressor advances toward us, we are always vulnerable, are we not? Even if we respond with violence we are still at risk of being harmed or killed. In Life Community we are looking for a way to end violence, not just on our part, but on the part of others as well." Nestor had listened intently to Grund and others with a furrowed brow. With wonder in his voice he asked, "Are you telling us you have found a way to stop violence?" Grund turned to face Nestor. "I cannot say that we have found a way to stop violence. We are working on a process to prevent it from spreading." "What about those times when you can't stop it?" Nake shouted. "Those times call for us to face violence despite our fear," Grund told him. "Death is always a possible outcome when we confront violence, whether we use violence or not. We plan to face violence with courageous endurance and hopeful patience." With a puzzled look on his face Nestor spoke again. "I have no idea how to respond like this and I don't see how I could learn." I watched as heads nodded vigorously in agreement. I was surprised to see Grund's head nodding too. He acknowledged the mystery of his words. "It is true, this is not within our present understanding, but that does not mean it isn't possible. For a long time the wise ones have been seeking to understand violence. We are giving you the fruit of our labors, which we take very seriously. Time and again we have seen how the use of violence to oppose violence does not bring peace or security."

Some of the color had faded from Nake's face, leaving a bright spot on each cheek which grew redder as he asked a pivotal question. "You haven't had a chance to try it out yet, have you?" Father rose to his full height and joined Grund. "Once again you are right, Nake," Father responded. "We have not yet had the opportunity to try out our ideas with outsiders. However, we have practiced nonviolence inside our community and we are encouraged by its success. What we are suggesting is simply taking our core value of nonviolence to the next step." Nestor rose again and I noticed how his presence commanded attention. "I have seen far too much killing in my life," he said with an urgency that filled the air around us. "You do lose a part of yourself when you kill. I should know because it turned me into a fearful, empty shell. Killing, and witnessing killing, is worse than dying, because sooner or later you become numb to life. It has taken me all this time to work my way back to life, and I am not going to risk losing it again! I am ready to stand up to violence and find a better way to live, even if I die trying." The tension in the group was thick. On one side stood Nestor, Quake, Stear, Moed, Vilet, Se, Flow, and most of the original group. Everyone else sided with Nake. Rather than force a decision, Father suggested we learn the skill of nonviolence and make our decision after that. His suggestion was met with sour looks, downcast eyes, and unspoken resistance. Suddenly, out of the blue, the sound of Lexy's laughter caught our attention. "Silly us," she said laughing, "we are not in a hurry. Why be so serious? Let's shake and dance and sleep on this tonight." Her laughter loosened fear's grip and I breathed a sigh of relief as the group rose to shake together. Afterwards, people wandered off to finish the day's work.

The wise ones stayed behind and Grund thanked Lexy for breaking the tension. "Really, I had no choice," she explained. "The laughter just bubbled up in me and I had to let it out." "Laughter is a gift from the Great Mystery," Grund acknowledged. "Perhaps this was the Great Mystery's way of working through you." We turned our thoughts toward the nonviolence training. Cean suggested we focus on the "why and the how" of nonviolence. He reckoned Grund had just scratched the surface. The group would need to be well informed before they could make a decision. "I'm not sure everyone wants to learn," I told them. "What will happen if some people choose not to accept nonviolence?" My question was reflected on the faces of the others, and Grund gave voice to what was in our hearts. The value of nonviolence is not one we can compromise. If we don't uphold nonviolence, community and connection will not be possible. Those who refuse to accept nonviolence will have to form their own community. I was saddened at the thought of this, and yet I knew Grund was right. Nonviolence lay at the heart of Life Community. We would, of course, help those who might choose to leave, but this was not what we wanted or hoped for.

After the meeting Cean and I slipped into the forest. We walked in silence until we came to a large tree not too far away from the community. "I'm thinking of building a tree house here," he said, "and I'd like your opinion." He helped me into the lower branches of the tree so I could get a better look. As I climbed higher, the magnificence of the tree's canopy settled over me. I could see the tops of other trees moving in the forest as the sunlight made its way around the leaves. It was love at first sight. "Cean, this place is magical," I whispered as I threw my arms joyfully around him. "Careful," he laughed, "or you will knock me out of the tree." "What shall we call the tree house?" I hardly had time to consider my answer before he continued: "Why don't we call it Cenmar? It would be the joining of our two names." "It's a good name," was all I said, although I smiled at his thoughtfulness. Warmed with the knowledge of our secret place, we walked back slowly. I wondered where all this was going.

Early the next day we met to discuss Father's proposal. Nake and Moed stood together, as they had before, to address the group. Moed's tiny body vibrated with energy and she electrified the group with her words. "We are the 'new ones' who know only violence. Indeed it is we who brought dissent, conflict, and violence into Life Community. It is unfair of us to hold you back because of our ignorance. We will not stand in your way." She turned to Nake and he continued. "I disagree with Moed, but I will agree to participate in the training and so will those who stand with me. We will make our decision after the training." "Fair enough," Father told them. I could see Nake was making progress—slow progress, but progress nonetheless.

The training on nonviolence began immediately. This was not a decision we wanted to delay. Roz began first. She said, "Violence requires us to use power-over, which leads to disharmony and imbalance. This is why we avoid it. Our everyday relationships have shown how easily violence can separate us from each other, and from ourselves. The Corpsety is a place where violence has been given free rein, and it has devoured all possible human connections in its path. Even when used for 'just ends,' violence perpetuates disconnection and revenge. Our goal is to create a strong, creative response to violence that is in harmony with the natural laws. We do not intend to go meekly to our deaths. And, we will not be forced into violence by the fear of death. We will be prepared to stand against aggression with tools that protect us and challenge the corruptive power of violence."

Cean joined Roz to explain our plan of action. "We have identified four tools that will serve as our protection. First and foremost is solidarity. This is our strongest and most powerful ally. Collectively, we can support each other and find the courage to resist violence. But this is not enough. Secondly, we must have a good defense system. We intend to expand our lookouts. This will give us more information about what is happening outside of Life Community. Everyone will be enlisted to watch for strangers. We have made flutes for you to carry and alert the community if you come across possible aggressors. And, we intend to build a series of underground tunnels which will allow us to leave if aggressors enter our community. The tunnels will lead to caves where we can take shelter until the danger is past. Third, we will post signs outside Life Community that explain our intentions to outsiders. Here is an example of what we might say:

Welcome to all who would enter. In this place people live in community. All are equal here. If you come in peace we welcome you. If you are hungry we will feed you. If you are thirsty we will give you water. If you are sick we will care for you. If you need shelter we will help you find it. We can teach you how to find food, clean water, build shelters, and live together peacefully. If you lay down your arms, let go of your hostilities, and embrace peace you may enter. If you come to steal, harm, kill, enslave, or use any kind of power-over, we will resist you. We will resist you to the death. We bow to no one. We share but will not be taken from. We are a Life Community, and any form of violence is unwelcome here.

Finally, we will create a small group of people to greet strangers should they arrive at Life Community. This group will be trained to assess situations quickly, defuse aggression, negotiate creatively, and remain calm in tense situations."

Father joined Roz and Cean to describe the inner

workings of people who are violent. "Those who use aggression and violence have put themselves outside the cycle of life," Father explained. "They are disconnected from themselves, from others, and from the spirit realm. They are focused on survival through violence, and they are vulnerable. The benefits of cooperation, community, balance, and spiritual support are not available to them. Violent aggressors are isolated; even when they join with others, distrust, dishonesty, and disharmony characterize their relationships. Because they are disconnected from others, fear dominates their lives. And, fear is an unstable foundation. Fear brings agitation and the inability to think clearly. This creates weakness. Furthermore, aggressors fear acknowledging the wrongness of their actions. They are still human and, at a deep unconscious level, have a sense of guilt and shame. Aggressors prefer to believe what they have been told—that they are superior to those they are killing. Only by glorifying their actions are they able to obscure the fact that they have done the 'unthinkable.' In this state of denial they will do anything, including killing, to avoid facing the truth of their actions. Having crossed over into the cycle of death, there they remain."

Roz's voice rang out loud and clear. She said, "Knowing these things gives us an advantage, and we have built our responses around this. Everyone is to be trained in nonviolent survival skills, even the children. We believe preparedness is our best protection. There are five basic survival questions we want you ask yourself when facing an aggressor: 1) Do you have something the aggressors want? If so, can you share it with them? 2) Have you done something the aggressors didn't like? If so, can you change your behavior? 3) Have you dealt with the aggressors fairly? If not, can you make amends? 4) What are the aggressors afraid of? Is there some way you can allay their fears? 5) Are they open to talking with you? These are the questions we ask ourselves when we are confronted." I joined Roz, and in a strong voice directed the group to consider how to present themselves when confronted by violence.

"We are not meek," I explained. "Facing the aggressor we show strength, confidence, friendliness, and fearlessness. We share our names and get as physically close as we safely can. We want them to look at our face and into our eyes. We do not willingly let our faces be covered, and we never turn our backs on aggressors. All the while, we continue looking for ways to use their violent, unbalanced position to disarm them. If these actions work we may be able to move into a place of negotiation, where power can be shared. If these actions do not work we must move to the next level, which requires courage and fortitude. Here, we face our fears and accept, deep in our hearts, that Life Community is worth dying for. In solidarity, we begin to challenge our aggressors, not with aggression, but by speaking truth to their violence. We speak of the universal law of connection and how violence violates this law. We speak of the powerful resistance humans have to killing because it breaks our connection to life. We point out that the Corpsety collapsed because its violence repeatedly violated the natural laws. We tell them they will collapse under the weight of their own violence. 'By your actions,' we announce, 'you will be alone, abandoned, and left out in the cold. You will become a pariah. You will carry the burden of violence for the rest of your life. And, when death comes, you will be held accountable for your actions.' We tell them we have learned how to commune with the natural world. 'If your violence persists,' we explain, 'we will speak of your deeds so that no plant, no animal, no person will welcome you.' Finally, we speak the truth that a part of them will die if they kill us. They will be carried into the realm of death, where they will stay until death comes. We will call for the aggressors to stop the violence, change their ways, and reclaim a good life with us. We repeat these truths over and over and over again. We do not back down and we do not silence our voices. In solidarity we stand our ground. Knowing that violence tears apart the web of life, we commit to preventing it at all costs—even death."

"If we are successful," Roz continued, "they may leave us alone or they may join us. If these actions fail, we move on to the last and most challenging level. In this situation, we look for opportunities to escape into the forest and hide. If we are unable to escape, we practice noncooperation. We refuse to move, work, or do anything. At this point, since we are of no use to them, they will either kill us or let us go. Remember, the most valuable thing we have to offer is our knowledge—we know how to survive in the Wild. We will remind them of our offer to share knowledge freely with those who ask, but to those who would use force we offer nothing." Roz ended with these words: "What we have described to you is, we believe, the only way to stop the cycle of violence. We hope you will join us in creating a pathway to peace."

After Roz finished, Grund cautioned the group. "You must

each search your heart. If you feel you truly cannot do what we are asking, then you must honor your truth. There is no shame in not following our nonviolent path if you feel it is too difficult or too radical. If you choose another path, it is time for you to begin creating your future. You are free to start your own community, and we will help you." Grund closed the teachings and told everyone we would hold a decision-making council tomorrow. People left with glum faces. The reality of what we would face in the future was a heavy burden for the new ones to carry. They had come hoping to find a safe haven. The rest of us had known all along we would eventually face the collapse of the Corpsety and the exodus of its people. Perhaps we had been preparing for this moment since we arrived.

The seven of us met in the sick shelter. We were working on making flutes and neck pieces to memorialize this second phase of entering Life Community. While we worked, we talked about tomorrow's meeting. Father and Roz felt sure it would be a long meeting. "As it should be," Grund told us. "This is certainly the most challenging of all the teachings we have given." We nodded our heads in agreement. Silently, we contemplated what the next day might bring. Night fell before we finished the flutes and neck pieces. Tomorrow everyone would pass through the threshold as newly anointed community members or as departing members. There was no room for the liminal now. The time had come to commit fully to Life Community and nonviolence or leave.

Cean and I watched the moonrise and ate our evening meal in silence. The moon was perfectly round and golden as it hung in the night sky and shared its light. We sat together and then moved slowly toward the sleep shelters. Cean broke the silence with a whisper, "Let the beauty of this night sustain us tomorrow." Then, he touched my face lightly before moving away. I hurried to my bed filled with moon glow and the warmth of his touch.

Morning brought a somber mood to the circle. People's faces were closed and their bodies moved slowly. Grund opened the council by asking us to take a few moments to gaze at the sun, the forest, and the mountains. Then, he invited everyone to close their eyes and take some deep breaths, reminding us that we breathe into and take breath from an ocean of air. We share the air with each other and with the trees and animals. The trees take in our breath and return it to us cleansed. "This is but one of the many ways we are connected to each other and to the Wild," he said wisely. After a time, he asked people to open their eyes, and I noticed their faces seemed softer.

Grund acknowledged the difficulty of our last teaching. "Nonviolence is new to all of us, and it is one of our core values. Nonviolence is the key to staying connected to ourselves, to community, to the natural environment, and to those we do not trust. Nonviolence allows us to maintain our connection to life. Without this we are doomed to repeat all the mistakes of the Corpsety." He opened the circle for discussion and I was surprised to see a young couple stand together with their baby. "Neither of us slept last night," the woman told us. "We discussed the teachings all night. I kept seeing men attacking our baby, while we did nothing to protect ourselves. I couldn't stand that picture." Then, her partner shared. "I saw us fighting and maybe even winning so that, when our baby grew up, he would have to continue the fight. In my picture the war would never really be won or finished." Each had struggled with their mental pictures, until they could see the possibility of a time and a place where violence did not thrive, where violence served no purpose and was not perpetuated. "This is the kind of place we long for and where we want our child to grow up. We know that violence leads to the Corpsety's way of life, which is not worth living. We are both willing to lose our lives and even the life of our child to avoid creating endless Corpsetys." They sat down with tears in their eyes and we allowed their honest words to pass through our hearts.

Next to speak was Nake. I braced myself to hear what he would say. "We are trying to take in the idea of nonviolence, but we have many questions," he began. "For example, when the Corpsety collapses, won't those who come have guns and knives and other weapons that will easily kill us? If all or most of us are killed, won't we have failed in our goal of creating a life sustaining community? Also, we believe violence is a natural state for humans, so isn't nonviolence going against human nature?" With these questions left unanswered, he sat down. Grund asked if anyone wanted to respond to Nake's questions and Moed stood to talk. "Although the people from the Corpsety might have guns at first, they will soon run out of bullets, and knives require some skill to kill. I think the plan outlined makes sense provided we focus on avoiding armed folks, especially at the beginning. I accept the nonviolent requirement and am willing to learn how to embody it." As Moed sat down, the thought crossed my mind that she might someday become a wise one.

We waited but no one else came forward, so Grund addressed the last two questions. "Our goal is to create a life-sustaining community and to spend our last breath supporting what we have given our lives in service to. We are not in control of our deaths. A howling storm or a disease could destroy us at any time. Does this mean our efforts have been in vain? I don't think so. If only one of us survives to tell the story, or if someone somewhere hears about our community, all we have worked for is not lost." He paused and then asked everyone a question. "Is violence a possible way for humans to respond to situations?" People nodded their heads. "Have you seen nonviolent responses to situations?" Once again heads nodded. "What are some of those responses?" he asked. One by one group members shouted out what they knew: "Sharing instead of grasping;" "Laughing at ourselves when we are prideful;" "Tending and befriending;" "Focusing on loving rather than resenting;" "Engaging our creativity and playfulness;" "Refusing to engage in gossip and acrimony;" "Replacing competition with cooperation." "Aren't these responses also part of human nature?" Grund asked. "If we cultivate violence it becomes our nature, but that is our choice. We can just as easily cultivate cooperation, sharing, and nurturing. In response to your question, Nake, I would answer yes. To be violent is part of human nature, but it's not the whole of it." After he had finished speaking, Grund opened the circle once again for discussion.

The talking continued through the noon meal and into the late afternoon. Like the other wise ones, I listened and watched, as the group shifted and settled. There were still a few who were not willing to join with the nonviolent requirement, but not many. Night descended and Father asked for the discussion to come to an end. Cean and Nestor played their drums and slowly people began to move as they warmed to the beat. In a short time, everyone began moving wildly, and I saw Nake's bald head bobbing up and down as he moved. Even Nestor and Cean were hopping around with their drums. When the shaking ended our bodies were flush with the heat of the moment, warming our beds as the night cradled us in its arms.

The next days were long and intense as people continued to discuss without coming to consensus. By the third day people were getting pressured to give in on both sides. Father pointed out that pressure and coercion have no place in our circle. "We are here to fulfill our promise to make decisions as a whole," he reminded them. "The process is not about any one individual, it's about the movement of the whole toward consensus. Let's begin today by going around the circle with these questions: Can you live with the nonviolence requirement and uphold it? If your answer is no, then what can we do to help you?" Around the circle people pledged to uphold nonviolence. Midway around the circle we came to Nake. He looked tired and haggard and his voice broke as he spoke. "All my life I lived with privilege. I had power-over others and I thought nothing of using violence. Now, you are asking me to make myself vulnerable to people who are like I was: uncaring and in denial about the harm they are doing. I have not felt that I could face them, knowing what the likely outcome would be. But last night I had a dream—a dream that I want to share with you. In my dream I saw frantic, desperate people running away from a Corpsety in flames. Children ran alone with no parent to protect them. In the chaos I picked up a young child and grabbed her pregnant mother's hand, taking them to a safe place. Their eyes were so full of gratefulness that I was compelled to go back and find more people, until I had a whole community with me. Then some wild-eyed men on horses arrived. They wanted my help and also wanted to join us, but their violence made that impossible. I moved close to them even though I was afraid for my life. 'Let me offer you a way out of your prison,' I told them. They laughed and reared their horses up as if to trample me, but I stood firm. 'I see your suffering,' I said, 'and I know a way out.' 'There is no way out,' they replied. In that moment, I threw up my arms and thousands of birds, animals, trees, and spirits suddenly appeared around us. 'The only way out is in,' the wild things sang. Awed, the men got down off their horses, bowed low to the ground, and began sobbing. 'Our fierceness and anger have brought us nothing but pain and suffering. We would be happy to live like the rest of you, but we don't know how.' I clapped my hands with joy and told them, 'It is my job to teach you.'"

With tears streaming down his cheeks, Nake told us, "This dream has awakened me to the possibility of finding peace by sharing what I have learned with others. My objections to nonviolence were based on my fear of confronting people who are incapable of peaceful actions. Now, I see that no one is beyond peace. I may have to die while serving the cause of nonviolence, but then I will die anyway, so it is not such a great loss. I don't think I have fully realized what the dream meant until this moment. I will join you in the cause of nonviolence, if you will have me." Nake had taken a giant step toward us and we were eager to meet him. We encircled Nake in our collective arms while a great healing presence held us.

Returning to our places, we continued around the circle. The last to speak was Stun, and he got right to the point. "I can see there are not enough of us to start a new community, so I really don't feel I have a choice. However, I admire your courage and know that fear is what holds me back. If you can help me develop courage and fortitude, I will join you." Grund acknowledged Stun's fear. He suggested our collective courage would be the foundation supporting each of us as we moved forward. And so it was settled. On this day, our community joined together in full acceptance of the value of nonviolence. The teachings were complete.

CHAPTER IX

Celebrating and Preparing

Father, Cean, and Thunar began setting up the wooden arbor outside the community circle and Roz and I brought baskets of good-smelling herbs. Everyone gathered around until Roz announced, "Let the ceremony begin!" Solemnly, each person passed through the sweet-smelling arbor to be welcomed and receive a flute and a clay amulet with a double spiral— signifying descent into the Corpsety's death cycle and ascent into Life Community's life cycle. Even the wise ones passed through the threshold. Now, everyone was a full-fledged member of Life Community. We would start anew, together. Great piles of food graced our table. Rich stews with vegetables from our garden, roasted deer, dried fish, nuts and berries, and sweet fruits had been lovingly prepared. In the midst of plenty we sat down to eat and gave thanks for our good fortune. After filling our bellies with food, we answered the call of the drums. Wild dancing and storytelling carried us late into the night. We wanted to squeeze every ounce of joy we could out of our coming together.

Father had planned to call a meeting the next morning but

he had not accounted for the lateness of the festivities. People were slow to rise, and it was afternoon by the time everyone had awakened and eaten their morning meal. He called the sleepy group together and announced, "Mariah has a dream to share." I wasn't sure they were ready for my dream, but I took a deep breath and began. "A few weeks ago I had a dream. In it I saw a smoking Corpsety, and large numbers of people wandering in the Wild. I also saw a small group of men on horseback terrorizing people. Those who wandered were carrying great boxes which slowed their progress and made them easy targets for the men." Nake interrupted me excitedly, "This is like my dream." "Yes, Nake, I have thought of that. I believe our dreams tell us the Corpsety has collapsed or will collapse soon." The words "collapsed" and "collapse" brought Father to his feet. "We must prepare ourselves," he said, "for we may soon encounter outsiders." Around the circle people nervously agreed. He asked for those who were strong to begin digging tunnels. Cean, Grund, and a few skilled builders would build the new lookouts. The rest of us would carry dirt and stock the caves, which would serve as temporary shelters. Each of us felt a sense of urgency. If we were to face people from the Corpsety, we wanted to be prepared.

We struggled through weeks of hard labor. Our hands were raw from digging and our bodies were blackened by carrying endless armloads of dirt. Weariness wound its way deep into our bones, but there was no time to rest. We could breathe a sigh of relief only when the caves were stocked with food, water, and blankets. The new lookouts were built. And, we could see a light at the end of the last tunnel.

Summer was fading and the days turned cooler. We carried firewood to the caves and tunnels. If someone came to steal from us they would find only a little food and empty fire pits. Our valuable tools, blankets, food, firewood, and fire starters were hidden from outsiders. In the midst of our work, we began preparing for our fall celebration and the joining together of Roz and Father, and Lexy and Thunar. This ritual would invite us into a time of feasting, dancing, singing, and giving thanks for all we had been given. We decorated the community room with branches and berries and a threshold was made out of young trees for the couples to walk through. I helped Lexy and Roz fashion dresses out of beautiful material given to them by Moed. Moed had brought bundles of cloth with her from the Corpsety. When we asked how she had managed this, she just smiled. It was her secret. There would be garlands of vines and berries for their hair and fragrant herbs for Lexy and Roz to carry. We would even sacrifice some of our scarce candles, which captured firelight. An air of excitement swirled around us. This would be our first partnering ceremony.

The days began to shorten as we waited for the last tunnel to be finished. I was busy and hardly noticed the changing cycle of the sun. Cean and I were given the task of training those who had volunteered to be greeters. I looked forward to working with such enthusiastic, creative people. Nestor, Stear, Moed, and Lexy joined Cean and me for the first training. They fulfilled my expectations and then some. In a very short time we had turned the nonviolent teachings into actions. Following Grund's suggestions, we came up with guidelines for greeting strangers. We would:

1. Face people with strength, confidence, warmth, and friendliness
2. Maintain a sense of humor and playfulness
3. Not react with fear or violence
4. Never turn our backs on aggressors
5. Work in solidarity
6. Speak in a low, firm voice while looking straight into the eyes of the aggressor
7. Use our knowledge of "the breath" to center, balance, and calm ourselves
8. Quickly absorb information about what was happening around us
9. Announce our community welcome statement
10. Ask ourselves the five survival questions (Do we have something they want? Have we offended in some way? Have we dealt fairly? What are they afraid of? Are they open to talking?)
11. When attacked, speak to the aggressors of the consequences of their actions.

Next, we would assess the people confronting us. Getting close to the strangers, we would look for these signs of hostility: not looking directly at us; not sharing names; not listening; and displaying anger. This assessment would determine our next steps. If a group seemed honest, respectful, and receptive we would share food and water. They would be asked to wait while we consulted with Life Community. We envisioned a series of steps for the community to consider. We could teach a group how to gather, hunt, clean water, and find shelter and send them on their way. Or, we might teach a group how to start a community. And, in a few cases we could accept a small group into our community. This gave us three good options to choose from.

Our work together created a positive flow of energy which held us close as we came to the difficult task of determining how to deal with a hostile, aggressive group. Maintaining solidarity while remaining relaxed, open, confident, and aware of our surroundings would continue to be the bedrock of our defense strategy. Now, we were challenged to consider what to do if violence erupted. What would our response to force look like? "Our first priority should be to identify an escape route," Nestor suggested. "Then we could leave at the first sign of aggression." "What will we do if we are unable to escape?" Lexy asked. Cautiously, our eyes met around the circle. Our faces were solemn yet our souls were resolute. We would follow the nonviolent path Grund had laid out . . . to the death. Yes, we were willing to die to protect Life Community and our way of life. But we would not go quietly. In our own way, we would resist the violence, aggression, and power-over that had corrupted the Corpsety. The plan we crafted was strong, flexible, and creative and would serve as a guide through the valley of death and destruction.

On a cloudless blue day, the tunnels were finished and we began our celebration. The air was crisp and just a bit cool with a gentle breeze that danced around us. A small group gathered wood for the bonfire which would burn all day and into the night. The forest called to us as the sun playfully danced between the trees. I wanted to stay and dance, but the celebration pulled me back. We sat down at the community tables anxious to eat. But before we could take even so much as one bite of food, we had to release the gratitude filling our hearts. Softly we named all that we were grateful for: plentiful food, good friends, new beginnings, healthy children, freedom from the Corpsety, recovery from illness, love, life, happiness, community, and the Wild. Like the curling smoke, our words ascended into the heavens, and we were free to eat with abandon all the fruits of our labor.

The sun slipped behind the mountains and we brought out the arbor to bless the new couples. Father and Roz went first. Roz's face was serene and aglow with happiness. Her dark eyes spoke of her love and loyalty. Father's strong face was filled with softness, and I noticed his hands shook a bit as he reached for Roz's hand. They passed through the arbor and I stood with them as they spoke of their commitment to each other and to life. Afterward they embraced as the community called out blessings for their life together. Now, it was Lexy and Thunar's turn. Their ceremony was much the same with one exception. They announced the arrival of their child in the spring. Blessings sprang from the community for Lexy, Thunar, and their expected child. Both couples were feted and arounded with joy, happiness, and friendship. Before the night's festivities ended, we accompanied the couples to the private shelters. Roz and Lexy looked beautiful in the candlelight, and I felt a little sad and lonely as I left them. Shaking my head to clear my thoughts, I reminded myself that I had a roomful of people to share the night with. I would not be cold or alone.

TEN

Confrontation

The next morning our bonfire was still burning and people were slow to begin the workday. I was in the forest gathering herbs when I heard a flute and saw Quake running toward me. "The farthest outpost has sighted a group of people moving this way," he hurriedly whispered. I returned to the community, while Quake alerted others. The new couples were called to the circle meeting and I was sad for them. Their precious time alone had been cut short. Grund solemnly conferred with Moed and me. "Will you travel with me to greet the strangers?" he asked. Everyone agreed that the three of us should go. Father pulled me aside to say, "I am proud of you for volunteering to go on such a dangerous mission." He hugged me and whispered in my ear, "Be safe, Mariah, for you carry my heart with you." Everyone in the community would prepare at home while we travelled to meet the strangers. Once again, we were entering into the unknown.

Wolf did not want to leave my side and cried when I commanded her to stay. I hated to leave her, but it was too dangerous to take her along. There were tears in my eyes as I left Wolf standing forlornly next to Father. We walked accompanied by our thoughts. The collapse of the Corpsety had come more quickly than we had hoped, but that was not a matter for us to decide. In a way, it was good the Corpsety had collapsed since it released people from their bondage. But, what would happen now? This was the question on all our minds. Would the refugees see the evil in the Corpsety's greed, violence, and corruption now that it had collapsed? Could they imagine and accept a different way of life? We had faced these questions and had helped others to face them. Now, we would be confronted by those who likely did not know there were questions to be faced. We spent the night at one of the lookouts, and early in the morning set out for the far lookout. Arriving at mid-morning, we asked the woman keeping watch about the group. "They are a short distance away toward the east," she told us.

We walked quietly, breathing deeply and affirming our courage as we moved to meet our first refugees from the Corpsety. It was a small group. They appeared to be cold, tired, and hungry. We approached and Grund called out that we meant them no harm. They let us come fairly close, but only because their guns were pointed at us. "What do you want?" a man asked. "We live in the area," Grund replied, "and we've come to greet you." "We come from the Corpsety," the man explained. "It has collapsed into chaos and is no longer a place where people can live." Grund continued, "My name is Grund and what is yours?" "I am Master Edward and these are my family and slaves." This told us he was a Corpse. "Will you sit with us?" Grund asked. "What is your station in life?" Master Edward wanted to know before sitting.

"In the Corpsety stations have meaning. Out here they are meaningless. We carry no stations around our necks," Grund replied. Hesitantly, the man sat down but kept his gun aimed at us. We showed him that we were unarmed and asked him to put down his gun. Reluctantly, and due to the urging of his wife, he dropped the gun. He began to tell his story: "We have been traveling for weeks and are running out of food and water. We escaped from the Corpsety but despair is all we have found. We are exhausted by our travels." "Where are you going?" Grund asked. "We heard talk of another Corpsety nearby and we were hoping to find it," the man replied. Grund shook his head. "We left many years ago and have built a community nearby; but we know of no other Corpsety. We can offer you the food and water we are carrying." Upon hearing this, the women started crying and offering their thanks, but the man and his son were more cautious. "Why would you do this? We mean nothing to you," he said coolly. Moed stepped up to tell him of our community guidelines. The man was shocked. "What kind of people are you? This is no way to live." "We do live in a different way, that is true," Moed explained. "We do not allow guns or slaves into our community. Everyone enters unarmed as an equal." The slaves were silent, but I could sense their eagerness. The man sat down and put his hands over his head. "The world is spinning around me," he cried out. Moed touched his arm gently and said, "I too was a Corpse and knew no other way of life, yet I have learned. It is possible to change." Master Edward lifted his head. "We will accept your help," he sighed. Promising to return in two days, we told him we would meet with our community and discuss the next steps. We left our extra food and water with them and began the journey back.

I had expected something different. I thought they would be more argumentative like Nake. Moed felt the man was "wrong somehow" but she couldn't explain why. "This experience is not necessarily the norm," Grund warned us. We had been gifted with an easy first encounter, or so we thought.

Upon our return, a community council was called. We gathered around the circle, but before we could tell our story, a runner brought news that the small group we met was actually part of a larger, heavily armed group. It seemed we should have taken Moed's intuition more seriously. Instead of deciding the small group's fate, the meeting would help us decide how to proceed. Father opened the council and Grund told everyone what we had encountered. Emotions ran high. People spoke out against the small group which had deceived us. Many were opposed to granting them any kind of help. Cean asked for ideas about how to go forward. Some wanted to ignore them. "What if they find their way here?" Cean asked. Then it would be a bigger problem, all agreed. Others wanted to send the wise ones to deal with the group. "Is it a good idea to send all the wise ones into a potentially dangerous situation?" Father asked. When put that way, it didn't seem like such a good idea. "Now is the time to put our nonviolent resistance plan into action," Grund declared. "The three of us should finish what we started." The mention of our resistance plan agitated the group, and a few came forward with ideas. "Why don't you meet the group at night?" Nestor asked. "That would give you some advantage." Vilet shyly reminded us to reach out to the women, and she was right. The women had been much more responsive than the men. We needed to find a way to connect with them.

If we were to meet the strangers at night, we would need to begin our journey back quickly. Grund, Moed, and I rested while the community prepared for our departure. I slept soundly and dreamed. I saw groups of people caught in a net of guns, holding their hands out for help in the darkness. I called out for them to break through the net, but they couldn't hear me. Finally, a young child jumped over the net and ran free. After a shocked pause many, but not all, followed the child and ran laughing and shouting toward me. I woke and looked for Father. I wanted to share my dream with him. He was with Roz preparing food for our journey. They hugged me with tears in their eyes. I told them of my dream and Father's brow, which had been furrowed, relaxed a bit. "Mariah, you have dreamed of the days to come. It seems you will have a good outcome." "Yes, it seems good," I replied, "but the darkness is disturbing. I don't have a good feeling about it." "What do you think it is?" Roz asked. "I'm not certain. The darkness could represent death or not being able to see clearly," I replied. I saw Father's brow furrow again and I knew he was worried. I touched his shoulder and told him I wasn't afraid of death. "I know, little one," he sighed, "but I want to hold onto you."

Quietly, we ate our meal and prepared to leave. The community held us as we swayed to the rhythm of the drums. The womb of community warmed and nurtured our hearts and souls. We left the circle feeling deeply connected and committed to protecting our way of life. Cean caught up with me as we were walking away. He gave me a small amulet he had fashioned out of a piece of green stone. It had a curious spiral cut into its face and was beautiful. Cean took my hands in his and looked deeply into my eyes. "Please come back to me, Mariah." Then, he turned and left abruptly. What did he mean by "Come back to me?" I felt a flutter in my stomach as heat spread throughout my body. Could it be that Cean—the strongest, most handsome, and kindest man I knew—wanted me? My body told me he did, yet my mind continued questioning. I had plenty to think about as I set out on this treacherous journey.

Again, I commanded Wolf to stay with Father. This time she howled when I left, and her howls followed us as we moved away from our home. We walked through the night and shared our thoughts. I spoke of my dream and wondered if death might be near. The others listened and agreed we must be ready to face our deaths. Grund lowered his head as if meditating. Finally, he spoke, "I have lived long and well and now I'm willing to go with death if it is my time. Moed told us she wasn't sure she had made her peace with death. She wanted to enjoy life a little longer. And, she was willing to die in order to save Life Community. I wasn't afraid to go with death either, but like Moed, I had hopes of experiencing more life. As I shared my thoughts, an owl flew past, and its wings touched my cheek. Had it marked me for death? The owl broke our train of thought, and we walked quietly the rest of the way. In the afternoon, we found a cave and built a small fire to keep us warm as we slept.

I woke to the sound of hundreds of black birds flying out of the cave. They had huge wings and made an awful screeching noise that was very un-bird like. I tried to stand but several of them got tangled in my hair, and I started screaming along with them. Grund awakened and helped me get them out of my hair. Moed had also awakened. Grund told us to lie quietly until they passed out of the cave. It seemed like an eternity before they all flew out. There must have been thousands of them. "What kind of bird is that?" I asked Grund. "They are not birds, Mariah, they are bats. Bats are strange creatures which live in darkness and come out at dusk to eat. I have seen bats flying in the night sky, but never before have I seen them up close and in such numbers. It seems we shared their home as we slept." It was an unsettling start to the evening and I was uneasy.

By the time we reached the strangers, the fading sky had turned into night. The women ran out to meet us. "We were afraid you would not come back," they cried. I looked into their faces. They seemed open and sincere. The man and his son held back, as if waiting for us to come to them. They did not meet our eyes. "What is your decision?" Master Edward asked. Grund greeted him and asked how their night had been. "What is your decision?" Master Edward said loudly. "We need to talk about that," Grund replied. He invited Master Edward and his family to sit with us, but they continued to stand. "We demand to know what the decision is," Master Edward repeated. By this time it was very dark, and only firelight reflected their faces. "We know you are travelling with a larger group," Grund began. "Can you tell us about that?" Even in the dim light I saw Master Edward's face freeze. He lunged at Grund and knocked him to the ground. Moed and I helped Grund stand up, and suddenly we were surrounded by men on horses with guns. While they circled, Moed, Grund, and I stood calmly, observing what was going on around us. The women had retreated and were watching anxiously. Master Edward appeared to be in charge.

We were held captive while another group of men slowly approached. I counted somewhere between twenty-five and thirty people, including children and slaves. A man stepped forward to speak. "Edward tells us you have built a community nearby that has food and water to share, is this true?" Grund shared his name and asked for the man's name. The group of women and children were drawing closer. "My name is of no consequence to you," he replied. "Answer my question." Grund smiled and continued, "Did Edward tell you we do not condone violence, nor do we hold with any kind of hierarchy?" "These things are of no importance to us," he growled. "Then we have nothing to offer you," Grund responded. The firelight reflected a growing rage in the speaker's face. He shouted, "You would deny us food and water when we are starving?" Grund remained calm as he recited our community statement: "Welcome to all who would enter here. In this place people live in community. All are equal here. If you come in peace we welcome you. If you are hungry we will feed you. If you are thirsty we will give you water. If you are sick we will care for you. If you need shelter we will help you find it. We can teach you how to find food, clean water, build shelters, and live together peacefully. If you lay down your arms, let go of your hostilities, and embrace peace you may enter. If you come to steal, harm, kill, enslave, or use any kind of power-over, we will resist you. We will resist you to the death. We bow to no one. We share but will not be taken from. We are a Life Community and any form of violence is not welcome here." Then he added, "We do not welcome those who bring death." There was a short pause after Grund spoke. Then the man shouted for the guards to tie us up. The men on horses dismounted and tied our hands. Grund, Moed, and I had a chance to speak to each other briefly. It was clear we had something they wanted, but would they negotiate with us? We observed the guards while chanting: "Using violence against others violates the natural laws of the universe. It will cause you to lose your connection. The Corpsety violated this natural law by killing and harming others and it collapsed. This will happen to you too if you continue to violate the natural law. You will be alone, forsaken, left out in the cold, apart from others and from the Great Mystery. We hold the power of the ancients, the medicine of people from the past, to commune with all the beings of the world, and we will tell them of your deeds. You will be burdened and cursed by your own actions. Stop the violence now, change your ways, and regain your life."

We continued chanting over and over again as the guards roughly pressed our bodies against a tree and tied us there. I looked into the eyes of the guard who was assigned to me and his gaze did not falter. He tied the rope gently around my wrists. Could he be sympathetic? The night grew cold but we were not defeated. We reminded each other to relax and let our minds warm and sustain us. In solidarity, we assessed our situation. Grund felt the male Corpses were unsympathetic and would not yield. Moed had been watching the slaves. She thought they were agreeable but afraid of the Corpses. I shared my insights about the women and my guard. I believed both were receptive to us. Grund suggested we focus our energy and attention on the women and slaves. No matter what happened, we would maintain our resolve. Escape didn't seem possible right now, but we would continue to look for opportunities. We slept off and on, waiting for the sun to bring a new day.

The guards loosened us from the tree soon after sunrise, and we watched as the male Corpses met briefly around the fire. The man who had spoken last night approached and offered us a way out. He would release us if we agreed to take them to our community. "Are you willing to lay down your arms and give up your power?" Grund asked. The man struck Grund across the face with a whip. I swallowed hard so I wouldn't shout out. "Trasher, you have no right to ask such questions. What is your answer?" "You have our answer," Grund replied. "We gave it to you last night." The Corpse moved in closer as he spoke, "You give me no choice but to use force. Take him to the tree and tie him," he commanded. Moed and I were freed but guarded with our hands tied behind our backs. Everyone came closer to watch what was happening, even the children. One of the guards began beating Grund with a whip. Grund's face was turned toward the tree so I couldn't see it. Moed and I would have to be his face for the crowd. We screwed up our faces in agony and began to chant: "The Corpsety violated the natural law against harming others and it collapsed. You too will collapse if you continue to violate the natural law with torture." As we looked into the faces of the women, slaves, and guards, we continued chanting: "Stop the violence now. Change your ways to save your lives and souls."

The guard continued lashing Grund and we continued

chanting over and over again, "You are cursed by your own actions," until the Corpse told the guards to gag us. We continued to look at the group as the beating went on and on. The women, children, slaves, and some of the men averted their eyes from our gaze. The beating didn't stop until Grund fell unconscious to the ground. I noticed some of the women were crying. The Corpse came over to us as the guards removed our gags and bound us back together with Grund around the tree. "One of you will be beaten tomorrow," he said. "Think about that. All you have to do is give us what we want." I stared hard at him before reciting our chant. "It is wrong to harm others. It is wrong to force others to do things against their will. You are acting contrary to the natural laws of the universe. You will pay for this," I promised, "for by your own deeds, you are cursed." He hit me hard across the face and shouted for all to hear, "This one will be beaten tomorrow."

At that moment, Wolf lunged out of the woods and attacked the man before he could draw his gun. One of the guards shot Wolf, but not before she had mortally wounded their leader. Oh, how I longed to hold Wolf in my arms as she lay dying. I called out my thanks and sang prayers, telling her we would always be together in the spirit world. She looked at me and I could swear Wolf smiled as she took her last breath. I sobbed for Wolf and for Grund, for I had a premonition that Grund wouldn't make it either.

Spent with crying, I dried my eyes and noticed I was loosely tied. I could slip my hands out of the rope. I whispered to Moed, "Check your rope knot." It was loose, too. When darkness fell, we could escape. We worked on Grund's knot, but it wouldn't budge. "I won't leave without Grund," I whispered. "I don't think he would want you to stay," Moed shot back at me. I knew she was right, but I could not imagine leaving him with these horrible Corpses. Darkness descended and the guards changed. I recognized one of the guards. They stood watching as we watched them. When it got darker the guard I was familiar with came over to check on us. "Are the ropes too tight?" he asked softly. "What are you doing with the prisoners?" a Corpse called out. "I'm checking the ropes," the guard responded. "Make it quick," the Corpse commanded. He bent down to look at the rope and whispered in my ear. "There are ten of us and one child who will agree to your terms and go with you. We will free you at midnight and follow your lead." "What about Grund?" I asked. Without hesitation the guard answered, "I will carry him." "How will you stop the others from following us?" I said. "Let me take care of that," he replied.

Grund slowly made his way back to consciousness. We had been given no food or water, and Grund desperately needed water. We told him the guard would help us escape, and though he was weak, he smiled. "It seems our plan has worked," he whispered. "We have won some of them over to the side of life." He instructed us to leave him behind. He was too weak and would slow us down, he reasoned. We tried to argue with him, but he refused to budge. The moon was high above us by the time the guard arrived. He cut Grund loose and we got a good look at him. His clothes were soaked with blood and his hair was matted into a red helmet. He only weakly protested when the guard put him over his shoulder.

ELEVEN

Paying the Price: The Wages of Good

Cautiously, we followed the guard and met those who were waiting for us outside the camp. The light of a full moon guided us as we moved toward the forest. We walked without making any noise until we came to a place where we could rest for a moment. "How did you leave the others behind?" I asked the guard named Rut. Gladly, he shared his story. While the other guards slept, he had taken their guns and hidden them. Working quietly, he went around the camp collecting all the guns and buried them among the rocks and plants. Finally, he led the horses away from the camp and set them free. "It would have been easier to kill the guards," he admitted, "but I was trying to follow your guidelines." His goal was to take away the Corpses' power to kill without harming them. Moed and I were amazed at his ingenuity and understanding of our values. "We could not have done it better ourselves," we exclaimed and praised his courage, creativity, and resolve.

Rut gave Grund some water and he revived a little. One of the slave women came over to join us. Her name was Iway and she was a touch healer. "Would you like for me to work on your wounds?" she asked Grund. He was barely able to nod his head, but his eyes said yes. We watched as she moved her hands over his body, sometimes touching, sometimes not, with gentle soothing movements. Before she had finished, Grund fell asleep. "This is good for him," she said shyly with her head bowed. I thanked her for sharing her gift and noticed a slight smile on her face before she faded into the shadows. Standing once again, we agreed to continue walking until we reached Life Community. We needed to put as much distance between us and the others as we could. Halfway home it began to rain. At first I worried the rain would slow us down, but then realized it would cover our tracks and remove all chances of being followed. I smiled to myself and kissed the raindrops as they fell on my upturned face. Surely the Great Mystery was with us on this journey.

Wet, bedraggled, and exhausted, we stumbled into Life Community. I began at once to apply herbs to Grund's wounds. Iway was curious about my work and I let her watch as the others built a fire. Soon we were warm, and I heated water for a nourishing herbal tea, which we all drank except Grund, who had slipped into unconsciousness. The small group looked at us and I noticed how young the women were. We soon found out that they were daughters. Only the child's mother, a widow, was an adult. It seemed the wives had cast their lot with their husbands. I couldn't help but think of the terror they must have felt when they woke to find their guns, horses, slaves, and daughters gone. I was sure this was on the minds of the daughters as well. The slaves had cut themselves loose from their masters, but they were unsure what the future held for them now. Even the guard wondered what would happen next. Father was the first to return from the caves. Others would follow now that the "all clear" signal had been given. He held me tightly to his chest and I felt the wetness of his tears. "I thank the Great Mystery you have returned," he whispered as he touched my bruised and swollen face. A community circle quickly formed to discuss what we would do now. The new ones were invited to join us, and Father welcomed them. He gave thanks to Grund, Moed, and me for the work we had done in service to the community. Moed and I recounted our journey, but our focus was not on the violence—Grund's wounds and my face spoke to that. Instead, we focused on the nonviolence plan. It had worked. I invited the new people to share why they had decided to break with the others and come with us. Cautiously, Rut stood and recounted how he saw the determination in our eyes and heard it in our voices. "You were not going to give in, and I didn't want to lose the opportunity you were offering me." One of the young daughters stood next to Rut. "I was so tired of the violence and living in constant fear. Your words gave me hope that there is another way to live." Two of the former slaves stood together to speak. "You offered us the impossible—the chance to be free, to be equal like the others. We would have followed you anywhere." One of the young daughters put her arms around the slaves as she spoke. "We were all slaves in the Corpsety, even the Corpses, though my father could not see it. I want to live where I can breathe and be happy. I want to live without the guilt of knowing that others are enslaved because of me." Their words gave us encouragement. Perhaps it was possible for people to wake up in the middle of violence. Certainly Grund's beating was a high price to pay, but then we knew we would have to make sacrifices. I shared the story of Wolf's valiant attempt to come to our aid, how she had watched and waited for the right moment to help. "We must never underestimate the power of the Wild," I said, as tears rolled down my cheeks.

The community quickly reached consensus on accepting the new people. They would stay in a shelter outside the community until the teachings allowed them to make the transition to Life Community. We would supply them with food until they learned how to hunt and gather. The new people were taken by surprise when we asked if this was acceptable to them. They had not expected to be consulted and expressed their gratitude. This would be the first of many surprises they would experience in Life Community.

We ended the council circle and moved to the common area where we shared our meal together. I caught up with Rut and searched his face for any sign of frustration or disappointment. "I hope you will be happy here," I told him. He grinned broadly. "I am already happier than I have ever been. This is my idea of paradise." I laughed and cautioned him about expecting perfection. "We have our flaws," I admitted, "but we do our best to be aware of them. How many people do you reckon have already left the Corpsety?" Rut believed this group of Corpses was among the first to leave. He guessed many more would arrive next spring or summer. I was relieved to hear his words, not because I feared facing another group, but because winter was coming. We arrived at the common area and I was just about to sit down when I heard Father calling me. I left Rut with the others and hurried over to Father. "Mariah, Roz needs you in the sick shelter right now," he said curtly. He looked distressed, which was unusual for Father. I was worried that Grund was failing. I ran toward the shelter and Iway followed me. "Please let me see if there is anything I can do," she begged. I motioned for her to follow as I entered the shelter.

The room was warm, but Grund was shivering. An infection has set in, I thought as I began mixing herbs to relieve his fever. Roz applied honey to his wounds, while Iway began working over Grund's body with her hands. She stopped when I gave him the potion and then began again. I noticed her presence and practice were oddly calming. When she finished, the three of us sat watching over him. All through the night we prayed and sat with Grund. He was restless until morning broke, and then he was calm. He opened his eyes and asked for Father, Se, Cean, Roz, and me to stay with him. He called Iway over and took her hands in his. "You gave me much relief," he told her. "You are a gifted healer. Thank you for sharing your presence with me." Then he called to me, "Mariah, see to it that Iway's gift is understood by the community." I put my arm around Iway and promised Grund I would do as he wished.

Grund motioned for me to come closer and whispered weakly. "You know what's happening, Mariah?" With tears in my eyes I nodded my head. "Ah, little one, I am not sad to be leaving this world. I have had a good, long life and am ready to begin the next journey like Illow before me. I would ask you for one last favor." "I am at your service," I promised. He spoke slowly and with effort. "If you are willing, I would like for you to take Se under your wing and watch over her after I am gone.

She looks up to you, and I think she has a talent for healing."
"I am honored that you trust me with such a precious gift," I
whispered in his ear. "I will be happy to be a loving presence in
her life. Consider it settled." He reached up to hug me but fell
back in agony. I gave him something to ease his pain and then
bent down to give him a tender kiss.

Father, Cean, and Se arrived and we gathered around
Grund's bed. We told stories of the past and named all the
wonderful ways Grund had touched our lives. We brought
broth and soft foods for Grund, but he was not interested in
eating. He laughed with us and cried a bit over some of the
memories. As he grew weaker and weaker, he was held fast
in the circle of our love. Father was holding his hand when
he sighed and slipped into a deep sleep from which he never
woke. Se was weeping softly and I put my arm around her
shoulders. "Would you like to sleep with me tonight?" I asked.
She nodded her head and we left together. Cean, Father, and
Roz would wash Grund's body and sit with him tonight. I held
Se in my arms as she sobbed until I felt her body relax and drift
off to sleep. It was strange to feel the joy of holding Se in the
midst of my sorrow. I had lost Grund and gained a daughter.
How mysterious the coming and going of life is.

The next day we told the community of Grund's passing
and a bonfire was started. I took the path over to the new
group's shelter and told them of Grund's death. They took the
news hard. They felt responsible and feared being blamed for
his death. "Is there anything we can do to help?" Iway asked.
"Come to the ceremony tonight. It will help you understand
how important each person's life is to the community. You will

see how the unnecessary death of anyone makes a difference in the world."

I spent the day with Se, helping her prepare for the ceremony. I listened as she expressed her grief and told her how I felt when my grandmother died. I spoke of my belief that Grandmother, Illow, and my mother watched over me. "What makes you believe that?" she asked. "It's more of a feeling than anything else," I answered. "I had a dream last night," Se said quietly, "and it made me feel good. Is that what you mean?" I invited her to tell me about the dream. Grund had appeared to tell her all would be well. "You are in good hands," he assured her. Shyly, she whispered, "I believe those hands are yours." "Is that what you want?" I asked gently. She threw her little arms around me and cried softly. This was all the answer I needed. "So it will be, little one, and, yes, I believe this is how Grund watches over you now." We walked hand in hand to the sick shelter where Grund's body lay. Grund was at peace now, his face was calm and his suffering ended. We were grateful for that. Illow and Grund had left us within a few months of each other. Now, Father and Roz would be the oldest wise ones. How strange it must feel to take on this mantle.

When it was time to place Grund's body on the fire, Cean joined us and carried one end of the pallet. The whole community, including the new arrivals, stood as we said our good-byes. We told of all the things we would miss about Grund: his mischievous sense of humor, his steadfast belief in the value of community, his knowledge of survival, his hard work and keen mind. Se told him she would miss the comfort of his sheltering arms. Father cried as he shared how he would miss the warmth of their friendship. I already missed his strong shoulder to lean on in difficult times. We sent him on his way to the Great Mystery with our blessings. Quiet overcame us as we watched the fire take the last bits of the body we knew as Grund. Later in the evening, we gathered to eat and continued sharing stories of Grund's life. We were nearing the end of the evening when Rut stood to speak. "I need to tell you that Grund was the first person I have known who acted with complete integrity. I helped tie him to the tree just before the beating which took his life. When I looked into his eyes, I saw no hatred or fear. All I saw was a look of peaceful, loving resolve which I cannot forget. Here was a man I desperately needed to learn from, and I helped to kill him. I will carry this knowledge with me for the rest of my days as a reminder of the sacredness of life. You have shared the importance of Grund in your lives, and now I see what a difference one life makes in the lives of others. I honor Grund for giving me life at the expense of his own."

Rut's admission was the perfect ending to a life lived in service to others. I could see Grund smiling at the paradox of his death giving life. "Just part of the mystery," I heard him say. Perhaps it was the lateness of the night, but we were more somber than usual. We moved with a slower sense of life's rhythm. I was walking, with Se by my side, when Cean suddenly appeared. I had not connected with him since my return, and I smiled as he took my hand. That night he slept in our shelter, and I was comforted to know he was nearby. Father and Roz had rejoined the shelter too, and I slept surrounded by those I loved.

The weeks and months passed quickly as we prepared for the cold and taught the new ones. Deep winter descended on us and everything slowed down. I gathered Flow, Iway, and Se around me to learn the art of healing. The three of them got along well and fell into a sisterhood. They teased me and called me Mother as I watched over and taught them. We had a great deal of fun and became a family of sorts. Cean was working his way into my heart, and though we had made no plans, we were exploring and deepening our relationship. I felt a growing excitement I could hardly contain and an unfamiliar fullness in my heart. I was confused and a little afraid. "What is happening to me, Roz?" I asked one day. "I really need to know." "This is how love begins and passion grows," she answered with a smile. "Cean has loved you from a distance for a long time, but he wanted to make sure you felt the same way. I am glad to hear you are thinking of partnering with him. I believe you would be very happy together." I blushed at the word partnering. I was sure I didn't know all there was to know about that.

TWELVE

Deep Winter's Thaw

The teachings were going well. The new ones were eager to learn and we were seasoned teachers now. We were settled into a comfortable routine when we got the news. Four men on horseback had been sighted at the distant outlook. This meant a group of us would have to trudge through the snow to meet them. We immediately held a council meeting where it was decided that the community would go into hiding. Father, Cean, and Stear would go out to greet the group. Visions of Grund's torture and death came back to me and I cringed as I thought about what they might face. I wanted to give Cean something to carry with him for good luck. As he was preparing to leave, I slipped in beside him. "Could we talk for a moment?" I asked shyly. He took my hand and we walked outside. I was about to speak when Cean swept me up into his arms and held me close. "Mariah, will you be my partner?" he shouted. "Shh, everyone will hear you." "I don't care. I love you." Laughing, I kissed him and whispered, "Yes, I will be your partner on one condition." "Anything for you," he said as he bowed low before me. "Promise you will come back to me."

"Don't worry, Mariah. A pack of wild wolves could not keep me away!" I gave him my mother's barrette for good luck. I had carried it with me when we met the first group and I wanted him to have it on this journey.

I walked alongside Cean as he joined the others. I hugged Father and told him Cean and I would be partnering. Father's face lit up and he congratulated us both on our good fortune. I watched as the three of them walked out of sight and out of my life. I prayed they would all return safely. Thy will be done, amen.

The community spent the next week stocking the tunnels and moving to the caves. We were reasonably comfortable, and I was reminded of our early days in the Wild. There was little work to do, so we continued with the teachings. Now that we had a whole community of teachers the learning came quickly. My thoughts often strayed to Cean, Father, and Stear. I wondered what was happening, but all I could do was send prayers. I believed in prayers. I knew they transcended time and space and brought the energy of the universe to bear on a situation. I did not pray for a specific outcome—that was in the hands of the Great Mystery—but I prayed for the well-being of all concerned.

As the days went by, I grew more and more concerned, and I could feel the tension rising in my body. Finally, Roz called for a shaking, dancing, and prayer ceremony. The thought of a group ceremony brought me some relief—I needed this. We all needed it. As my bare feet touched the ground again and again, its pulse moved through my body, clearing my mind and lifting my fears. I caught Roz's eye as we danced and she smiled at me. Sometimes it was easy to forget that she needed ease and comfort as much as the rest of us. Being the oldest elder didn't erase human needs. We gave our prayers and our fears over to the earth and reconnected with the will of the Great Mystery. Now, I could endure the wait.

Perhaps our prayers worked their magic. The next day we got word that a group of six, some on horses, had been sighted coming this way. It took several days for the group to be identified, and even longer for them to arrive. Roz, Nestor, and I were there to greet them. Cean lay draped over a horse, and my heart stopped when I saw him. He was unconscious. Nestor lifted him gently off the horse and laid him near the fire. I ran to get herbs and blankets, while Roz went to prepare and warm the shelter. There was no time to think; I could only do. Cean had been wounded in the chest and he was hot and shivering. We moved him into the sick shelter where I began ministering to him. I sent for Iway to come and work her healing magic. While I was working with Cean, Father brought a woman for me to look at. She had also been shot, but her injury was not serious. I dressed her wound and gave her some herbs to drink. I suggested she come back tomorrow since she didn't need to stay in the sick shelter. She thanked me and left. I continued dressing Cean's swollen wound, which was sending angry red tentacles down his arm. I was concerned about the spread of infection and tried to give him a potion of garlic, honey, and herbs, but he was unresponsive. Roz, Father, Iway, and I stayed with him through the night. We watched over Cean, while Father told us what had happened.

"After arriving near the place where the men had been

sighted we set up camp," Father began. "We built a fire and were cooking a small animal when the horsemen arrived. The men appeared to be unarmed and seemed friendly, so we invited them to share our meal. They sat down to eat but did not offer their names. The men told us they had left the collapsing Corpsety and were seeking a new one. I explained that we lived in the area and knew of no Corpsety save the one they had escaped from. 'You must know the area,' they declared. 'Won't you help us find the Corpsety we have heard others talk about?' I told them we had no idea where to look and could not be of any assistance. They did not believe me and angrily demanded we help them. When we refused, they pushed us to the ground and tied our hands behind our backs. We began calling out our nonviolent refrain until they placed gags over our mouths. The next two days we were made to walk, tied together, until we arrived at their camp. The rest of their group came out to greet the men. 'Who are these people?' someone shouted. The men started to explain when they were interrupted by another of the group members with, 'Did you say they lived around here?' 'Yes,' the men answered while laughing, 'And they say they know the secrets of the ancients.' 'Stop laughing,' commanded a decidedly feminine voice, 'you must let them go at once.' The four men were not impressed. 'We will do no such thing,' they growled. The woman took off her hat, letting her long, black hair spill over her shoulders as she spoke: 'I was with a group who came through here some time ago. We met up with a small group of three who said the same thing to us. Within a few weeks the men who had beaten and tortured the group were dead. I believe it was no coincidence. What they say is true—they do know the secrets of the ancients.' The men looked warily at us and backed away. The male leader asked us if we had killed the men. I told him we knew nothing of the men's death, but that the curse would have been brought on by their own violence. 'Nonetheless,' the woman responded, 'they *all* died. I say let them go as they are of no use to us.' The leader disagreed. He felt we could be forced to help them. At that point, we began saying our refrain in unison. The woman put her hands over her ears and then drew a gun and pointed it at the leader. Suddenly, there were seven guns pointing at each other. The leader and his men stood together, while the woman and two others opposed them."

"'I can take care of this problem,' the leader shouted. He turned toward the three of us tethered together and shot Cean. I'm certain he would have shot Stear and me too, but the woman fired her gun and the leader fell to the ground. More shots rang out, and the woman slumped over her horse. The two sides continued shooting until everyone was on the ground. Stear struggled to help the wounded, but only the woman who had saved our lives survived. I lifted Cean, who was now covered in blood, and tried to stop his bleeding as best I could. When the woman revived she told us how she and her two female companions had been wives of the Corpses who tortured Grund. Everyone else in their group had perished. Alone in the Wild, the women had taken up with this group of men in order to survive. She told us her name was Mun and asked if she could join us. We were doubtful, and yet she had saved our lives. 'You would have to commit to following our community guidelines,' I told her. Even though she was wounded, Mun straightened her back and fixed her gaze on us. 'We were not in agreement with our husbands, none of the women were. We saw the futility of continuing to act as Corpses in a strange land. Still, we believed our place was beside our husbands. I was wrong and must atone for my mistakes.' 'We are not looking for atonement,' I explained. 'We ask that you work with us to release the violence you have unleashed within yourself.' Without hesitation, she laid down her gun and said she would follow any guidance we gave her. After that, we put Cean on a horse, and I rode with him until we reached home."

Though the story ended with their return, it gave us much to think about. Our plan for nonviolent confrontation was working, but not without casualties. Father reminded me that fighting would also bring casualties and possibly more deaths. I knew he was right, but somehow I wished we could avoid the business of causalities. One thing we knew. Women were generally more receptive to our plan. Men who were armed, or had an advantage such as leadership status, were decidedly unreceptive.

As we talked, Cean roused and tried to sit up. I was at his side in a heartbeat. He recognized me and smiled a crooked smile. "See," he said weakly, "I did come back." "Yes, you certainly did," I replied as I smoothed his forehead. "And now you must rest and get better." I gave him the herbal drink and tried unsuccessfully to quiet him. "I just visited with Illow and Grund," he continued. "They were so happy to see me. I wanted to stay but they told me I had to go back because Mariah was waiting for me." He drifted back to sleep while Roz, Father, and I looked at each other. It seemed Cean had had a near-death experience. Only a miracle sent him back to us. We thanked the Great Mystery (and Illow and Grund) for allowing him to return. Though I knew Cean would have a long recovery, I felt sure he would live now. I was filled with gratitude and said my own silent prayer of thanksgiving.

We took turns sitting by Cean's bedside while he slept. In the morning, he was less feverish and seemed more comfortable. I went to the community shelter to eat and got a good look at Mun. Her black hair and brooding eyes caused her to stand out from the others. She was beautiful and yet seemed unaware of it. I sat down next to her, and though she did not speak, I could feel her good-heartedness. "Mun," I said softly, "thank you for saving the lives of my father, Stear, and Cean." She looked at me with tears in her eyes. "You mean you don't blame me?" I put my arm around her shoulders and said, "There is nothing to blame you for. These are difficult, strange times with circumstances we cannot predict or control. You are here now and will become a part of Life Community. This is what is important." She reached out and grasped my hand tightly and said, "Thank you so much for your kindness. I've been thinking of leaving because I feel so guilty." I continued holding her hand as I spoke, "You are welcome here, Mun, and I want you to stay. You will be a great asset; I can feel it." She smiled at me, and I knew she would stay. In that moment, I learned what a difference a simple gesture of goodwill can make in someone's life.

Father called a council meeting to decide the fate of the newest arrival. Even though Mun had saved Father, Cean, and Stear, she had violated our ban against using violence.

Father asked if she would agree to work with Roz and Moed to regain her connection to life. Mun gratefully agreed and no one opposed her. She would learn our ways along with the others and work with wise ones to enter the life cycle again. The outside shelter would be overfull now, but sharing a crowded living space would be a good lesson in community. After the meeting, I caught up with Father and Roz. "I am troubled by something," I told them. "I know what Mun did was wrong, but I can't help thinking that you would all be dead if she hadn't acted. How do you reconcile that?" Father was silent, so Roz answered, "We don't know that death would have been the outcome without violence, Mariah. We live and die by the Great Mystery's will, not the human will. Violence did not save your father. It was not his time to die. When we put the outcome into the hands of the Great Mystery, it frees us to follow our hearts. In our hearts we know that violence is an illness to be avoided at all costs." Roz's explanation was clear and I needed to hear it. Something that harms cannot truly save—this was my lesson.

I tended to Cean daily, and he improved slowly. It was clear that he would need the remainder of the winter to recover. When he was well enough to sit and receive visitors, the community began to come. A prayer pole had been set up outside the shelter, and people were generous with their prayers for Cean's recovery. Now they could give their blessings in person, and a steady stream of visitors came to encourage Cean.

Nestor, Stear, and Moed joined the wise ones as we met to plan our strategy for spring. We had much to discuss: how to minimize our casualties; training more greeters; and preparing for the possibility of intruders coming into Life Community. All of these issues needed to be addressed, and soon. As usual, the wise ones had their hands full.

One day the sick shelter was unusually quiet, giving Cean and me some time alone. "Mariah, I want you to know how grateful I am that you saved my life. I will always be indebted to you." I responded thoughtfully, "Cean, I can't take credit for your healing. It was a team of us who cared for you." "Say what you will, Mariah. I know it was your heart and skill that called me back from the other side. Sometimes I think you don't know your own power." He pulled me to him and asked when we would be partnered. "When you feel well enough," I said laughing. "How about in a month?" he asked. Tenderly I took his face in my hands. "Cean, whenever you wish it to happen, I am ready." And, so it was that Cean and I planned our commitment to life together in the shadow of death.

The wise ones studied the challenges confronting us and, when they were ready, called a council circle. "In the spring more people will arrive from the Corpsety," Father told the group. "We must prepare for this. Our experiences have shown that men in leadership roles are not responsive to us. Therefore, we suggest using a tactic of 'avoidance' when confronted by such men. This means our greeters will not engage them and we will relocate to the caves until they move on. In the unlikely event they should decide to take over our community, we would leave and establish a new site." There were groans from the group when he mentioned moving. Roz lifted her hands. "I know, I know," she said. "It would be a lot of work, but we have the skills and the will to do it." People nodded their heads in agreement and even laughed at their newfound laziness and desire for comfort. "We did it once, we can do it again!" some shouted.

"We must also confront the possibility a group could come into our community," Roz acknowledged. Just the mention of this created restlessness among the group. Instead of the usual buzz, there were moans tempered with a shrill resistance in people's voices. "We will be overwhelmed by their sheer numbers." "We cannot let them destroy us." "Why can't they just leave us alone?" Roz raised her arm as if to ward off the negativity. "Yes," she admitted, "our whole community could be overcome and wiped out. This is a possibility we face. However, we have found that our nonviolent tactics work, and I believe a whole community using them would be powerful. We would like for everyone to be trained as greeters in case we are confronted." People continued to talk around the circle for some time, and I could see the influence of the new ones. They gave powerful arguments for the effectiveness of our nonviolent process. After a time, the group quieted. Each person agreed to play a role in protecting the community. They had worked hard to create Life Community, and now they would work equally hard to preserve it. A community training was embraced in the hope that, together, they could face whatever the future brought.

Cean had attended the circle today against my better judgment. He was still weak, and I feared the excitement of the meeting might be too much for him. Frankly, I didn't know if he would ever fully regain his strength and health. This didn't matter to me. I loved him no matter what, but I wondered how he would feel about being an invalid. By the end of the meeting he was pale and shaky. People drifted off to eat their noon meal, while father helped Cean back to the sick shelter, where he collapsed on the floor.

That night his fever returned and he was restless. For the next several days, Cean struggled with fever and pain. I didn't dare leave his side. I consulted with Iway, who came to give him healing each day. "He is weak," she said, "but not beyond help." I noticed the community had gathered again at the prayer pole. I was grateful to them, for Cean needed all of our prayers. It went on like this for several more days and I began to lose hope. My dreams had been hidden in darkness for weeks and I felt lost. One afternoon, I slipped away to visit the tree Cean and I had named Cenmar. Under the tree I wept and spoke of my love and longing for Cean's recovery. Leaning against its trunk I felt a loving presence, and some of my darkness lifted. That night my dreams returned and I saw Cean running through the forest.

I woke with a feeling of peace and joy. I was certain Cean would recover. Without stopping for breakfast, I ran to the sick shelter and opened the door. Cean was awake, and though he was shaky, I could see the sparkle had returned to his eyes. I cautioned him to take life slow and easy from now on and said, "I think something inside has been damaged by the bullet and needs to rest until your healing is complete." Cean smiled weakly and promised to follow my instructions. "After all, you have saved my life twice now," he said. I sat down beside him and stroked his hair as we talked. "I think we should wait to partner until you are healed," I murmured. A strange look

passed over Cean's face and he was quiet. "What is it, Cean?"
I asked. He was silent, and after an uncomfortably long time
he responded, "That's a good idea. We should wait to see if I
am going to recover fully before partnering." "Cean," I shouted,
"that is not at all what I meant. I am concerned that the
excitement and festivities might be hard on you." He looked
into my eyes. "All the same, it is better to wait," he said grimly.
I felt a chasm open between us that I didn't know how to close.
Father returned and I ran out of the shelter. I needed some
comfort from Roz. "It's natural that the stress of his illness is
taking a toll on you both," she suggested. "Perhaps it's time for
the wise ones to spend more time with Cean. This may help
him regain his perspective, and you can get back out into the
community." Roz was right; I needed to reconnect with my
daily life. I gave her a warm hug of gratitude. Where would I be
without my friends?

Cean's convalescence continued to go well, but it was clear
it would take months, not weeks, for him to recover. Much of
his time was spent talking with the wise ones. I visited regularly
but didn't venture into intimate conversation. I didn't know
what to say that wouldn't make things worse. For his part,
Cean was quiet and reserved when I was around. The distance
between us was festering, like a wound that refused to heal.
One day, I heard Cean laughing as I walked up to the door of
the sick shelter. Maybe today he will smile at me, I thought. I
opened the door and was surprised to see Mun sitting on his
bed. They both had tears in their eyes they were laughing so
hard. Cean froze when I entered, and I quickly turned and ran
out the door.

Tears streamed down my face as I hurried up the mountain path. I sat in the cold for a long, long time and tried to commune with Illow. "I have lost the love of Cean and I don't know why. Well, I do know why, but it's a misunderstanding. I didn't mean to offend him. I guess I don't understand how to love someone. Oh, Illow, please tell me what to do now." I waited, but there was only silence. I had never felt so lonely. Cean had turned away from me, and I was lost in his shadow. I walked slowly back down the mountain. I didn't want to see or talk to anyone tonight. I had taken a roundabout way to get to the sleeping shelter and was almost there when I ran into Mun. "I've been looking for you," she said calmly. "Can we talk?" I wanted to be angry with her, but I wasn't. I was hurt and sad. "Mun, I'm not angry. If you and Cean love each other, I can accept that that is how it's meant to be." She grabbed my shoulders and forced me to look into her eyes. "I swear by all that is good Cean and I are not in love. We are friends and that is all." I relaxed a little and then started to cry. "I don't think we are friends anymore," I sobbed. "Cean never laughs when I'm around." "Sit down," Mun commanded. "I have been married and can tell you a thing or two about men. Cean is still very much in love with you. He is afraid his injury has made him less of a man. He doesn't want you to be saddled with an invalid for the rest of your life." "I'm confused," I said. "I told him that doesn't matter to me." "Yes," Mun answered, "but it still matters to him." "What can I do?" I asked. "He will have to work through this on his own," she advised. "And, there is no reason why you can't cajole him into being close again. Why don't you try being affectionate and playful? I predict he won't be able to resist you." I thanked Mun for her advice, even though I wasn't sure I could do as she suggested. She gave me a kiss and told me not to let fear get in the way of love. I slipped into the sleeping shelter and lay there thinking about her words—don't let fear get in the way of love.

In the morning I was subdued yet determined. I found Mun and gave her a grateful hug. "You held up a mirror for me yesterday, and though I didn't like what I saw, it has given me the strength to face Cean." She cocked her head to one side and smiled at me. "You are a wise woman, Mariah. You will find a way to reach him." I marched over to the sick shelter and opened the door. Cean was talking with Father. "Can Cean and I have some time alone?" I inquired. Father got up abruptly and took his leave, even though the look on Cean's face said, "Stay." When we were alone, I walked over to Cean's bed and sat down. Taking his hand in mine, I began, "Cean, we cannot let fear get in the way of our love. I backed away because I was afraid of hurting you. I felt my words had made you feel 'less than,' even though that was not my intention. My fear of saying the wrong thing kept me at a distance. Now, I see how I let my fears come between us."

Tears filled Cean's eyes as he took in my heartfelt words. "I too have been afraid. My fear is of the future and what the injury may have taken from me. I withdrew from you so that you would not feel obligated to stay with me. Perhaps I was blinded by my pride. Now I see that this was not the right thing to do. I have missed you so much. My heart aches all day every day, and I long to touch you. Can you forgive me for causing your suffering?" He moved in the bed to reach for me, but I slipped onto the floor. Laughing, I got up and fell into his arms. It felt good to laugh and to be back in the circle of love.

Our relationship settled into a pattern of talking, dreaming, and planning together. Cean continued to consult with the wise ones, and I helped teach the nonviolence skills to the community. This time, the group was eager to learn. In fact, I was surprised at their enthusiasm. During one of the practice sessions, I was overwhelmed by the force of their voices as they shouted the refrain. When I told them how it felt, their faces glowed with delight. They were proud of their accomplishment. Spring arrived early and we got busy building two additional sleeping shelters. There was little time for worrying.

The weather warmed, and so did Cean's body. He no longer stayed at the sick shelter. He was up and doing things around the community. We set the date for our partnering ceremony and Roz, Lexy, Se, Flow, and Iway offered to help me organize and plan the event. Once again, Moed shared some of her magical material for my dress. The beautiful cloth she had smuggled out of the Corpsety continued to fill us with awe. No matter how many times we asked how she managed to do it, it remained her secret. I cried when my eyes caught sight of the colors and patterns. Moed had given me a treasure. The material reminded me of the forest, with its dappled light and subtle colors. Cean was busy working on a project he was secretive about, and though I was curious, I let him have his mystery.

THIRTEEN

Unexpected Blessings

I busied myself gathering herbs and helped Roz prepare for Lexy's birthing. Lexy was strong, but we both had a feeling this might be a difficult birth. Unfortunately, when Lexy's time came we were proven right. Her labor lasted for two days, and then she began bleeding heavily. Finally, the child was born, but Lexy's bleeding continued. I ran to the place where we kept the dried plants. Illow had told me about an herb that could stop bleeding in childbirth. I searched frantically but couldn't find it. I consciously slowed down and looked carefully at each container on the shelf, but there were hundreds of them. I tried to eliminate those I knew, but this was taking way too much time. Then, I remembered the technique Illow had taught me to find plants. Maybe it would work for dried ones too. I closed my eyes and called to the plant, although I didn't know its name. Soft as a whisper, I heard Illow's voice say, "Look in the container on the third shelf by the garlic. There you will find what you are looking for." I called and Illow had answered! I stood mute for a moment and then I heard her voice again: "Hurry, child. Time is of the essence." I ran back to the birthing shelter with my prize, giving thanks to Illow along the way.

After giving the potion to Lexy, we massaged her stomach for hours. The bleeding finally slowed, and Lexy roused enough to ask for her baby. He was a strong boy with brilliant red hair. We gave him to her and she managed a small smile. "We will call him San," she said and closed her eyes to sleep. Thunar looked after San, while we took care of Lexy. It was wonderful to witness Thunar's tenderness. He picked up the child, wrapped him in a blanket, and began singing quietly to him. He was welcoming his son into the world. Surprisingly, Lexy made a quick recovery. Both Roz and I counseled her not to have any more children. "Next time," Roz told her, "there is a good chance you might not survive." I gave her medicinal herbs that would prevent pregnancy and hoped she would take them. Lexy was strong-willed, and I could tell by the look on Thunar's face that he was doubtful she would listen to our advice. I drew Lexy aside to remind her that there would be many children arriving in the years to come—including mine, I hoped—and I wanted her to be there for them. With a wistful look on her face, she pulled me close and whispered in my ear, "You always know how to get to me. I will be there for you," she promised.

The community was full of flowers and good smells on the day Cean and I were to be partnered. I still did not know Cean's secret. The others had built an arbor for us to pass through made of flowers and vines. Father gathered everyone together while Cean and I began to walk. We stopped before the arbor and shared our vows. "Together we will stand, and no matter what forces blow against us we shall not part. Our strength is in our partnership. In the beauty of relationship we will spend the rest of our days." As we stepped through the arbor Father and Roz stepped forward to hug us. Then Lexy, Thunar, Se, and Flow moved in to give hugs, and soon the whole community was dancing around us and we were dancing and laughing inside their circle. We spent the rest of the day eating, dancing, and making merry. As the evening began to draw to a close, Cean took my hand and led me into the forest. "Where are we going?" I asked. "It's a surprise," was all Cean would say. We walked until we were in front of the tree Cean had shown me so long ago that we had playfully christened Cenmar. High up in the branches of the tree was a tree house. It shone with candlelight, and as I climbed the ladder I caught a glimpse of the inside. Cean had covered the floor with animal pelts, and the sleeping pallet was raised up off the floor. Brightly colored cloth covered the walls, and I gasped when I entered the room. I could see the tops of trees and the stars. Cean had remembered how I loved sleeping under the stars. It was a magical place, and I hugged Cean with tears streaming down my face. "This is the most wonderful sight I have ever seen," I said breathlessly. Cean had tears in his eyes too as he whispered, "It's my gift to you, Mariah—my gift of beauty to a truly beautiful woman who has brought the magic and wonder of love into my life." We spent the night exploring the mysteries of our bodies and woke with the flickering of sunlight through a veil of leaves. We wandered aimlessly through the forest and delighted in each other for several days. Community members brought food and water but did not intrude. We were free to enjoy our time alone. When we were ready to return to community life, I told Cean that this place would always be ours. Even though it would be shared by many others through the years it would be ours, because we knew it first. Cean smiled and pronounced, "Cenmar belongs to us and we belong to it."

The community welcomed us back with laughter, teasing, and hugs. It was good to be back in the embrace of those we loved. We continued with our daily routine, but the anticipation of more people coming weighed heavy on our minds. I was in the forest collecting herbs with Se and Flow when I heard the flutes sounding. I sent Flow and Se to the tunnel, as was our plan. I should have gone with them but I could not contain my curiosity. I moved closer and climbed up in a tree to watch. I saw ten men on horses with guns drawn facing the community, which had spread out along the length of our living space. I heard the man who appeared to be their leader introduce himself as Reawk and ask for food and water. "We can pay you," he added. Father asked them to put down their guns before we could help them. The leader refused to give the order for his men to disarm, even though Father told him we were unarmed. "How do we know you are telling the truth?" he asked. They moved forward on their horses as if to break though the line, and everyone began speaking in unison. Even from my vantage point the community of voices was a powerful force. Oh, how I wished to be there with them. I repeated our refrain quietly, though only the birds could hear me. Then, a few minutes later and much to my amazement, I saw large birds circling over the group, lending their presence. Had the group's calls drawn them? Had they heard my voice? I would never know.

The leader held up his hand as if to protect himself from the words and agreed to disarm in exchange for some food and water. The men dismounted and laid down their guns and knives. Their leader apologized and thanked Father for his help. This group felt different to me, and Father must have sensed it too, for he proceeded to recite our community welcome to them: "Welcome to all who would enter. In this place people live in community. All are equal here. If you come in peace we welcome you. If you are hungry we will feed you. If you are thirsty we will give you water. If you are sick we will care for you. If you need shelter we will help you find it. We can teach you how to find food, clean water, build shelters, and live together peacefully. If you lay down your arms, let go of your hostilities, and embrace peace you may enter. If you come to steal, harm, kill, enslave, or use any kind of power-over, we will resist you. We will resist you to the death. We bow to no one. We share but will not be taken from. We are a Life Community and any form of violence is unwelcome here."

After he finished, Father announced that we would not take their money, as we had no use for it in the Wild. "Can we do something to repay you?" the leader, Reawk, asked. Father was silent and Reawk went with Mun to collect food and water for his men. While they were gone, I could see the other men talking with people and laughing. After quite a long time, Reawk and Mun returned with the supplies. He thanked Father again, picked up his gun, and got on his horse. He ordered his men to load the supplies and take up their arms. Sheepishly, the men looked down at the ground and told him they wanted to stay. 'We have nowhere else to go," they complained, "and this seems like a good place to live." Reawk raised his gun and looked at them silently for a tense moment. Then he let out a great laugh and said, "Well I'll be, if it's good enough for my men it's good enough for me." Throwing down his gun, he got off his horse and asked if they could stay with us. He was very handsome, with black hair graying at the temples and a strong, wiry build. His blue eyes were full of intelligence and wit. I liked him immediately and so, I thought, did Mun. Had she intentionally been slow to gather the supplies in order to delay him? I could see a relationship developing between them in the future.

I joined the group just in time to hear Father asking the men if they could agree to our community guidelines. These fierce men, who had leveled their guns at us just moments ago, easily agreed. "There will be a period of learning and adjustment before you are welcomed into the community," Father told them. Reawk said he would see to it that his men followed the guidelines. Father reminded him that we are equals here and no one is above anyone else. Reawk's face reddened and he apologized for getting it wrong already. "I guess my men will have to watch over me," he joked. It was clear that the men liked him and followed him out of respect, not power-over. "A man who can laugh at himself knows how to lead," Father announced, and Reawk and his men were warmly welcomed.

We took their guns and destroyed them with axes. We had a pile of broken guns at our community entrance which we hoped would send the message that "guns are not welcome here." Father collected their knives but did not destroy them.

Knives were work tools and would be returned once the men became full-fledged community members.

Life Community was getting close to the limit we had set of a hundred people, but we had larger problems to confront. Reawk told us there was another group of men, perhaps as many as thirty, who were likely to be coming this way within a day or two. Father called a council meeting to consider what we should do. The group decided everyone but Nestor, Cean, Father, Roz, Nake, and I would move immediately to the caves. The six of us would stay behind to put things away, and then we would join the others. The tunnels were not mentioned because we did not yet trust the new ones. Everyone began to gather supplies, and within a few hours they were gone. Working into the night we stocked the tunnels with supplies from the community center. By sunrise, we were working on removing the last of the food when we heard the sound of horses' hooves. We hurried to the tunnel's entrance, hoping they had not heard us. This was cutting it a bit too close for comfort. We caught our breath as we entered the tunnel and listened to their footfalls. They shouted, "Come out or we'll shoot," and then we heard gunfire. Our decision to use avoidance was clearly the right one! We quietly moved along the tunnel. Nake accidentally knocked over a jar, giving us a fright, but we needn't have worried. All the shouting and shooting prevented the men from noticing. At one point we heard someone shout, "There's been a fire here but all the rooms are empty. Where have the people gone?"

We hurried to the caves and told the others to put out their fires so the smoke would not give us away. We would not take any chances with this group. Reawk told us guns and ammunition were becoming scarce and those who had them were mostly caravan workers, Corpses, or policemen. His group had been policemen, but he reckoned this group was likely caravan workers. Reawk figured the number of people with guns would diminish greatly after this summer. If only we could make it through the summer, I thought.

We waited without fire for days. Our food was limited to nuts, berries, and dried meat. The nights were cold, and even though we slept close to one another we could not get warm. Finally, the need for water sent a group of us back to the stream. Father, Thunar, Stear, Reawk, and Mun volunteered to get water for us. Just as they were leaving, Stear turned her ankle on a rock and was unable to go. So, I stepped in to take her place.

FOURTEEN

Earthquake

The men were eating the remains of the food we had left behind. We could see at least thirty of them sitting around fires. We edged up to the stream with our bags and began to fill them. We were almost done when a dog started barking and running toward us. They had brought dogs with them. We retreated, but it was too late. The dogs followed us, and the men followed them. Thunar and Mun had moved further into the forest and went undetected while the three of us were roughly pushed up the hill to the community center.

The violent men had taken over, and what was once a welcoming community was now a cold and forbidding place. Shaken, I realized a community is not about the buildings or even the natural setting. Community is about the people you share it with. The leader stood while we were pushed to our knees. "Where have you hidden the others and your supplies?" he demanded. Father introduced himself and asked for the leader's name. The leader struck Father across the mouth and ordered him to answer his questions. Father began to recite our community welcome. He was struck again and I began to call out our refrain. I didn't get any further than Father when a hand was placed over my mouth. "Take me to the others or I'll kill the girl," the leader shouted. Just then I felt a slight tremor. The others didn't seem to notice but Father had. "All right," Father said, "I will take you to them, but we will have to move quickly or they will be gone along with the supplies." Father rose and began running toward the mountain. I thought I knew what his plan was. If the trembling got stronger the rocks would fall and cause chaos. It would be dangerous, but it was a brilliant plan. As we ran, I told Reawk to watch out for falling rocks. He looked at me strangely but nodded his head. We reached the base of the mountain and a great trembling began to shake the earth and move rocks off the mountain. Many of the men were killed by giant falling boulders. Dropping their guns and pleading for mercy, those who survived ran away. The horses had taken flight as soon as they felt the tremors, so everyone was on foot. The leader had been hit in the head and lay dying. Father lifted him up to offer some comfort. "Who are you?" the man asked. Father repeated his name and told him he had left the Corpsety long ago. "I should have listened to you," he said before he died in Father's arms.

The earthquake and death of the men caused me to think of Grandmother's prophesy. *The true promise of the Corpsety is death, destruction, and suffering brought on by wanton greed and corruption. When the natural balance of the world is broken madness is released.* These men had called the stones from the mountain down on themselves just as surely as the Corpsety had caused its own collapse. Greed and corruption prevented them from finding a peaceful solution to their problems.

They carried the madness of the Corpsety with them. Only by working with the mountain had we managed to save ourselves from the insanity. The Wild had rescued us from the sinking lifeboat that was the Corpsety. I said a silent prayer of thankfulness to Grandmother for sharing her story, for encouraging Father to take me into the Wild, and for trusting me to "hold the course."

We walked back to the stream and found no one there. After we collected the guns, hid them, and filled our water bags, we disappeared quietly into the forest. It would not be possible to go back until we were certain no one was following us. We spent a cold, miserable night sleeping on the hard forest floor. In the morning, there were no signs of dogs, men, or horses, so we returned to the cave and waited for the lookouts to give the "all clear" signal. When it finally came, we returned to our community. We smashed the weapons and added them to our growing pile of broken guns. Now we were free to create our own story.

FIFTEEN

Nothing Stays the Same

Once we were settled and had reclaimed our community space, the wise ones met to discuss our growing numbers. We agreed that one hundred was as large as a community could be and still maintain its integrity. Roz noted that she had felt the difference when we moved past fifty. Father asked how we felt about starting another community and I was surprised to hear Cean speak first. "It's a good idea," he reasoned, "and I would like to help make it happen." This was news to me! Others were not sure, and neither was I. We had worked hard to create this community we loved. I didn't relish the idea of leaving it. Father continued, "It could be an asset to us. If the community were built near enough we could even connect to it with a tunnel." I needed to think about his words—would a tunnel make a difference? Father suggested we call a community council to discuss the possibility.

After the meeting ended, I asked Cean why he had responded with such certainty to Father's suggestion. He told me he had been thinking about this for quite a while. "We would be the natural ones to start it," he explained. "We are wise ones and have experience in building community. Have you forgotten that part of our vision is to create Life Community in many places?" I took a long time to consider what he had said. The Great Mystery had been clear about our responsibility to share the gifts we had been given, and creating community was surely one of them. Cean waited patiently for my response. Unconsciously, I had moved away from him, and he moved closer to me. "Wouldn't you miss the fellowship of Life Community?" I asked. "Mariah, I believe the beauty of Life Community is in the fellowship we create when we live by life-affirming values. A new community would broaden our opportunities for fellowship and community." "When do you think it would be built?" I asked. "Right away," he answered. "We would need to get started this summer." "But," I blurted out, "we are going to have a baby." "I know, Mariah," he said softly. How could he know? I had just discovered it myself. Cean put his arm around my shoulder and pulled me to him. "I know your body like my own, and it's been changing," he laughed. "Don't worry; we will be close to Roz when the time comes."

Our next community council brought everyone together in the spirit of growth and achievement. Creating another Life Community was an idea people were ready for. Everyone agreed we should start the planning process immediately. Others wanted to join Cean and me. Lexy, Thunar, Iway, Reawk, Mun, Moed, and Nake—among others—pledged themselves to the new community. Of course, other people would arrive from the Corpsety. Some would remain to help us build our vision of a new world that cultivates life, while bringing balance and joy to all who live there. Perhaps they would have things to teach us. I remembered my long-ago dream of the ancients. We resembled them now with our unkempt hair, strange clothes, and smiling faces. The ancients were surely in our blood and in our bones. It was their wisdom that guided and sustained our vision. It was the old ways that had allowed for life to begin anew.

In my new home I would be responsible for telling children the stories of the ancients, of the Corpsety, and of "those who walked away." I could already see myself, nestled in blankets, sharing the stories that had graced my life. For it is through stories that we create the future. Our child would be born in the new community, in the middle of the Wild. Perhaps we should call her, for I already knew my child was a girl, Wilder. Knowing only the Wild, her life would be as different from mine as my life was from Grandmother's. I had fulfilled Grandmother's prophesy of finding a way to escape the Corpsety, and now Wilder could fulfill Mother's prophesy of living in a place where people are free. What dreams, adventures, and mysteries would her story hold? I would have to dream on that.

And now, dear friends, my bundle of stories rests in your hands. Hold them close, for they carry the seeds of a new life waiting to be born.

ROSTER OF GROUP PROCESSES

The Natural Laws: Cooperation, Community, Connection, and Conservation

Communion of the Forest:
Trees live together in a community called a forest. No matter how strong or large or beautiful a tree might be it can never compete with a forest. You see, the forest is a place of refuge where trees grow together by nurturing, supporting, and protecting each other from the vagaries of wind, rain, and

sun. Wrathful winds do little damage to a forest because of the support trees offer one another. Torrential rains that might uproot a single tree find it difficult to move a tree in the forest. When the sun's heat bears down and there are no clouds of relief, the trees share water and are saved. The forest is a sanctuary, a place where trees can grow and thrive. Any tree deprived of its forest is less than it could be and is infinitely vulnerable. And so it is with people, too. We are all more when we are together in community. We are a place of refuge for each other when we grow and nurture and support one another. Our collective presence offers us safety from the vagaries of nature. Together we are wise, we know things that none of us could know individually, because our collective mind is joined with that of the Great Mystery. We may all act as leaders or followers at times, but we must never forget that it is the whole, the community, that sustains us and provides the wisdom and strength we need to survive.

Community Guidelines:
1. Respectful relations with people and the natural environment
2. Equality
3. Cooperation and sharing
4. Group problem-solving and decision-making
5. Nonviolence in words and actions
6. Valuing differences
7. Valuing community
8. Wise resource use by taking only what you need.

The Ceremonies:

Ceremony of Leave-Taking. Each person is asked to consider the wounds they suffered while living in the Corpsety and share with the group. Everyone else listens as witnesses. Then a large fire is lit in the middle of the circle. Each person searches for an object they can imagine putting their wounds into. Next, they throw the object into the fire and shout farewell as they watch their wounds turn into smoke and ashes. Drumming while people step forward, everyone shouts good riddance to the wounds. The burden of suffering lifts with the rising smoke, and shaking and dancing follows. We move away from the tragedy of the Corpsety and into the arms of community.

Circle of Renewal. People are asked to think about their life story and look for areas of growth and change. In silence they reflect on their stories and then share them with the group. When each person finishes the group responds with the phrase, "I see you." This is the beginning of genuine connections and true intimacy.

Ceremony of Reclamation. In this circle, we call back the parts of our spirit lost in the Corpsety. Calling these parts back is essential to becoming whole again. After each person speaks the group will call out with the individuals, if asked, as they "call their spirits back." Swaying together ends the ceremony.

Transitioning Into a New Life. As each person passes through the arbor (made of branches, flowers, and fragrant herbs) everyone chants, "You have turned toward life and are returning to wholeness." Each person chooses something to leave outside the arbor that represents all they are leaving behind. Singing and blessings are bestowed as people pass through the sweet, smoke-filled arbor. After everyone has passed through the arbor the things left behind are burned. A new life has begun.

The Old Ways and Vital Life Skills:
1. Valuing our unique "self."
2. Use of boundaries in relationships.
3. Acceptance of feelings and discovery of their insights.
4. Communicate through listening and giving honest feedback.
5. Creative dancing with conflict.
6. Engaging in deep relationship.
7. Relaxing the body and mind.
8. Allowing death to accompany us throughout life.

Vital Community Skills:
Work—You are encouraged to follow your heart when selecting work. All work is valued and each person is accepted whatever his or her level of ability. Beyond basic survival work (provision of food, shelter, water, and essential needs), no one is forced into labor. Satisfied people meet the needs of community joyfully. That joy spreads out to touch everything and everyone and this is what Life Community thrives on.

Councils—Councils are what we use to make decisions, find resolutions, problem-solve, and address community issues. Anyone with an issue can convene a council meeting. In the council circle we speak from our hearts and listen with openness. This allows us to find our deepest truths together. Speaking and listening from the heart creates a sacred circle, a group energy field, which wraps us in a blanket of empathy for ourselves and others. In this place it is easy to see how each person holds a piece of the truth. And the artificial boundaries between us begin to dissolve. The wise ones have a special responsibility in regard to council circles. Community members are free to stay or leave a council meeting, but wise ones stay with the process until decisions or resolutions are crafted.

Violence—Any form of violence, physical, verbal, and emotional, is treated as an illness. Violence occurs whenever someone tries to exert "power-over" another person or group. Attempts to use "power-over" are an indication that something is out of balance. When violence erupts in Life Community, a community member is given the task of accompanying the offender until learning, change, and justice are served. This is true of all kinds of violence, including self-harm, harming of community members, and unnecessary harm done to animals and the natural environment. Justice is sought that restores the balance between the aggressor, his or her own self, those harmed, and the community. We believe everyone in the community is harmed when violence occurs.

Healing Circles—Healing circles help us find our way to a just resolution and forgiveness. Forgiveness must be asked for and received before healing can occur and balance can be restored. Even when we kill an animal or take from plants, we ask for forgiveness. Acknowledging our violent behavior in front of others removes the temptation to become self-righteous and arrogant and forget our place in the whole of life. Healing circles allow us to confront violence and opens a space for those who have been harmed to talk about their experience. A healing circle is a safe and nurturing place where all are respected, even those who commit violence. In the circle, people speak of their feelings and the harm done to them while the aggressor listens. After all have spoken, then, and only then, is the aggressor asked to share his or her story. The aggressor is expected to have reflected on what led him/her to commit violence and how he or she was harmed by the violent act. When the sharing is finished, the aggressor asks for forgiveness from everyone touched by the violence. In a healing circle, there is no room for judgment, and we do not judge the aggressor. We listen with compassion, just as we have listened to those who have been harmed. Finally, people begin to speak of what they need in order to heal. Now, a resolution is possible. Carrying the understanding of the healing circle in their hearts, the community is now ready to enter into a council and find justice.

Leadership—We believe true leadership is serving and working with others. In Life Community leadership is a shared responsibility. You will all be called upon to act as leaders at some point in time. In the Corpsety leadership is based on being better than others and exerting power over them. Life Community requires leaders to serve the whole. Though we may be called upon to lead in many small and large ways, when our task is finished, we return to our regular duties. Moving back and forth between leading and following helps us maintain humility and balance.

Real Community—For us community speaks to the reality that we are a unified whole working together for the good of all. We are in essence one body in an ocean of wildness. A city is simply an inhabited place where people live as disconnected individuals. We do not intend for Life Community to ever grow into a city. Cities become Corpsetys and Corpsetys become agents of death. We intend to remain small enough to maintain our connections and provide these things to our members: a sense of order which everyone is engaged in; leadership that is not corrupt; equality and fairness; a slow pace of life where there is time for contemplation and reflection; close relationships which nurture us from birth to death; education for everyone; peaceful relations; and balance between play, work, learning, and solitude. In Life Community we cultivate a nurturing environment with interactions based on compassion, acceptance, and shared learning.

Ritual—The death ritual is but one example of how we celebrate life. When a baby is born or a person recovers from an illness, we celebrate. When two people partner, their new life together is celebrated. We hold rituals that connect us with the changing seasons, the earth, our food, and our community. We celebrate in our hearts and together with song, dance, drumming, and prayer. It is ritual that helps us shift and move from the ordinary into the sacred and then back again. This is how we stay connected to the Great Mystery and to each other.

Nonviolence—Violence requires us to use power-over, which leads to disharmony and imbalance. This is why we avoid it. Our everyday relationships have shown how easily violence can separate us from each other, and from ourselves. Even when used for "just ends," violence perpetuates disconnection and revenge. Nature shows us there are many possible responses to violence such as: sharing, laughing, tending and befriending, caring, nurturing, loving, playing, refusing to engage, and cooperating. Our goal is to create a strong, creative response to violence that is in harmony with the natural laws. We do not intend to go meekly to our deaths. And, we will not be forced into violence by the fear of death. We will be prepared to stand against aggression with tools that protect us and challenge the corruptive power of violence. We recognize that solidarity is our strongest and most powerful ally. Collectively we can support each other and find the courage to resist violence.

Life Community Welcome: Welcome to all who would enter. In this place people live in community. All are equal here. If you come in peace we welcome you. If you are hungry we will feed you. If you are thirsty we will give you water. If you are sick we will care for you. If you need shelter we will help you find it. We can teach you how to find food, clean water, build shelters, and live together peacefully. If you lay down your arms, let go of your hostilities, and embrace peace you may enter. If you come to steal, harm, kill, enslave, or use any kind of power-over, we will resist you. We will resist you to the death. We bow to no one. We share but will not be taken from. We are a Life Community and any form of violence is unwelcome here.

ABOUT THE AUTHOR

The author lives in Chattanooga, Tennessee, with her life partner. She is a wanderer, a healer, and a dreamer. Her travels have taken her through the valley of despair and hopelessness to transcendence and compassion. Along the way she picked up knowledge of lifelong education, anthropology, community and organizational development, adult non-formal education, community organizing, teaching, counseling, art and movement therapy, mind-body medicine, and standing for peace and justice. Her dream is to teach others how to create Life Community in their lives, not necessarily in the Wild (although that is a beautiful dream), but where they are at any moment in time and space.

To contact the author, address e-mails to: **TurnedTowardLife@gmail.com**

CPSIA information can be obtained at www.ICGtesting.com
Printed in the USA
LVOW01s1257181014

409218LV00003B/3/P